B48 713 7

KT-231-917

ROTHERHAM LIBRARY & INFORMATION SERVICE

BR

RYG1

BRINSWORTH
114

25 FEB 2017
27 JUN 20
11 JU **KIVETON PARK**

RW   b114

22 AUG 2017

20 DEC 2019

DINNINGTON
115

3 NOV 2017

27 JAN 2020

Foulds
Myers

MALTBY

5 AUG 2021

GREASBROUGH

7.18

20/1/17

- 6 JAN 2020
5 AUG 2021

KIVETON PARK

1123

- 4 FEB 2017

0 4 JUN 2024

This book must be returned by the date specified at the time of issue as
the DATE DUE FOR RETURN.
The loan may be extended (personally, by post, telephone or online) for
a further period if the book is not required by another reader, by quoting
the above number / author / title.

Enquiries: 01709 336774

www.rotherham.gov.uk/libraries

THE WRONG SIDE OF HAPPINESS

It is 1887 and times are lean. When West Country farm labourer Emmanuel Ladycott and his daughter, Tresca, lose their jobs, they head for Tavistock where Emmanuel hopes to join hundreds of navvies working on the railway line. Lodging together in a tiny attic room, Tresca is determined to forge a new life among the overcrowding and poverty of Bannawell Street. But when Emmanuel is dismissed from the railway, Tresca doesn't know whether to blame her father or his Irish foreman, Connor O'Mahoney. Torn apart by her conflicting emotions, events spiral out of control leaving Tresca broken and on the brink of despair.

THE WRONG SIDE
OF HAPPINESS

The Wrong Side Of Happiness

by

Tania Crosse

Magna Large Print Books
Long Preston, North Yorkshire,
BD23 4ND, England.

British Library Cataloguing in Publication Data.

Crosse, Tania
   The wrong side of happiness.

   A catalogue record of this book is
   available from the British Library

   ISBN   978-0-7505-3707-0

ROTHERHAM LIBRARY &
INFORMATION SERVICES

F

B4871376 37

First published in Great Britain in 2011 by
Severn House Publishers Ltd.

Copyright © 2011 by Tania Crosse

Cover illustration © Gordon Crabb by arrangement with
Alison Eldred

The moral right of the author has been asserted

A catalogue record for this book is available from the British Library.

Published in Large Print 2013 by arrangement with
Severn House Publishers Ltd.

All Rights reserved. No part of this publication may be reproduced,
stored in a retrieval system, or transmitted in any form or by any
means, electronic, mechanical, photocopying, recording or otherwise
without the prior permission of the Copyright owner.

Magna Large Print is an imprint of Library Magna Books Ltd.

Printed and bound in Great Britain by
T.J. (International) Ltd., Cornwall, PL28 8RW

Except where actual historical events and characters are being described for the storyline of this novel, all situations in this publication are fictitious and any resemblance to living persons is purely coincidental.

To all our wonderful Dartmoor friends,
but especially to
THE HAIRY BEARS.
What amazing times we have spent together!
And, as always, to my darling husband
for sharing the tears and the laughter.

Acknowledgements

With many thanks to all those who have contributed to this novel: my Irish cousin, Peggy O'Sullivan, for her help with the Irish Gaelic; retired physician and co-founder of the Berkshire Medical Heritage Centre, Marshall Barr, for his advice on historical medical matters; my friend Geri Laithwaite, who lives in part of the old dairy and kindly shared her knowledge of the building's history; Tavistock historian Gerry Woodcock; and last but not least, my friend Paul Rendell, Dartmoor Guide and historian and editor of *The Dartmoor News*, for his help and support.

One

'Here, you, give me that back!'

The young girl buying a pasty at the stall in Tavistock's Market House grabbed the arm of the youth who had snatched her purse, her reactions as quick as lightning. The lad tried to shake her off, kicking at her shins, but she replied by smashing her fist across his face. He dropped the purse, which was back in her possession in a trice, and disappeared into the crowd before anyone could stop him.

'Yes, that's it, run away afore I call the constable!' the girl shouted after him, flushed with rage, and turned back to the stall with an angry jerk of her shoulders. 'Now then, where were I?'

The stallholder had his hands on his hips, laughing uproariously. 'Got a proper right 'ook on you there, cheel! Wouldn't 'ave expected it from a little thing like you! 'Ave the pasties on me. It be worth it for the entertainment.'

'Oh, right, thank you,' the girl replied as the fury slid away from her.

She took the pasties gratefully, although she wasn't going to tell the man that there was barely enough in her purse to pay for them, the rest of her money being prudently sewn into her bodice! It wasn't a very good start to their life in the small market town. Still, at least they had got a free meal out of it, she considered as she made her way back to the main square where she had left her father guarding her basket and his own bundle, which contained the few possessions they had in the entire world.

'Here,' she said, handing him one of the pasties, but not telling him that she had managed to acquire them for free. She held the purse strings, and if her father thought there might be some money going spare, he would want to spend it on a bottle of beer.

They munched on the pasties, both of them ravenous since they hadn't eaten for two days. They had been on the road for weeks, traipsing through the countryside searching for work and sleeping rough, until that afternoon when they had arrived in the vaguely familiar town of Tavistock.

'What we'm goin' to do next then, cheel?' her father pondered, scratching his unshaven jaw.

Tresca felt so much better now she had eaten and her brain snapped back into action. The prospect of sleeping in a proper bed again filled her with ridiculous excitement and she suddenly sprang across the square and approached the first likely looking passer-by.

'Excuse me, ma'am,' she said politely. 'Would you know where my father and I might find a suitable room? We can't afford an inn, but somewhere clean and dry?'

To Tresca's relief, the young woman's plain but serene face broke into a friendly smile. 'Well, it isn't easy with all the railway folk here,' the modestly attired stranger replied in a well-spoken voice, which nevertheless had a West Country lilt.

14

'The railway has two hut villages a way down the track, but it isn't nearly enough. The town's bursting at the seams. But try Mrs Mawes in Bannawell Street. She can be somewhat brusque, but her rooms are very clean. Tell her Vera Miles sent you.'

Tresca nodded her gratitude. The railway ... that was the reason they had come into the town. The Great Western Railway had arrived in Tavistock in 1859, but now, nearly thirty years later, a rival company was building an alternative line and, like many unemployed farm-workers, her father was hoping to be taken on as a labourer.

'Thank you very much,' Tresca said to the young woman. 'Can you tell me the way, please?'

Vera Miles gave her directions and then, wishing her luck, went on her way. Tresca turned back to find her father. There he was, sitting on the churchyard wall and leaning against the railings, enjoying the autumn sunshine. Tresca crossed the square to join him, irritated that he hadn't been doing anything more useful.

'Come on,' she said tersely. 'I've found out where we might find lodgings.'

'Aw, cas'n an ol' fellow 'ave a rest?'

'No, you can't. And you'm not old. You'm just lazy.'

'No, I's not! I's an 'ard worker, you knows that!'

'Yes, I do,' she replied, suddenly grinning as her love for this exasperating man broke through her annoyance.

Emmanuel realized she was teasing and laughed back. 'Cheeky so-and-so,' he chuckled. 'Let's find this yere lodgin's, an' then us'll see 'bout earnin'

15

some money.'

They set out, arm in arm and full of hope. Rounding the corner of the churchyard, they walked up the side of the imposing church. Opposite, on a street corner, was a footwear shop stretching through several old and rickety buildings. It was evidently a thriving business, with thousands of pairs of boots and shoes on display.

'That must be the biggest shop I've ever seen!' Tresca declared, suppressing a smile. 'Maybe they need an assistant in the Ladies' Department. I'll go in and find out later.'

'That's my girl!' Emmanuel crowed with pride. 'So where does us go now? Up this 'ill with all the shops?'

'No. The lady said to turn up by the shoe shop. Come on.'

As they turned the corner, the narrow road of Market Street was littered with other smaller shops. It quickly opened into the square Vera Miles had described, and Tresca noted it all with satisfaction. Tavistock was a flourishing town, and surely she would be able to find work, either in one of the shops or as a servant in one of the more prosperous houses?

Go up Lower Back Street on the far side, Tresca remembered, and further up it turns into King Street and then Bannawell Street. She noticed that all the shops and houses gave directly on to the road, but as they climbed steeply upwards they left the grander buildings behind; now each side of the narrow street was lined with smaller houses forming one long terrace. Back in the town centre, elegant ladies and gentlemen in top

16

hats had rubbed shoulders with all and sundry, but Bannawell Street instantly gave the impression of poverty and overcrowding. Tresca noticed paint peeling off the woodwork of many a neglected house, and here and there a broken windowpane had been left unmended. Ragged children with bare, filthy feet played in the street among the muck in the gutters and the horse dung in the middle of the road. Women loitered in doorways, calling across to one another or yelling at their offspring as a rumpus broke out.

Tresca's optimism sank at once. It was an unfamiliar world, one she had never experienced before. To someone who had only ever known the quiet of the countryside, the noise was horrendous. And the smell... Fresh manure with its good, natural aroma was the worst odour she had ever come across, but here the stench of what appeared to be rotting vegetables hung in the air like a fog.

A woman, arms folded across her stained apron, was gossiping with another lounging against the wall of a house. They scowled at the strangers as they passed as if blaming them for interrupting the conversation, and Tresca felt so many eyes boring into her back. Even a dog, guarding an open doorway, snarled at them – until the unseen owner threw a well-aimed shoe at the animal from somewhere inside and it slunk back into the depths of a dark hallway.

'Everyone's looking at us,' Tresca whispered from the corner of her mouth, even though her head was held high.

'Lookin' at my beautiful darter,' Emmanuel

winked back, although Tresca could tell it was forced and that he was feeling as uneasy as she was.

Oh dear, had they made a terrible mistake coming into this town whose centre, on the odd occasion they had been there, had always appeared so attractive and prosperous? But what choice did they have when the harvest was over and they had been thrown out of the permanent jobs they had secured at Tremaine Farm? But a moment later, a woman with an infant in her arms and a hoard of little ones around her skirts gave them a pleasant smile, and Tresca nodded back, feeling encouraged as they trudged on.

'Arternoon,' a friendly voice said, and Tresca turned to see an elderly man on crutches whose leg ended just below the knee. 'Strangers in town, are us? Can I 'elp at all?'

Tresca felt fired with confidence again. 'We'm looking for a Mrs Mawes. We were told she has rooms to let.'

'Mrs Mawes, eh? Near the top she be. But whether 'er 'as any rooms, I cud'n say. All the railway folk, see. Good luck, anyway!'

''Er seemed nice enough,' Emmanuel said as the fellow stomped off on his crutches.

'Yes, he did. Perhaps it won't be so bad. As strangers, we'm bound to arouse curiosity. Come on. It can't be far now.'

The houses, including Mrs Mawes's, now had tiny but pleasant front gardens, and Tresca experienced a surge of hope. The face of the woman who opened the door, however, was as hard as nails, and Tresca braced herself to enquire about

18

a room.

'I's sorry,' the sharp voice answered, not sounding sorry in the least. 'All my rooms be taken.'

Tresca was filled with disappointment at the frosty reply. It might be the first place they had tried, but they didn't want to traipse all over the town if they could help it. She trawled her brain for some words to change the woman's mind, and suddenly remembered the modest young lady she had spoken to in the town square. 'We'm to say that Mrs Miles sent us,' she announced hopefully.

'Mrs Miles? Oh, you means Vera? *Miss* Miles. Oh, why didn't you say? Friends of hers, are we?'

Tresca hesitated. 'Well, not exactly–'

'Us doesn't like strangers, see. Us has to be careful with all they railway folk about. Now I've one room in the attic free. Small, an' it's only got a single bedstead, but there's a mattress on the floor your father can sleep on. You really *are* father an' daughter, I take it?' she added, looking them up and down suspiciously.

'Indeed, ma'am.' Emmanuel gave his most winning smile. 'The name's Ladycott, by the way. Emmanuel Ladycott, an' this be my darter, Tresca.'

'Well, you looks respectable enough,' Mrs Mawes conceded, hitching up her bosom. 'Come in and I'll show you the room.'

Emmanuel met Tresca's eye dubiously as they entered the dark little house. It reeked of stale, boiled cabbage, and as Mrs Mawes led them up two flights of stairs, the bare wooden treads creaked under Emmanuel's weight.

'There. What d'you think?'

Tresca's eyes swept over the room. It seemed so tiny compared to the accommodation over the byre that they had been used to at Tremaine Farm. But it was a roof over their heads and she should be grateful for that.

'How much?' Emmanuel finally spoke.

'Two shilling a week.'

Tresca was so shocked that the words were out of her mouth before she could stop them. 'What? That's daylight robbery!'

'You'll not find cheaper, missie, with all the railway folk in town.' Mrs Mawes nodded emphatically, her lips compressing into a stubborn line. 'They reckons over two thousand navvies and their families have come yere since work began on the line back in the spring, to say nort of the blacksmiths and foundry workers. My price includes clean sheets once a fortnight. You do your own cleaning, mind, and coal's extra when you wants it,' she concluded, jabbing her head at the grate.

Tresca glared back, equally determined. 'One and sixpence,' she said, her chin tilted defiantly.

The woman frowned. 'One and ninepence. And two weeks in advance. That's my last offer. Take it or leave it.'

Tresca glanced at Emmanuel, hoping he might try to negotiate further, but he didn't. 'All right,' she answered. 'We'll bring the money down to you in a minute.' For she wasn't going to show their new landlady where she kept her money!

Mrs Mawes grunted, and then left them alone as she clomped down the stairs. Tresca turned back into the room. Her father had already sat down on the bed, looking about him as if expecting some fascinating feature to emerge from the stark walls.

A weary sigh escaped Tresca's lips as she sat down next to him. 'Oh, well,' she murmured. 'It's better than nothing, I suppose.'

Beside her, Emmanuel's face twisted with remorse. 'Aw, I's that sorry, cheel,' he breathed. 'I knows 'ow you loved it at Tremaine Farm. It were a good summer there, an' I knows it were all my fault us 'ad to leave. But I'll make it up to you, princess, I promises.'

Tresca gave a weak smile. Oh, yes. She'd heard that one a thousand times. He was a good man, her father, kind and well meaning. He had brought her up single-handed since her mother and little brother had died of fever when she was but five years old. It couldn't have been easy for an itinerant farm labourer, and she appreciated how he had always insisted she went to school wherever they happened to be, never begrudging the pennies he had to pay as she seemed to have such an aptitude for learning. It had been the two of them against the world; they were the best of friends as well as father and daughter. She had loved him with a passion. She still did. But as she grew older, she had begun to realize that he wasn't the hero she had always believed him to be.

Tresca got to her feet and went to open the roof light. She was just tall enough to see out. It overlooked the narrow street, and Tresca pressed her forehead against the glass. Children still played in the dirt, kicking a stone aimlessly along the

21

compacted earth or idly scrapping among themselves. A woman was dragging herself up the hill with a heavy basket on each arm. A mangy cat ran out in front of her, nearly tripping her up. A man was staggering along in the gutter, a bottle swinging from his hand. Tresca drew back with a shudder. It was the last thing she wanted to see.

Welcome to Bannawell Street, she whispered bitterly to herself. And girding up her courage, she turned to her father with a determined smile.

Two

'Oi, look where you'm going, you!'

Tresca had gone down to pay Mrs Mawes the precious two weeks' rent. The landlady had taken the coins grudgingly and nodded to a pile of bedclothes on the table. Tresca had expressed her thanks through equally tight lips and begun to make her way back up the dark, narrow staircase armed with the bundle of bedding. There was shouting from one of the rooms on the first floor and then a door slammed loudly. The sounds of a baby crying, other children playing noisily and a woman swearing came from a second open door, making Tresca cringe. Above all the din, she did not hear the man storming down the stairs and she bumped into him as he passed.

'Sorry, but I couldn't see over the top of this lot!' she called indignantly at his back, but he had already thundered down the remaining flight of stairs and out of the front door. Tresca sighed wearily and was almost sent flying again as a hoard of small children clothed in little better than rags streamed past her, chased by a woman with a screaming baby in her arms.

'An' don't come back till your dad comes in!' she hollered after them. Seeing Tresca pressed against the wall, she glared at her with hostile eyes. 'What you'm staring at?' she snarled, and then her door, too, was slammed shut.

Tresca stood for a moment, letting the misery wash through her. Oh, Lord. She didn't want to live in a house like this, crammed into one room with her father – although by all accounts an entire family occupied the larger room below theirs. She took a deep breath and climbed the second staircase, wondering with trepidation who rented the other little room in the attic next to theirs.

Emmanuel was staring down at the spare mattress he had pulled from beneath the bed, and Tresca dropped her bundle on to it. 'There. You can make yours first,' she told her father frostily. This was all his fault, after all. She sat up on the bed, watching him and feeling as if her courage had been torn to ribbons.

But this would not do. After a few moments, she set her jaw stubbornly and glanced round the room again, determined to turn the place into a home of sorts. They could store the second mattress under the bed during the day to give more room. Hopefully, though, they would soon both be out at work earning money in the daytime, and perhaps they might then be able to move somewhere better.

23

'Come on,' Tresca said resolutely. 'We need to buy some food and start asking about work.' When she saw Emmanuel open his mouth in protest, she quickly shut it for him. 'No grumbling or putting it off until tomorrow. The sooner we start, the better. Our money's not going to last long at this rate.'

They walked back down the hill and Tresca felt more of a stranger than ever. But there was only one way to deal with a situation like this, and that was to face it full on. She was summoning her courage to address the next person she saw, when as luck would have it she spied the young woman with the babe-in-arms and the tribe of children who had smiled at her in the street earlier.

'Good afternoon,' Tresca said, encouraged. 'My father and I have just arrived in town.'

The woman gave another welcoming smile. 'So we're going to be neighbours, are we? Well, my name's Assumpta Driscoll, and this is Caitlin and Niamh, the two eldest, then that's Brendan, Patrick and Liam, and isn't the baby Maeve.'

'Pleased to meet you, Mrs Driscoll.' Tresca smiled down at the two little girls. The taller one stared back at her without blinking, while her sister turned her head into her mother's skirt. 'Oh dear, I hope I haven't frightened her.'

'Sure isn't she the shy one. So what can I do for you?'

'Actually, I were wondering if you might know where my father and I might find work? My father were hoping to do labouring on the railway.'

'Sure, that's easy. Connor O'Mahoney's the chap you want to see. Isn't he one o' the gangers

24

for this part o' the line. That's foreman to you. Hasn't my Rory worked with him for years. All over the country. Fair man is O'Mahoney, doesn't my Rory say. Won't stand no nonsense, mind. Be back this evening, so he will. Lodges at number eight. More respectable than the rest of us can afford.'

'Thank you very much,' Tresca nodded. She had never heard anything like Mrs Driscoll's accent before, and she found it rather pleasant. She guessed it must be Irish for it was said many of the navvies came from the Emerald Isle. All those names had a foreign ring to them and O'Mahoney certainly sounded Irish to her!

'Sure you'll recognize him easy enough. Giant of a man with hair as red as a holly berry, so it is.'

'Oh, right, thank you.'

'Not at all. And call in any time. We're at number twenty-nine.'

'I'd be delighted. In a day or two when we'm settled. We must get on now, if you'll excuse us. Need to buy some food.'

'Go to Pearce's in the square. Best value in town.'

'Thank you, I'll remember that. And I'll see you soon.'

'I hope so,' Assumpta Driscoll smiled again. 'Come on, you,' she ordered the children as she turned away. 'Goodbye for now'

'Good day to you. And thank you again. That's good, isn't it?' Tresca said, turning to Emmanuel as they continued down the street. 'Mind you, sounds pretty formidable, this Mr O'Mahoney, doesn't he?'

Emmanuel scratched his stubbly chin. 'Maybies I could find summat else, like. I's not certain I fancies working for—'

'Oh no you don't. We'll go and see him this evening. And in the meantime, I'll see what work *I* can find.'

They came down into Lower Back Street and Tresca bought a small loaf in the bakery. Then she crossed the square to Pearce's, Emmanuel trotting behind her. A slice of ham and a couple of ounces of cheese; they could do without butter and there was no point in buying anything that needed cooking until it turned cold enough to light a fire in the room. For the same reason, they need not get any tea. They would have to make do with cold water for now – once Tresca had checked with Mrs Mawes that the water supply to the standpipe in the backyard was safe to drink.

'Is that all we'm 'avin' to eat?' Emmanuel grumbled. 'If us was still at the farm...'

Tresca had to bite her tongue. If it weren't for her father and his ... well, his *weakness,* they would still have been there. Tamping down her frustrations, she repeated to the shopkeeper the question she had asked in the baker's. 'I'm looking for work,' she said in her most polite voice. 'You wouldn't by any chance have a position, would you, sir?'

Her voice had risen expectantly, but then her hopes tumbled as the man's kindly smile faded. 'Sorry, maid. I doesn't need anyone. Have you worked in a shop afore, like?'

'I'm afeared not. But I'm very quick to learn.

On the farm, I could do almost anything.'

'Farm girl, then?'

'Skilled dairymaid.' Tresca waited as he frowned thoughtfully. Perhaps he knew some-one...? 'I helped in the house and kitchen as well,' she added, since she would be happy to be taken on as a domestic. 'And on the farm I looked after the hens and helped with the harvest as well as being the dairymaid. I delivered the milk in the local villages, so I'm used to dealing with money. And, of course, I can tack up horses and drive a cart.'

'Quite an accomplished young lady, then. Wish I could help. But I tell you what. There be two dairies in Bannawell Street. Only small, but why doesn't you try them?'

'In Bannawell Street?' Tresca's eyes stretched wide in amazement. 'But ... where are the cows?'

'In fields at the top of the hill,' Mr Pearce answered with a chuckle. 'Brought down for milking twice a day, they be. I doesn't know if the dairies need anyone, mind, but don't do no harm to ask, do it?'

Tresca thanked him as she paid her small bill. Outside again, she stood for a moment or two, wondering what to do next. Emmanuel hovered at her side and Tresca could see that his eyes had locked on to the loaf and the little packets of folded greaseproof paper that contained their supplies. Could she trust him to take them back to the room while she went in search of work? He was almost salivating even though they had only recently had a pasty each, and his face had taken on that pleading, lost-dog expression she knew

27

only too well. No, it was best she kept the supplies safely in her basket.

As they trudged back up the steep hill, they found the first dairy in what looked just like one of the houses, which was why they hadn't noticed it before. Inside it was cool and dark, and Tresca's eyes took a few seconds to adjust. On a marble counter was a little handbell, which echoed in the silence when she rang it. An elderly woman shuffled through a door at the side.

'What can I do for you, cheel?' she asked with a warm smile, and Tresca repeated her question, but even as she spoke she knew the answer. 'I's proper sorry, my lover,' the woman replied. 'We'm only a small dairy an' I has a maid already. Try the other dairy up the hill.'

'Yes, I will. Thank you.'

'I's mortal sorry, but I wishes you luck.'

Tresca smiled back, though her heart felt as heavy as lead. What now? She would try the other dairy, of course, and if there was no luck there, she would visit every shop in Tavistock.

By the time they were ready to go and wait for Connor O'Mahoney outside number eight, Tresca had indeed been into every shop in the little square and Market Street, including German's Footwear and a huge ironmonger's and builders' merchant on the opposite corner – where the man she had spoken to had laughed at the idea of a *female* working there. It seemed that despite the boom in the town from the influx of the railway workers, all the extra jobs it had created had already been filled; they were six months too late.

Tresca wasn't disheartened yet; she hadn't even

touched the main shopping area of the town. And she could always go in search of domestic work. But just now, her hopes were focused on Emmanuel being taken on by this Connor O'Mahoney.

As they waited outside the house, the sun was going down and no longer shone into the narrow street. Tresca pulled her shawl more tightly about her shoulders, and as the evening chill descended, the women lingering by the doorways and the children playing in the gutters disappeared inside.

'If 'er don't come soon, I's goin' 'ome,' Emmanuel grumbled. 'My belly's rumblin' like a traction engine.'

Home? Fine home they had found! Tresca's bitterness spurred her tongue into action. 'Oh, no – you'm staying here until this fellow comes back!'

She bunched her lips mutinously, praying that Connor O'Mahoney wouldn't be long. But just as she, too, felt like giving up, the figure of a man who could be no other than the said railway works foreman strode up the hill towards them.

Assumpta Driscoll's description was a little exaggerated, but it was unmistakably him. He was certainly tall, well over six foot, with broad, muscled shoulders that strained beneath his jacket. A red neckerchief was tucked into the top of the waistcoat that hugged his firm waist, and his heavy trousers were splattered with mud from the knees downwards. He cut an altogether overwhelming figure, and out of the corner of her eye Tresca saw Emmanuel's head shrinking into his shoulders. But if he wouldn't make the approach, then she would have to.

She stepped resolutely forward. 'Excuse me, sir, but are you Mr O'Mahoney, foreman on the railway line?'

The man blinked in surprise at the young girl who blocked his path. The corners of his generous mouth twitched humorously and his bright blue eyes danced beneath the thatch of ginger hair that showed under his battered bowler hat.

'I am so,' he answered in the same lilting tone as Assumpta Driscoll. 'But one of many. Sure I'm not building the railway on me own.'

It was as if his mouth could not help breaking into a smile, and Tresca felt herself relax. He was nowhere near as terrifying as she had imagined.

'I'm glad to hear it,' she found herself smiling back. 'Cuz my father here's looking for work.'

'Is that so? Worked as a navvy before, have you?'

'No, but I's a farm labourer born an' bred, an' I doesn't see as shiftin' one sort o' muck be any different from anither,' Emmanuel answered, and Tresca was glad that he drew himself up to his full height. He might be dwarfed by the Irishman, but he was half a head taller than the average man.

'Used to hard physical work, then.' Connor O'Mahoney voiced his thoughts aloud. 'Still takes a year or so to harden someone up, mind. Picks and shovels, so it is. Twenty tons of dirt you'll be expected to shift each day, and when you can do that, you'll get paid three and sixpence for it. Can I be asking how old you are?'

'I's forty-two, sir,' Emmanuel replied at once, and Tresca inwardly squirmed. Emmanuel was *fifty*-two, having married and had a family late in life – which was perhaps why her mother had been his world. Tresca mentally crossed her fingers. Working on the land aged people's faces prematurely, and she hoped her father could get away with the lie.

'Tell you what,' she was relieved to hear Mr O'Mahoney say. 'Meet me here at daybreak tomorrow and I'll take you along. Work hard and I'll take you on at two and six a day to start off. But I need good, reliable men to turn up six days a week. If you can't do that, you'll be out, so you will.'

'Oh, I'll be there, sir,' Emmanuel assured him, doffing his cap. 'Thank you very much.'

'Hadn't I better know your name, then?'

'Emmanuel Ladycott, sir,' he replied, almost scraping the ground.

'And have you and your daughter somewhere to live? We have a couple of hut villages down the line, but sure it's not suitable for a young lady.'

Tresca was aware of the blush in her cheeks. During the weeks they had tramped the countryside and the few hours they had spent in Tavistock, she had felt like a vagrant, the lowest of the low, so to be treated with such civility was a real tonic.

'Us 'as a room yere in Bannawell Street,' she heard Emmanuel telling him. 'Arrived yere this arternoon, us did.'

'Well, there'll be work here for two or three years, so I reckon. There's tunnels and cuttings to dig and a massive viaduct over Bannawell Street here. So we'll be neighbours for some time and I shall look forward to that.'

Connor O'Mahoney raised his hat, his eyes

31

flashing meaningfully in Tresca's direction, and then disappeared inside, closing the door behind him. Another poor fellow wanting to work on the railway, he thought, as he unlaced his muddy boots. Well, he looked strong enough, although not as young as Connor really liked his men to be. Farm labourers were usually pretty tough, though. He would just have to see how Emmanuel Ladycott shaped up.

It was the man's daughter who had really caught Connor's eye. The look of determination on her face had almost made him want to smile, but there was something else about her, something he couldn't put his finger on, that intrigued him. She was a beauty, that was for sure, petite and slender yet somehow strong-looking – to match her character, he mused. Her eyes, almost like silver, had a keenness about them, and her hair had hung enticingly in a thick, tawny plait down her back. Oh, what a glorious mane it must be when it was loosened...

Connor pulled himself up short. Sweet Mother of Jesus, she was a child, and he old enough to be her father. Well, not quite, he was sure, but she had done something to his heart that he reared away from.

He turned with a sigh and padded up the stairs to his room.

Three

Tresca watched the big Irishman shut the front door behind him, then turned to her father, straining to hold her emotions in check, and saw his eyes gleaming like bright buttons in his face. Neither of them noticed the peeling paintwork or the pungent smell as they entered Mrs Mawes's boarding house and climbed the creaking stairs again. It was not until they reached the little attic room and shut the door on the outside world that Emmanuel spun round, grinning from ear to ear as joy exploded on to his face.

'Three an' six a day!' he crowed incredulously. 'That be a guinea for a week's work! Us didn't earn ten shillin' a week between us on the farm.'

'But we did have free board and lodging. And remember it'll only be two and six to start. But – oh, it's still a fortune, so you be certain to behave yourself!'

'Oh, I will, cheel, I will. Promised you I'd make a good life for us, didn't I, like?'

His joy was infectious and Tresca could not help but laugh at his antics as he perfected a little jig on the spot. She shook her head, finally releasing her own happiness and falling back on the bed with a buoyant sigh.

'If I can earn that sort o' money, *you* won't need to find a job at all!' Emmanuel announced, puffing up his chest like a preening peacock. 'My dear

Emma would've bin proper proud o' me. If only I'd found this sort o' work back along an' could've afforded somewheres decent to live, maybe she an' the little fellow wouldn't 'ave ... 'ave...'

His voice faded into the trail of desolation Tresca knew so well. It was rare that a day went by without him mentioning her mother and her little brother, even though they had died ten years ago.

'Let's not think about that now,' Tresca said gently, for she knew how maudlin he could become when he started to talk about his lost family. It was almost an illness with him, a kind of despondency he couldn't shake off. Tresca couldn't help but feel deep sympathy for him. He had clearly loved his wife passionately, and Tresca had never known him so much as glance at another woman. She scarcely remembered her mother except as a smiling blur in a blue dress, but perhaps even that was a vision she imagined rather than an actual memory. For her father, though, the memories were all too real. But it was when he became lost in that overwhelming sadness that he turned to drink, and that was the last thing they needed now.

'Let's have this little feast of ours,' Tresca suggested brightly, taking the items of food from her basket.

'Mmm!' Emmanuel's face lit up again. 'I's starvin'! Pity us didn't know for certain I'd get such a good job, else us could've bought more. But maybies the shops'll still be open. Shops in towns doesn't close till really late as I believes.'

'No, we still need to be careful. Let's see how

34

the job works out afore we start spending any more than we have to. We've not much money left and Mr O'Mahoney didn't say if you get paid each day or at the end of the week.'

'Aw, right as ever, you, cheel,' Emmanuel chuckled, sitting down beside her on the bed and tearing a chunk from the loaf of bread. 'I's that 'ungered, I could eat an 'orse.'

'I'm afeared horse isn't on the menu,' Tresca answered with a straight face, and then the two of them fell about laughing. Life was looking up again – at last!

They munched their way through half the loaf, the slice of ham and half the cheese, washed down with cold water. The rest of the food would have to sustain Emmanuel through his strenuous day's work, and Tresca would get in more supplies the following morning.

'You will work hard, won't you?' she said, chewing thoughtfully. 'And you promise me you won't get drunk again?'

Emmanuel's face coloured. 'Aw, you knows 'ow 'ard I tries to keep off the bottle. It were just with the 'arvest supper bein' the same day my dear Emma died, it made us feel so sad, I just 'ad to 'ave a little drink to cheer us up a bit.'

'But it weren't just one little drink, were it?' Tresca persisted, taking the bull by the horns. 'It lost us our jobs.'

She saw her father's mouth twist with guilt. 'Aw, I's mortal sorry 'bout what 'appened, you knows that. Worst thing I's ever done, an' proper shamed I feels 'bout it. But you knows I've niver 'urted no one when I've bin in my cups. I've oft

35

times seen men brawlin' really violent like when they'm drunk. Or beatin' their poor wives black an' blue, or their chiller. I've niver *ever* done ort like that.'

'I know, Father, I know,' Tresca assured him, patting his hand fondly.

It was absolutely true. So many times since she was a child she had waited for Emmanuel outside a village public house, watching men stagger out at closing time and lurch down the road. She always found somewhere to hide herself out of harm's way, for she had seen how some men could behave when they were blind drunk. But when her father was the worse for drink, he just became morose and ravaged by memories of his dear departed wife. When he emerged from whichever hostelry it happened to be, even if he could barely stand, the first thing he would do was look for his little girl, and he would shield her protectively from the abusive inebriation that was going on around them. He would quietly slink off to wherever they were living, deliberately avoiding any trouble – even if Tresca had to show him the way.

'So let's make this a fresh start, eh?' she said, turning to him, determination shining from her eyes. 'And you promise me that even if you have a little drink occasionally – and I *mean* little – you won't ever get drunk again,' she concluded fiercely.

Emmanuel's face moved into a solemn mask. 'I promises on your mother's grave,' he declared with sincerity.

Tresca hoped and prayed that he meant it.

It was virtually dark and time for bed, especially as Emmanuel had to be up early in the morning. He mustn't be late on his first day. If Mr O'Mahoney didn't find him waiting on the doorstep as they had arranged, he would hardly be likely to offer him another chance.

They had lit the candle in the one enamel holder in their possession, and Tresca took it to see her way down to the water closet in the backyard. It had all seemed so normal in the daylight, but now the shadows made her heart beat nervously. She could bump into any of the other lodgers, and from what she had seen of them, she wasn't at all sure she wanted to.

Out in the yard it was almost pitch black as the street lamps didn't penetrate that far. Tresca had never been afraid of the dark before. In the countryside you were only likely to come across a worker from the same farm, but heaven knew what dangers lurked out here in the yard. She clenched her jaw resolutely as she lifted the latch to the privy, and then once inside set the candle holder on the concrete floor to push across the bolt. At least Mrs Mawes kept the place relatively clean, and it smelt of bleach rather than anything else.

Tresca was relieved to go back inside the house and climb the stairs without meeting a soul. Not a sound came from behind any of the closed doors, except for loud snoring from the room where the couple had been arguing earlier that afternoon. Tresca hurried up to the attic, releasing a deep sigh of relief – and collided with a figure emerging from the room next to theirs.

It was a young woman, but nevertheless Tresca experienced a flush of alarm. In the flickering candlelight the human form took on a ghostly appearance, the bush of dark hair wild and unkempt and falling loose about the shoulders. What shocked Tresca even more was the ragged blouse half undone and revealing the top of the girl's full, ripe bosom.

'Oh.' The young woman started and visibly jumped back, and for a moment they stared at each other in silence.

'We've just moved in next door.' Tresca spoke first, her voice firm and assured now. 'My father and me.'

'I's sorry to 'ave startled you,' their neighbour replied. 'I's just goin' out.'

Going out? It seemed a funny time to be going out, especially on her own and dressed like that – or rather in a state of undress. But Tresca stood back, letting her new acquaintance pass and watching her hurry down the stairs.

'How very odd,' she mused as she went back into the room, where Emmanuel had pulled out the mattress. 'I've just met our neighbour, a young woman, and she's just going out. All on her own, too.'

'None of our business.' Emmanuel shrugged casually. 'Well, us must get some sleep if I's goin' to work in the mornin'.'

'You'm sure you don't mind sleeping on the mattress?' Tresca asked as she undressed down to her underwear. 'You'll need a good night's sleep if you'm going to be working hard during the day.'

38

'No, I's quite 'appy for you to 'ave the bed, my little princess. An' I really promises we'm goin' to 'ave a new life from now on!'

Tresca gave a wry smile as she climbed into bed. She hoped he was right. But it was so lovely to be in a proper bed again, even if the mattress was a little lumpy. It wasn't long before her father's rhythmic snoring told her he was asleep, but it wasn't disturbing her. After all, he would need a good night's rest before the strenuous day ahead, and he would need to impress Connor O'Mahoney with his strength.

Tresca closed her eyes, but the day's events kept whirling inside her head. All the strangers she had met conjured themselves up in her brain: Vera Miles, Assumpta Driscoll and her brood of children, the nice lady in the dairy, the one-legged man and, of course, Connor O'Mahoney – all of whom had made their arrival in the town less daunting. But then her thoughts moved to the less savoury characters: the boy who had tried to rob her, the staring women in the street, and above all the other lodgers in the house. She wasn't at all sure about them, but if Emmanuel kept to his promises, they could hopefully move on to better accommodation in a few weeks' time.

Yet Tresca's heart ached; it would have been so much better had they been able to stay on at Tremaine Farm. She could picture now the night it had all come to an abrupt finish – the peaceful, idyllic harvest supper that had ended in disaster.

'Well, everyone,' Jethro Tremaine had announced, 'you've done a good job and the corn's all in. It's not been the best of years and times are hard, but I reckon we'll survive. So sup up and enjoy yourselves. My wife and young Tresca've been busy in the kitchen and we've been blessed with a fine evening. So my thanks to you all, and let supper begin.'

A jovial cheer lifted from the small group seated around the long trestle table in front of the farmhouse. Over the last two weeks, the wheat and barley had been reaped and bound into sheaves, left in stooks to dry in the fields, and then brought in and stacked either in the barn or in the two carefully constructed and weatherproof 'mows' in the rickyard. But Jethro would not need to employ outside workers any longer. It was not a huge farm and he and his two sons could probably manage to strip the fruit trees and thresh and winnow the corn themselves – in between ploughing and sowing, harvesting turnips and storing mangolds, and everything else that had to be done on a mixed farm in the autumn. It was by being thrifty that they had survived and could afford to pay a fair rate for a good day's work – and provide a harvest supper that was second to none.

Tresca's heart lifted with contentment as her eyes swept down the laden table and convivial chatter broke out once more. Behind them, the late summer sky was almost aflame as the sun floated downwards, and everyone was in a happy mood as they helped themselves to hard-earned food and drink.

'My missus tells us you're really good in the kitchen,' Jethro said to Tresca. 'And we need a good dairymaid and just one hired hand through

40

the winter. So I'm hoping you and your father will stay on.'

'Oh, yes, please!' she cried delightedly.

'I be thankin' you kindly, sir,' Emmanuel nodded with his mouth full of pie, and Tresca wished vehemently that he had better table manners. It had dawned on her as a young child that most yeoman farmers conducted their eating habits in a more genteel fashion, and she had begun to copy them. She had even tried to mimic their more refined speech a little, since one day, she hoped... Well, she wasn't quite sure what she hoped. To marry a farmer's son and become a farmer's wife, she supposed. But a yeoman rather than a tenant farmer ... maybe even young Alex Tremaine who she got on so well with. Oh, yes, she was determined that she wasn't just going to be a travelling dairymaid all her life.

Before too long, the table was scattered with the remains of the meal Mrs Tremaine and Tresca had laid out so painstakingly. But as the night went on the earthenware ale pots continued to be refilled, and lively banter and gentle laughter wafted across the balmy evening air. Then Obadiah Burrell fetched his old violin and his lively jigs soon had them all on their feet, making wheels of eight, skipping under arches of joined hands and weaving in and out of opposing circles. Tresca was dancing with Alex, the laughing faces flashing past her in a blur as she dreamed that the night would go on for ever.

Then Alex stopped abruptly, wrinkling his nose and sniffing. 'Can you smell smoke?' he whispered, and walked off in the direction of the yard.

41

An acrid whiff wafted into Tresca's nostrils, too, becoming stronger as she followed him around the corner of the farmhouse. The darker silhouette of the barn was outlined against the open, star-scattered sky, and Alex was a grey figure moving in a pale, low mist drifting from a crack below the great barn doors.

Tresca froze. It wasn't mist, of course it wasn't. It was smoke.

As if to echo her stunned thoughts, she heard Alex scream at her across the space that separated them. 'Fire!' he yelled. 'The barn's on fire! Get help!'

Dear Lord. Tresca's legs felt imprisoned in their own leaden weight, but with a supreme effort she forced herself to run back towards the scene of celebration. 'Mr Tremaine!' she cried above the clamour of merrymaking. 'There's smoke coming from the barn!'

Jethro's mouth dropped open in appalled disbelief, but an instant later he was rushing past her, shouting over his shoulder as he went. Tresca ran after him. She had seen that Alex had opened one of the barn doors just enough to squeeze inside – so as not to fan the flames, she realized instinctively. Jethro, too, had disappeared into the expanding cloud of smoke, and Tresca followed him without a second thought.

It was difficult to see through the thick, grey veil that stung her eyes, but she could make out the murky shapes of Jethro and Alex frantically beating with their coats at the flickering fingers of orange that were darting through the edge of the corn stack. Tresca at once picked up an empty sack and began beating at the flames herself. It was then that she spied the familiar figure lying on the barn floor. Emmanuel was fast asleep, snoring heavily in a drunken stupor. Beside him was an empty jug of ale, and where his arm had flopped away from his body, his pipe had fallen from his open fingers, charring the corn stalks around it.

Oh, God. Tresca's blood froze in her veins. Emmanuel had set the barn on fire.

She saw Jethro turn and jabbing his head at the prostrate form, he barked at his son, 'Get him out of here!'

Alex swung round, and for an instant his streaming eyes met Tresca's. Then between them they dragged Emmanuel outside. He grunted in protest, his incoherent words slurred and incomprehensible. They abandoned him out of harm's way and then Alex turned to the group of horrified faces that by now had assembled in the yard and began issuing instructions.

Tresca stood, locked in shock, as people rushed all about her. It was a nightmare. Her eyes moved from Emmanuel to the smouldering barn and back again, but the time for recriminations would come soon enough.

A human chain was being formed across the yard from the pump to the barn and Tresca took her place, passing buckets full of water in one direction and returning empty ones in the other. It was unreal, voices becoming hoarse from both shouting and the smoke, and the faces on either side of her smeared with sweat and black smuts. She must look just the same, hands filthy and the

43

new frock she had stitched from some material bought cheaply at market totally ruined. No matter. Her heart was pumping furiously, every muscle strained and aching. But she must keep on. For her father had done this and she must help to put it right, even if it killed her. And just as she felt she couldn't go on, they were told to stop.

Everyone collapsed, exhausted, to the ground, bone-weary and eyes bloodshot from the billowing smoke that only now was drifting away. But Tresca could not rest. She stumbled through the darkness to the now open door of the barn. The floor was awash with water and wet, slippery stalks of ruined corn, but it looked as if the hungry flames had at last been extinguished. Jethro and Alex had evidently dragged the burning sheaves from the stack to stop the whole lot going up in flames. Though the stack was partly demolished as a result, most of it remained intact and the danger appeared to be over.

'We'll need to keep a vigil all night,' Jethro croaked. 'It'd only need a stray spark somewhere for the whole barn to go up.' When he saw Tresca standing there, his blackened face moved into a scowl. 'Best keep your father out of my sight or I'm likely to throttle him for this!' And he stomped past her out into the yard.

Tresca shrank on the spot. Jethro was furious, and justifiably so. But not as angry with Emmanuel as Tresca was herself. He had committed the cardinal sin for a farm-worker of smoking in a barn. It was beyond belief – and when Jethro had just offered them permanent positions. Well, they could say goodbye to those! Tresca's dreams lay shattered at her feet and she sank down into the broken pieces, hands over her face as she wept.

And that was indeed the end. The next morning they were dismissed, and as Tresca followed her father along the rutted lane from the farm, she swallowed down the despair and humiliation that burnt her cheeks.

'Us'll find summat soon enough,' Emmanuel had assured her, but they hadn't. Harvest was over and there was no long-term work to be found, even here in Cornwall, where the mixed farms were so labour intensive. Then they had heard about the railway and had pinned their hopes on that. And so they had crossed back into Devon. Though her heart ripped when she thought of Tremaine Farm, Tresca was determined that they would make a good life for themselves in Tavistock. Feeling content at last, she drifted off to sleep.

The knocking sound that came from the next room in the middle of the night cut sharply into her dreams. Her eyes sprang open, staring into the darkness. The knocking grew louder, faster, filling her with uncertainty. As the noise increased further, Emmanuel stirred on the mattress on the floor beside her.

'What the devil–?' Tresca heard him mumble, and then a man's cry echoed through the wall and the knocking stopped.

'What were that?' Tresca asked in alarm. 'Be someone hurt, do you think?'

It was a moment or two before Emmanuel

45

answered. Reluctantly, it seemed. 'No. No one's hurt, cheel. Now go back to sleep.'

His voice sounded odd, ashamed almost. Tresca obediently tried to snuggle down again, confused. There were sounds of movement coming through the wall still, but quieter and different from before. What on earth was going on, Tresca wondered, imagining the older girl she had met earlier on the tiny attic landing?

'You bitch!' A man's voice shouted through the wall. 'Promised us more than that for me shillin', you did!'

The unmistakable thwack of a vicious slap speared into the night and Tresca shuddered. The feelings, the thoughts, the *realization* that thundered in her head made the nausea rise in her throat. No wonder Emmanuel had encouraged her to go back to sleep.

'Father...'

'Aw, I's sorry, princess. Tiddn what I wants fer you. P'r'aps us can find somewheres else to bide. In a while, when I's taken on permanent, like.'

Tresca swallowed hard. And in those few seconds it was as if she had grown up and become a woman. In knowledge if not experience. Oh, God, perhaps the world was not so good after all.

Four

Tresca took a deep breath and hurried down the stairs. Emmanuel had got off to work on time, excited at the prospect of being gainfully employed again. Tresca had stood on tiptoe to look out of the roof light and watched him walking down the street as a grey dawn broke over the town. Bannawell Street wasn't as deserted at that hour as she would have imagined. Several men were setting off to work, and further down the hill Tresca could just see the unmistakable figure of Connor O'Mahoney emerge from his lodging house. Excellent timing, she congratulated herself – since she had been the one to wake first and had prodded Emmanuel's sleeping form into action.

Twelve hours it would be before she saw him again, and here she was, a young girl alone in a town full of strangers. And strangers they would remain unless she did something about it. She washed in the little enamel bowl, dressed and tidied the room. She fixed her old felt hat on her rebellious hair, wrapped her tattered shawl about her shoulders, and made for the outside world.

'Good mornin', miss!' a voice greeted her almost as soon as she stepped into the street. 'Find a room at Mrs Mawes's place, then?'

Tresca turned, and at her shoulder stood the one-legged man they had met the day before.

'Yes, thank you, we did. And my father's got a job labouring on the railway, so we'm mighty pleased.'

'That's good. Goin' to take some years to build, so 'er'll 'ave a job fer some time. Goin' my way, are us? Down the 'ill?'

'Yes, I am actually.'

'Then us can walk together,' he said, setting off, and Tresca fell into step beside him. 'The name's Elijah Edwards. Cas'n shake your 'and cuz I needs them both fer the crutches. I's a saddler. Works fer the big place in West Street, I does. Doesn't need two legs fer that. Lost my leg in the Crimean. Wud've died if it 'adn't bin fer that Florence Nightingale woman. Course, she weren't so famous then. So when I gets back 'ome, I trains as a saddler an' bin doin' it over thirty year now.'

'Really? We'm farm-workers, so we know all about tack an' the like. Used to drive the milk cart, I did.'

'Well, us makes all sorts o' saddles an' 'arnesses yere. Fer gentle folk what rides their 'orses or drives their traps. An' then all the commercial vehicles fer the brewers an' all the coal merchants, like.'

'You don't think they'd need anyone to see to customers, do you? I'm looking for work as well, an' as I know all about that sort of thing–'

'I doesn't think so, and I doubts they'd consider a woman even if they did. But I'll ask anyway. Have a good day, then, cheel.'

'Yes, I will, thank you.'

She stopped outside Pearce's and watched Elijah continue across the small square. Nice

48

fellow, she thought, but a pity he didn't think there might be any work for her at the saddler's. She'd have liked that, and she knew as much about tack as any man. But never mind. If Emmanuel's job on the railway became permanent, finding work herself wouldn't be as essential.

She bought some more supplies and then made her way back up to the dairy. Perhaps they could afford a little milk on the strength of Emmanuel's expected wages.

'Good day, my lover,' the pleasant woman greeted her cheerily. ''Ow's you today?'

'Very well, thank you. Can I have a gill of milk, please?'

'Course you can. Got ort to put it in?'

'Yes, this,' Tresca replied, handing her one of their enamel mugs. 'Hmm, has a certain smell, doesn't it, a dairy?' she observed, sniffing delicately. 'Don't make cheese, though, do you?'

'No, my lover,' the woman chuckled as she measured out the pure white liquid. 'We sells most of our milk, an' we turns the rest into butter. Sally's churnin' it now. Not found any work, then?'

'No, but my father has. On the railway.'

'Ah, good. But if I 'ears of ort fer yersel', I'll let you know.'

'Oh, thank you, Mrs, er…'

'Ellacott. Jane Ellacott. An' you?'

'Tresca Ladycott. So how much is that?'

She paid for the milk and carried everything carefully home to the little attic room where she made herself some breakfast. Things were falling into place now, and she didn't feel quite so much of a stranger. Perhaps she should call in to As-

49

sumpta Driscoll and let her know that her father had been taken on by Connor O'Mahoney. But much as she would have liked to see the friendly woman again, it was really more important for her to look for work. And so, feeling quite confident, she set off down the hill once more.

She explored Bank Square, Market Street and Lower Back Street, just to make certain that she hadn't missed anywhere the previous afternoon. The only place she hadn't been into was the Tavistock Mineral Water Company, but they didn't have any vacancies either, so instead Tresca turned up West Street away from the town centre.

She decided to work her way up one side and down the other, enquiring at every establishment she passed. She found two butcher's shops, two boot and shoe makers, a baker's and a grocer's, but none could offer her any work. The coal, corn and manure merchants scoffed at her for being a young girl, even though she insisted with spurning contempt that she had worked on farms since the cradle and knew as much about the relevant commodities as they did. She stood outside, fuming with anger. Perhaps she would have better luck in the florist, but the woman there turned her away when she couldn't name the beautiful, exotic blooms in the shop – all grown in hothouses, Tresca supposed, since it was autumn. Seasonal chrysanthemums were the only ones she recognized.

Oh, Lord, things weren't going too well, were they? She certainly wouldn't try the hairdresser's or the gentleman's tailors. She could sew a shirt for Emmanuel or a simple dress for herself, but you needed to be apprenticed for years in tailoring proper. She stopped next outside a confectioner's shop, and her mouth watered at the display of delicacies in the window: fine, intricate work requiring artistic skill as well as knowledge of ingredients. She would love to learn how to make such marvellous treats.

The two ladies inside were very interested in her, and Tresca's heart lifted on a crest of hope, but they had only just taken on a new girl to train up. Disappointment showed clearly on Tresca's face, and they gave her a chocolate truffle to make up for it. All done up in a tiny box of fancy card and tied with a little ribbon, Tresca had never had anything like it in her life, but it only served to deepen her sadness.

She went outside and her despondent gaze searched about her. It didn't seem that there were any more shops further up the hill, so she crossed over the road. Perhaps luck would be on her side in the extensive hardware and ironmonger's shop that she came to next. Tresca glanced up at the name over the door: Trembath and Son. From the window display, it appeared they specialized more in household goods, with prettily decorated china and glassware, cutlery and kitchen appliances as well as hinges, door handles, screws and nails and such.

An elderly man in a calico apron approached her as she strode into the shop, and a little bell over the door clanged tunelessly. 'What can I do for you, miss?'

Tresca came straight to the point. 'I'm looking for work, actually. I'm used to–'

'Aw, it'll be young Mr Trembath you want to see. You hold on here and I'll fetch 'en for you.'

The fellow called through a door behind the counter and Tresca waited patiently, avidly taking everything in: furniture polish, beeswax, blacklead, shoe polish, brushes and brooms. Items as familiar to her as the back of her hand. She turned, her face a study of confidence, as a figure emerged on the other side of the counter.

'I understand you're looking for work, miss?'

The young gentleman gave her an affable smile. At least that was a good start. He was somewhat older than she was, in his mid-twenties, she reckoned, and had an open, approachable face. With any luck, she could persuade him of her worth.

'That's right,' she replied at once. 'I've never worked in an actual shop before, but I've been doing a milk round for some time, so I'm used to dealing with customers and handling money. I'm a dairymaid really, but I've often worked in farmhouses as well, as a maid and in the kitchen, so I know all there is to know about the sort of merchandise you have here. So I'd be as good an assistant as any man.'

She held her breath, lips pursed softly, as she watched the young man's reaction. She had worded her approach in the most professional manner she could, and she observed as the man's face broke into an amused but not unkind smile.

'I'm sure you would, and I'd have no objections to a young lady serving in my shop. In fact, I think it would brighten things up a little. But the fact is that we don't require anyone at present. I really am sorry.'

Tresca sucked in her lips and nodded. At least he had given her the time of day – but not a job. And she supposed he couldn't just invent one any more than any of the other shopkeepers could. Thank heavens Connor O'Mahoney had taken her father on. She just prayed that the job became permanent.

She hadn't realized how much time her fruitless search had taken, but there weren't many more shops before she would be back where she'd started. At the back of her mind lurked the old saying that you always found what you wanted in the last place you looked, and she felt convinced that she would be taken on in one of the remaining establishments.

She wasn't. She stood outside the last shop, defeat gnawing at her heart, but still she refused to give up hope. There was Duke Street that led into Brook Street, both lined with shops and other commercial concerns. But it was getting late now, and her stomach cramped with hunger. Children who had been at school earlier were playing outside, the narrow streets in shadow and the air turning chilly.

Tresca pulled her shawl more tightly about her shoulders. She had completely grown out of her coat last year and hadn't had one for the whole of the previous winter. But if matters went their way, she could buy a second-hand coat at a stall she had noticed in the Market House.

The steep climb up Bannawell Street warmed her up, and she let herself into the house. It was much quieter today, with only the faint sounds of young children coming from the crowded family room on the first floor. The stairs creaked as she went on, and as she turned the corner she came face to face with the lady of the night who occupied the attic room next to theirs.

Tresca stopped dead, feeling so awkward that crimson flooded her cheeks. The realization of what had been going on through the flimsy dividing wall had shaken her to the core. She mumbled some evasive greeting under her breath, averting her head and squeezing past as she tried to make her escape. Her heart turned a cartwheel, though, when the woman grasped her arm.

'I's proper sorry if I disturbed you last night,' she apologized, her voice low and hesitant. 'I ... I doesn't usually bring ... bring people back yere. Only last night, there weren't nowheres else to go, an' I were ... I were desprit. Please don't say ort, I begs you. Mrs Mawes'd throw me out an' I've got nowheres else to go.'

Tresca lifted her eyes to the older girl's face. She really did look as desperate as she claimed to be. There was a burgundy mark on her cheekbone, spreading towards her eye. A result of the clout she had been given by her client, no doubt.

Tresca felt herself soften. 'No, I won't,' she found herself saying. 'But please don't do it again. It's not very nice when you'm just next door.'

'Oh, bless you.' The girl's taut face sagged with relief. 'I promises not to bring anyone back yere again.' She held Tresca's gaze, making her feel uncomfortable, but then the girl's full mouth moved into a smile. 'Bella,' she said, nodding her head so that her halo of unkempt hair bounced up and down. 'Best you knows no more 'bout me

54

than that.'

Tresca felt a twinge of sympathy. 'I'm Tresca,' she introduced herself. 'And my father's Emmanuel. He's been taken on on the railway. I just hope it works out. I've been looking for work all day but I've not found any.'

'Well, good luck. You'd 'ave a better chance than me, I can see that. Not too bright, me. That's 'ow I ended up... But you doesn't want to 'ear 'bout that,' she ended wryly. 'I'll see you later, I expects.'

'Yes, I expect so,' Tresca murmured in reply.

Prostitute, she pondered as she went inside. She wasn't too young to know what that was. The idea appalled her, and she had imagined some coarse and bawdy trollop, foul-mouthed and legless from drink. Bella, if that was her proper name, was nothing like that, and a touch of pity brushed against Tresca's bemused heart.

But it wasn't her problem and she had things to do. Emmanuel would be tired and hungry after his long day. It would be a pleasant welcome for him to have his meal set out ready and waiting, and the truffle in the little box would be a nice end to their meal.

'How did you get on today?' she asked, dancing with enthusiasm when he eventually came in.

'Mighty well. 'Ard work, mind, an' look at us. Niver bin so muddied in all my born days, not even pullin' mangolds. Let me wash mysel', an' then I'll tell you all 'bout it. An' what 'bout you, princess? Any luck wi' a job?'

'No,' Tresca sighed dejectedly. 'I went all up West Street. Took me all day and no luck. But I'm

55

getting to know some of the neighbours. And I bought a drop of milk from the dairy. Mrs Ellacott, she is.' She paused, wondering if she should tell him about Bella; she knew his opinions on morality. She was saved from the dilemma as she looked down. 'Oh, your boots *are* muddy, aren't they?'

'An' my trousers. Bound to be when you'm shiftin' so much earth. That Connor O'Mahoney were right. I cas'n quite keep up wi' the regular navvies. 'Er drives them pretty 'ard. An' 'er won't stand no nonsense, I can tell you. Mind you, 'er's only one foreman out o' many, so p'r'aps others isn't so strict.'

'And are most of them Irish?'

'No, not at all. I means, lots o' them is. But I's 'eard all sorts o' different accents. An' they'm not a bad bunch. O'Mahoney couldn't be standin' over me all day, so the others showed me what to do, Rory Driscoll especially. I cud imagine some o' them gettin' drunk an' causin' a right aud uproar, but most o' them is decent enough. Now then, my stomach thinks my throat's bin cut, so let's 'ave this supper afore I faints from 'unger. An' what's that there?' he demanded, frowning at the little coloured box that contained the chocolate truffle.

'Oh, that's a surprise!' Tresca answered, tossing a carefree laugh into the air since Emmanuel's day appeared to have gone so well. 'You'll have to wait and see!'

56

Five

When Tresca knocked at number twenty-nine, the door was opened by the child she recognized as Assumpta's eldest daughter, Caitlin.

'Good morning. Caitlin, isn't it?' Tresca smiled. 'Do you remember me? I'm—'

'I do so,' the little girl said flatly. 'Are you wanting to see Mammy?'

'Yes, please,' Tresca answered, taken aback at her directness. Poor child seemed aged beyond her years.

She led Tresca down the hallway to a door at the back of the house. Tresca took in the room at a glance. It was a decent size, with a small range in the chimney breast, but a double bed on either side left little enough room for the rustic table that stood in the middle. Assumpta, Rory and their six children evidently lived in this one room, just like the noisy family who lived in the room on the first floor at Mrs Mawes's house. But this space at once radiated with a sense of calm and happiness, and Tresca noticed a large crucifix hanging on the wall.

Sitting on one of the beds with the baby in her arms, the young woman looked up and her drawn face at once brightened into a smile. *'Failte!* Come in! Sure it's pleased I am to be seeing you again. Rory says your daddy talks about you such a lot, and haven't I been wanting to get to know you meself.'

'Really?'

'Oh, yes. So will you be sitting down,' Assumpta invited her, gesturing towards the other bed.

'Thank you.'

The small children who were sat on the bed shuffled along to make room for her. She noticed there were pillows at both ends, so the children must sleep head to toe. It was something Tresca had heard about but never seen. She supposed it was little different from sleeping in a barn on a bed of straw shared with the mice and the occasional rat – which she had done often enough herself.

'Are you settling in well? Do you mind if I feed the babby? She has a bottle sometimes, but I'm feeding her as long as I can meself.'

'No, not at all.'

Nevertheless, Tresca tried to avert her eyes for the sake of Assumpta's modesty, but her gaze was drawn back by the serene picture of motherhood and the little snuffling noises made by baby Maeve as she sucked greedily from her mother's breast. Meanwhile, the other children were staring at Tresca as if they expected her to perform some magic trick. Even Niamh managed a shy smile. So with Assumpta busy with the baby, Tresca felt it was up to her to start a conversation.

'Now, let me see if I can remember your names,' she said, putting on an exaggerated frown. 'Caitlin I remember, and I think you'm Niamh.'

The little girl nodded, her eyes wide, but her elder sister put in solemnly, 'Bet you can't spell

58

it, mind.'

'Spell it?' Tresca raised her eyebrows. 'Well, let me see. Is it N...E...V...E?'

'No, sure it's N ... I ... A ... M ... H.'

'Really? Well, I can see you've a lot to teach me!' Tresca gave a hearty chuckle and was pleased to see Caitlin's serious face move into a half smile. 'Is that Irish spelling? You must be very clever. And what was that word your mother said just now? Fail-something?'

'*Failte*. Means welcome.'

'I must try to remember that.'

'We try to teach them their mother tongue as much as we can,' Assumpta told her, 'even though none o' them has ever been home.'

'Never been to Ireland?'

'Rory and me, we came over here looking for work as newlyweds, so we did. Never been back, though me heart aches fer the place. Met Mr O'Mahoney on the boat over. A fine man, even if he were so young then. Already been working on the railways, he had, and took Rory along with him. Rory works hard, but Mr O'Mahoney always understood the engineering side o' things. And sure that's why he's a ganger now and Rory's just a labourer. We could do with his wages, mind, but there we are.'

Assumpta paused to change the baby over to her other breast, and Tresca's gaze wandered about the cramped room again.

'It must be hard for you to manage,' she sympathized.

'Sure it is, but isn't each little soul a blessing from above. I wouldn't have it any other way, and

59

Rory's a good man. Never goes out getting himself drunk or thieving like some o' the navvies do.'

'Do they? I know they have a reputation for it, but I've not seen ort like that.'

'Not been here of a Saturday night yet, have you? Stay indoors, so you should. It's not all the navvies, o' course it's not. But many o' the bachelor laddies from the hut villages come into town, and can't they run amok when they've been drinking. Well, now, *acushla macree,* I think your mammy's run dry.' She moved Maeve on to her shoulder, doing up the buttons of her blouse with the other hand. 'Shall you be having a cup o' tay with us, young Tresca?'

'No, thank you. I just came to thank you for telling us about Mr O'Mahoney. I don't know what we'd have done if he hadn't taken my father on. I spent all day yesterday and the day afore looking for work in a shop but without success. So I thought I'd try some of the big houses next week. Try and go into service. It couldn't be a live-in position, mind. I couldn't bear seeing my father for just a few hours each week.' Tresca bit her lip at the half lie. The truth of it was that she needed to be there all the time to make sure Emmanuel kept on the straight and narrow and didn't succumb to his weakness.

'Ah, yes.' Assumpta gave a heartfelt sigh. 'Don't I miss me own mammy and daddy something terrible. Not having seen them for eight years, and they've never met the children. Though haven't me brothers and sisters given them enough grandchildren between them to populate the whole of Ireland. Some o' them has gone to America, mind, and we'll never see them again.'

'America? Oh, that must be hard for you. But at least you *have* family. It's just my father and me.'

'That must be hard, too. Sure I'm lucky having all the little ones around me. And Caitlin's so good at looking after her brothers and sisters.'

'But...' Tresca hesitated only for a moment. 'Shouldn't she be at school?'

'So she should. And so should Niamh. But the Holy Mother knows we can't spare the pennies for school. And doesn't Miss Miles call in most days to give them some lessons and she's as good as any teacher.'

'Miss Miles?' Tresca glanced at her in astonishment. 'You don't mean Vera Miles?'

'Why, would you be knowing her?'

'I met her the day we arrived here. It were she as directed us to Mrs Mawes.'

'Ah, wasn't she sent by the Lord Himself to help us all. A lovely lady, even if she is a Protestant. Didn't himself object to her coming into our home at first, until he saw what a saint she is. Works among the poor of the parish, even though she's as poor as a church mouse herself. Parents died when she was young, and ever since she's lived on a tiny allowance from some rich uncle in Bath, provided she never sullies the family name by going out to work.'

'Well, next time you see her, please would you tell her we found a room at Mrs Mawes's house, and thank her for me?'

'Why not have that cup o' tay? Then you can

61

thank her yourself. She'll be here before too long.'

'Do you know, I think I will! And we can all get to know each other better. Now, you'm Niamh and you'm Caitlin,' she said, deliberately getting them the wrong way round. 'And your brothers are Tom, Dick and Harry.'

Caitlin frowned. 'No, they're Brendan, Patrick and Liam.'

'That's what I said. Tom, Dick and Harry.'

'No. They're...' And then the grave child started to giggle as she saw the teasing expression on Tresca's face.

As Tresca hurried back up the hill, rain battered down from the sky, turning the road into a filthy stream as horse dung and other debris were washed away. Within those few minutes, the rain had soaked through Tresca's shawl to her shoulders, but it was worth it for the few happy hours she had spent with Assumpta and the children. Vera Miles had appeared as predicted, although not a great deal of instruction had taken place. Tresca had told tales of her life on farms in the area, which Vera declared was as much a part of their education as learning their letters. Now Tresca's heart was lighter than at any other time since she had come to the town.

She hurried indoors and up the stairs, leaving a wet trail behind her. Emmanuel would be drenched working out in this all day, but at least he had a thick jacket and a waistcoat underneath, rather than her shawl and thin, flimsy dress. She shivered as she reached the first-floor landing.

Should she dare to light the fire yet? The previous evening they had bought some coal and lit a fire in the small grate. The cramped room had soon warmed up, the coals glowing a comforting orangey-red. Tresca had been back to Mr Pearce for some tea and a couple of slices of bacon, and they had feasted on their first hot meal for days. She had planned a simple stew for tonight, and the idea made her mouth water. It would seem like a banquet – until she remembered the tasty and unlimited fare they had enjoyed at Tremaine Farm. She shook her head, driving the regret to the back of her mind.

It was as she was climbing the second dark and narrow staircase that she met the lanky figure coming down. She was used to Bella now, though the older girl kept herself to herself. So her words took Tresca completely by surprise.

'Aw, you'm wet through. I's got a fire goin' in my room. I's just goin' down fer the privy, but does you want fer go in an' warm up?'

It only took Tresca a moment to make up her mind. She could easily have declined, but she found herself rather liking Bella, and it was hard to associate her with her *profession* – if you could call it that.

'Thank you,' she smiled back. 'I'll just change into some dry clothes.'

How very strange, Tresca reflected, as she let herself into the tiny room that was home – at least for the time being. She had spent the morning in the company of two devout women who shared their dedication, if not their religion. And now she was about to befriend someone who lived the most ungodly life imaginable. But that was Bannawell Street for you, and Tresca found herself caught up in its mysterious web. Vera had explained that, since the clearance of the slums several decades ago to make way for the grandiose Town Hall and the new Market House, Bannawell Street was possibly the oldest and poorest area in the town. It was certainly known for being overpopulated, and so it followed that its inhabitants would be a mixed bunch, from Elijah Edwards and the homely Mrs Ellacott, to the unfriendly woman in the room below theirs ... and Bella.

Tresca hung her wet clothes over the bottom of the bedstead to dry and put on her spare set. Oh, wouldn't it be marvellous one day to have a larger wardrobe of clothes? She said a little prayer that her father's job would become permanent. She had spotted a coat on the second-hand stall in the Market House, and could purchase a length of a warm woollen material to make herself a dress for the winter. And she could work herself up a night-dress, too – a luxury she hadn't enjoyed for some time, either!

She felt uneasy as she entered Bella's room, but she need not have worried. It was a little untidy, but no different from their own. It was only when Bella invited her to sit down on the bed, since there was not a chair in the place, that the bile rose in her throat as she envisaged what had gone on there a few nights earlier.

'Would you like some tea?' Bella asked casually. 'Or summat stronger?' she added, jabbing her head towards a half-empty bottle of gin.

Tresca gulped. 'No, thank you. I've just come from a friend and I'm awash with tea.'

'You 'as friends yere, then?'

'I have now. Didn't know them afore we came here.'

'That's good, then.' Bella spoke on a wistful sigh. 'Niver 'ad no friends, me.'

'Oh, why's that?' Tresca asked, bitten with curiosity. 'You seem friendly enough to me.'

'No, I's not really. I 'as fer keep mysel', well, *apart*, you might say. 'Ave fer in my line o' business. Fer keep mysel' safe. An' when folk larns what I does, well, they treats us like the dregs o' the earth. An' that's what I is. But *you*.' She paused, fixing Tresca with dark, penetrating eyes, and Tresca saw the livid bruise that had spread over her cheekbone. 'You'm different some'ows. Underneath you was afeared when us fust met, but you was determined not fer let it show. An' when you larns what I be, you didn't shun us like most folk does. In one so young, you'm either naive or very grown-up.'

'Grown-up, I'd like to think,' Tresca replied. 'But have you no family either?'

'If I 'as, I doesn't know where,' Bella scoffed. 'Fust I knows o' life were in a tumbledown cottage where a woman took in foundlings. Treated us like animals, she did, until one day I runs away. An' bin lookin' arter mysel' ever since. Ten year old, I were.'

A spear of pity and horror stabbed Tresca somewhere below the ribs. 'That's dreadful. But how on earth did you survive?'

'Slept rough. Stole. Picked apples off trees and

pulled carrots in the fields.' Bella shrugged, but then her eyes hardened fiercely. 'Wasn't niver goin' in no institution agin, not arter bein' in that orphanage. Rather slit my throat than go in the work'ouse.'

She jerked her head towards the top end of Bannawell Street where the huge, formidable building of the Tavistock Union Workhouse stood guard like a fortress. But surely it couldn't be that bad to be an inmate – and certainly preferable to earning a living lying on your back. Tresca couldn't imagine anything so heinous and degrading. Poor Bella, to be reduced to that.

'So did you never go to school?' Tresca ventured.

Bella gave a derisive cackle. 'School? 'Ow could I 'ave gone fer school? Wish I 'ad. Mightn't 'ave ended up like this. But you'm a clivor maid, I can see that.' She narrowed her eyes as she met Tresca's gaze. 'Don't you iver end up doin' what I does, no matter what. It's disgustin', and I 'ates mysel' cuz of it.'

For a moment or two, Tresca didn't know what to say. She felt strangely touched and wanted desperately to help, but what could she do when she herself had been traipsing round the town for two days in a vain search for work? 'What about going into service?' she suggested lamely, but she wasn't expecting Bella's reaction.

'Huh, got mysel' a job in service, all right,' she snorted. 'But then the son decided 'er fancied me. An' 'er, well, 'er forced me, you might say. Said 'er'd find a way to 'ave me dismissed. But I were dismissed anyways. They said I were leadin'

66

on their precious son. All o' thirteen, I were. An' out on the streets agin. An' then I discovered men'd pay fer what 'er took from me fer nort. An' that were it.'

Tresca stared at her, appalled. 'Oh, I'm so sorry,' she breathed, her voice trembling with compassion. 'That's a terrible story. But I tell you what,' she added, suddenly decisive. 'One day, if I ever have a big house – and I'm determined I will one day – I'll take you on as my housekeeper and no one will ever hurt you again!'

Bella turned to her, a rueful smile on her face. 'It don't do no 'arm fer dream, I s'pposes. But ... can us be friends anyways?'

'Of course we can! But right now, I must start preparing the dinner.' She made for the door, but glanced over her shoulder with her hand on the latch. 'I'll always be here for you, Bella.'

And as she went out, she saw tears collecting in her new friend's eyes.

By the time Emmanuel came home, the room smelt tantalizingly of the stew Tresca had cooked. She turned to her father in happy anticipation, but the smile slid from her face as she saw him.

'Oh, no,' she barely had the voice to utter. 'Don't say you haven't been working? You hardly look wet at all–'

'I's bin workin' all right. But Mr O'Mahoney 'ad a spare waterproof in 'is 'ut, an' 'er lent it to us.'

Tresca breathed out a sigh of relief. 'That were kind of him.'

'Well, 'er could see I were workin' real 'ard, like.

Most o' the men 'as waterproofs, but I niver 'ad one. There be usually summat that needs doin' indoors on a farm if it's that bad. But fust thing I's doin' when us 'as a bit more money, like, is fer buy mysel' one o' they waterproof. An' you'll 'ave a proper warm coat an' all.'

'Oh, you gave me a fright, then,' Tresca laughed. 'So, it's still going well?'

'It is that! An' I's famished an' that there stew smells mortal good. Eh, my little princess!' Emmanuel laced his arm about her shoulders and hugged her tightly. 'You an' me, us is good together, bain't us?'

Tresca's mouth moved into a smile, but somehow it didn't reach her eyes – or her heart. Yes, their situation was improving, but she would far rather they had still been at Tremaine Farm. Most of all, Bella's tragic tale was haunting her. Later, when Emmanuel had eaten, she would relate it to him. Much as he would abhor Bella's way of life, she knew he would be as appalled as she was when he heard how the poor girl had ended up that way. Oh, yes, he was a good man, her father, despite his faults, and she was so lucky to have him.

Six

'I reckons this calls for a celebration!' Emmanuel grinned, cock-a-hoop, as he emptied his pockets on to the bed. 'Fifteen shilling fer a full week's work. On top o' the four days' pay from when I started midweek last week. Us is rich, princess, proper rich! An' O'Mahoney says I can stay on proper, like.'

'Oh, that is good news. I'm mortal proud of you, Father. But we can't afford to be complacent yet. You need that waterproof and I bought that coat–'

'Two shillin' in the market! You could 'ave treated yersel' to a fancy new one. My princess deserves–'

'No, Father. We've a long way to go yet. The rent's due again and there's coal to buy now it's getting colder. And I still haven't been able to find a job. You know the only one I were offered were as a live-in housemaid, and I didn't want that.' She looked at him fondly, trying to hide her true thoughts. The image of him lying drunk in the barn while the hay smouldered around him had faded little over the weeks. Though her insides screwed in protest, she knew that she couldn't trust him to keep sober.

'Look on the table,' she told him.

'Oh, my little princess, some baccy an' a bottle of beer!'

'Now, you make it last all evening. I'll not have you go out tonight. It's Saturday, and I know what Assumpta said. You'll get mixed up with some of the lads you know on the railway and I won't see you till the morning.'

'Aw, you'm an 'ard woman,' Emmanuel teased. 'But you'm my treasure, an' all! Let me wash my mucky 'ands, an' then you can tell us what you've bin doin' all day. Apart from cookin' this fine smellin' meal. Now, 'as you seen that Vera Miles agin?'

'I have indeed. And I think she'm expecting us in church tomorrow.'

'Church? Oh, you knows we'm chapel–'

'We'm not anything in particular, you old fraud! I want you brushed up in your Sunday best for Matins.'

'Huh, *what* Sunday best would that be, then?'

'I washed your other shirt and it's ironed and ready. And I shall wear my new coat so you've no excuses.' She lifted her head haughtily as she dished out a plate of sausages and creamy mashed potatoes that she had managed to cook on the fire during the afternoon. 'Now get yer chops round that!' she cried in the most common way she could, and they both burst out with laughter.

Sunday dawned bright and clear. After all the recent rain, such a dry and sunny day was most welcome. Although the fallen autumn leaves were soggy beneath their feet, those that were still on the trees in the churchyard glinted copper and gold in the sunlight. The difference in the weather made the town centre appear fine and inviting,

70

and Tresca felt her heart lift as they came out of the church. She had spoken briefly to Vera, who had been delighted to see them in the congregation, but she told Tresca that she had to discuss something with the vicar.

'Good morning to you!'

'Good day to you, Mr O'Mahoney, sir,' Tresca heard Emmanuel return the greeting.

She turned to the tall, broad figure that had appeared beside them. Mr O'Mahoney looked so smart in a well-cut suit, a grey cravat folded about the winged collar of his snowy shirt, and shoes polished to a mirror-like shine.

'Miss Ladycott,' he smiled, revealing strong, even teeth.

'Mr O'Mahoney.' She dipped her head, feeling awkward at her own humble attire and almost wishing she *had* bought herself a new coat at the outfitters instead of the slightly worn second-hand garment she had settled on. But then she pulled herself up short. It was all right for Connor O'Mahoney. He was doubtless well paid and probably had no one else in the world but himself to spend his wages on. 'I didn't see you in church,' she added somewhat coolly.

'Sure you wouldn't,' he answered quite affably. 'I'd have gone to confession and then to mass if such a thing were to be had hereabouts.'

Mass? Oh, of course, how stupid of her. He must be Catholic like Rory and Assumpta. Tresca felt quite foolish and found herself muttering something about the weather.

'It surely is a fine day,' Connor replied, seemingly oblivious to her embarrassment.

71

'Would you care to take a stroll along the old canal? Or have you other plans for the morning? In which case, I shall detain you no longer.'

His eyebrows lifted above his intense eyes, which in this light appeared an almost peacock-blue, and Tresca considered that, despite his heavy brow and angular jaw, he was actually quite a good-looking fellow. She glanced at Emmanuel and was disappointed at the shuttered expression that came over his face. But this was his boss, and though she herself would have preferred to have made some excuse, she could also see that it might be to their advantage to socialize with him.

'Yes, we should love to, wouldn't we, Father?' she replied enthusiastically, throwing Emmanuel a glance that told him he must obey. 'It'd be grand to take some fresh air. I've been cooped up indoors these past two weeks nearly.'

'Don't I know how you feel,' Connor agreed. 'Sure I'm outdoors working all the time, but you don't get the views and don't I miss the mountains at home. It's this way,' he gestured, indicating the opposite side of the churchyard.

Tresca followed, wishing Emmanuel wasn't dragging his feet as they reached the road on the far side. 'Mountains?' she asked, smiling sweetly.

'Beautiful, so they are. Take your breath away.'

'But we have Dartmoor. Some of the tors are quite high.'

'So they are. And didn't I help build the railway that goes up to Princetown. Wasn't a ganger then, I wasn't, but I really enjoyed working out on the moor. The most scenic line I've ever worked on, and haven't I worked all over the country. But sure, it's not home.'

They had crossed over the road and reached the large open space which the disused canal cut through as straight as a mine rod. The land was used for grazing, but the owner, the benevolent Duke of Bedford, allowed public access, so Tresca had heard. As Connor had implied, it provided a pleasant spot for a stroll, ambling alongside the ribbon of water that had once bustled with commercial activity when copper mining had thrived in the area.

'Do you ever go home, Mr O'Mahoney?' Tresca asked, willing Emmanuel to join in the conversation, but it seemed he had his mouth resolutely shut.

'Once every few years if I can make it. The important thing is to make as much money as I can while the railways are still expanding. There's not much work at home. But I'd rather not think about it on this fine morning. Here.' He drew a brown paper bag from his pocket and held it out towards them. 'I come to feed the ducks when I can.'

'Thank you, sir.' Emmanuel spoke at last, taking a slice of stale bread from the bag. 'The little divils'll be hungered this chillsome morning.'

Tresca, too, took some bread and began to break it up and throw it in the water. At once, several ducks descended in a flurry of feathers and wild quacking, and Tresca reflected that not so long ago, she and her father might have fallen on such a handout with equal zeal.

The big Irishman was chuckling now at the

ducks' antics. What a complex fellow he was, Tresca thought. Dominant, self-assured, intimidating almost, and yet here he was, enjoying such a small pleasure as feeding ducks and talking ruefully of the home he missed. Tresca was glad of the interlude, but she really could not think of anything else to say to him.

'Ah, Mrs Trembath, good morning to you, and Mr Trembath.'

Tresca could not have felt more relieved as Connor turned to the couple walking towards them along the path. The young man sported a good-quality jacket with grey-striped trousers, and the older lady, whose gloved hand was placed delicately on the crooked arm of her companion, was wearing a fine, tapered coat and matching velvet hat. Tresca had noticed them in church and the young fellow had looked familiar, though she couldn't think why. But she had made so many acquaintances since they had come to Tavistock that it wasn't surprising.

'Good morning, Mr O'Mahoney. A fine one it is indeed.' He raised his hat, but Tresca noticed that the woman looked on sourly, frowning at his friendly attitude. He went on eagerly, 'I hope those lamps proved adequate.'

'Indeed they did. And I thank you for your help. I'll soon be putting in an order for another couple of barrels of lamp oil, so I will. I trust Pethicks paid the last bill promptly?'

'They certainly did. A pleasure to do business with you, Mr O'Mahoney.'

He lifted his hat once more, and as he shifted his gaze from Connor to his two companions, Tresca saw his eyes rest on her for longer than was polite. But an instant later, the woman tugged surreptitiously on his arm – although Tresca had seen the small movement – and with a forced, haughty smile, directed him away. Connor touched his fingertips briefly against the brim of his hat and watched them move off.

'Who were they?' Tresca asked. 'Trembath, you say? I recognize the name.'

'They have the ironmonger's and hardware shop in West Street.'

'Oh, I know where you mean. Of course. I went in there asking if they had any work. It were him I spoke to and he were very pleasant.'

'So he is. But I did give him a big order. I've bought other things for the railway from the other ironmonger's, too – Bakers, on the corner of Market Street. All the big items come from the foundries in Tavistock we've taken over, but for smaller things, well, it's good to make allies of the locals. Mind you, it'd be difficult to make a friend of the old mother there, it would. Face like a shrew, wouldn't I be thinking.'

Tresca blinked at him in shocked embarrassment. Thank goodness Mrs Trembath and her son had walked on out of earshot. Then she saw Emmanuel grinning impertinently as he enjoyed the joke, and she found herself laughing, too. For she was beginning to see that there was more to Connor O'Mahoney than met the eye.

Seven

'Tresca, are you there? Oh, pray sweet Mother of Jesus you are!'

Tresca looked up with a start as the door flew open and a young woman, eyes wild as her hair, burst into the room, a squealing babe in her arms and several small, bewildered children at her skirts.

'Assumpta! Oh, God Lord, whatever's the matter?'

Assumpta's face turned paper white. 'There's been another fall at that Shillamill Tunnel. And, oh, Holy Mother of God, isn't my Rory buried beneath it all!'

Her bloodless lips were trembling and Tresca felt her own chest squeeze with horror. The very same thing had happened a few days previously when the facing of the tunnel had collapsed, but the men had been eating their lunch so mercifully no one had been hurt. Boring had been suspended while the tunnel had been shored up securely. It had brought it home to Tresca how dangerous the work could be, and she had feared for her father's safety. But it had been Rory Driscoll, with his tribe of young children at home, who had been caught in this new fall.

'Oh, Assumpta, my poor lover.' Tresca's voice shook with pity. 'Sit yoursel' down here and–'

'No. I must go to him. Must be there. In case ...

in case… Could you be looking after the children for me? They like being with you. I can't take them with me. I don't want them to see … see their daddy…'

She choked on the last words, her eyes brimming with pleading tears. Tresca put an arm about her shoulders, could feel her juddering with fear.

'You don't *know*,' she said firmly. 'But of course I'll look after the children. Give me the babby–'

'Weren't you sent by the Angel Gabriel himself. Thank you so much,' Assumpta faltered, handing over the rag-clothed infant.

'Good luck,' Tresca answered, her own voice quivering.

'Pray for us, Tresca.' And making the sign of the cross, Assumpta fled the room and raced down the stairs.

Tresca stood for a minute, jiggling the baby in her arms, while the other children stared up at her, wide-eyed and expectant. She gulped hard. Poor mites. Did they understand?

And she, too, said a prayer.

The priest in his long robe led the lugubrious procession out of Tavistock's new cemetery back towards the town centre. Assumpta, so frail and on the brink of collapse, leant on Connor O'Mahoney's arm while Caitlin and Niamh walked behind, solemnly holding hands. Tresca held Brendan and Patrick by the hand, Emmanuel was carrying Liam, and Vera Miles had taken charge of the baby.

Behind them, a dozen or so navvies who had

77

worked with Rory Driscoll had come to see him laid to rest. They would need to get back to work now, as would Emmanuel, as they were officially paid by the hour and Mr O'Mahoney did not have the authority to stop their wages from being docked. They headed off in the direction of work, Emmanuel handing Liam into Tresca's arms. The priest had a final word with Assumpta before hurrying off towards the existing station to catch his train back to Plymouth, leaving the remaining mourners to find their way home. Caitlin took charge of the boys and Tresca felt her heart tear at seeing the small girl having been turned into a world-weary little mother, since Assumpta seemed to have fallen apart.

'Thank you so much, Mr O'Mahoney,' Tresca heard Assumpta murmur in an old, cracked voice as they reached their lodgings back in Bannawell Street. 'Sure, if it weren't for you, Rory wouldn't have had a holy priest to bury him.'

'Think nothing of it, Mrs Driscoll. Shall I be coming in with you?'

'No. That's very kind of you but I'd prefer to be on me own with the children, so I would.'

Tresca exchanged glances with Vera, who had been a tower of strength to the young widow. Surely it would be better for Assumpta to have some company at this terrible time?

'We'll go with her,' Tresca assured Connor O'Mahoney, nodding sombrely.

But Assumpta was having none of it. 'Sure you won't. You've all been wonderful, so you have, but I really need to be on me own.'

For the first time since that dreadful afternoon

when the broken body of her husband had been dragged from beneath the tons of fallen earth and rock, Assumpta spoke with some strength in her tone. So perhaps it was time for her to be alone with her children.

'Well, you know where I am if you need me,' Tresca said doubtfully, standing Liam on his feet.

'And let me give you this.' Connor pulled two five pound notes from his pocket. 'Your widow's compensation from the company.'

Assumpta nodded her thanks, took the baby from Vera and disappeared inside with the children. Vera took her leave and Tresca stood facing Connor, watching as he shook his head sadly.

'You gave her ten pounds,' she said curiously. 'She's only entitled to five, isn't she?'

Connor shrugged. 'Sure I can round it up from me own pocket if I want. If she knew some of it had come from me, she might not have taken it.'

A rueful smile pulled at Tresca's lips. Connor O'Mahoney was a hard taskmaster, Emmanuel had told her. He drove his men with his own vigour during their daily twelve-hour shifts, not letting them slack for a minute. But he was highly respected not only by his own gang of labourers, but by his fellow foremen. He was able to consult with the engineers on almost a level pegging, it was said, and often interpreted what was needed to the other gangers. But when it came down to it, he was a man of hidden compassion. His gift to Assumpta must be the equivalent of at least two weeks' pay. And apparently when the tunnel wall had collapsed, he had led the rescue with no thought for his own safety and working with

79

twice the strength and determination of any other man.

'I must change and get back to work,' he told Tresca now. 'Will we walk up the hill together?'

'Yes, of course.' And she fell into step beside him.

'It's a sad day, so it is,' Connor went on. 'Yesterday a fellow broke his leg further down the line. The first navvy to be admitted to the town's new cottage hospital. Dangerous work, so it is, and then there's all the explosives. That's why we have to be so strict with all our men, for their own sakes. And why it can be a lonely job as a foreman. The engineers, like Mr Szlumper for instance – isn't he the chief engineer for the Bere Alston to Lydford section of the line – they're far enough away from the labourers. But gangers are like pigs in the middle, so I'm inclined to keep meself to meself. Which is why it's good to have company such as yourself now and then.'

'Mr Szlumper, did you say?'

'Of Messrs Galbraith and Church. But don't we need a good man with the line being such a challenge. Well, here we are then.'

He stopped outside his lodging house but seemed to hesitate. Tresca was not sure why, so she said the first thing that came into her head. 'Thank you for being so kind to Assumpta, Mr O'Mahoney. I'm sure she appreciates it.'

'Sure, it was nothing when she's lost the love of her life. But … seeing as we're likely to be neighbours for some while,' he faltered, 'would you be after calling me Connor? Mr O'Mahoney sounds so formal.'

'Oh, well, yes, of course, if you like, Mr ... I mean, Connor,' she corrected herself.

'And ... and may I make so bold as to enquire as to your given name?'

He suddenly looked almost bashful and she was sure he flushed slightly. 'Tresca,' she answered, a trifle amused.

'Tresca? Sure that's mighty pretty. I've not heard it before.'

'It's Cornish. After my great-grandmother. Father always liked it.'

'Then he chose well. A pretty name for a pretty girl. But I must get back to work if you'll excuse me.'

He raised his hat and then opened the door behind him and went inside. Tresca continued up the hill. Mr O'Mahoney, *Connor,* was a man of secret depths. Some feeling she could not quite fathom came over her, but she carefully put it to one side as she set her mind to the task of preparing the evening's supper.

Some time later, with the stew simmering away in the pot worked into the bed of coals in the small grate, Tresca felt she could relax and picked up the book she had borrowed from the public library. Thomas Hardy, one of her favourites. She was soon engrossed in *Far from the Madding Crowd,* her mind transported by the relationship between Bathsheba and Gabriel to the far away countryside of Dorset, her heart gripped with turbulent passion.

Oh, where *was* Emmanuel? It had long been dark outside and Tresca had put down her book and lit their one candle some time ago. Connor's words echoed menacingly in her head. Dangerous work. Oh, God, surely nothing had happened to Emmanuel. Bad things came in threes. Rory, and the man who had broken his leg – not her father as number three? He should have been home, what, two hours ago.

As another ten minutes ticked by, Tresca was just putting on her coat to go down and see if Connor was back from work and could shed any light on the matter – what if he, too, had not returned because there had been another accident? – when she heard heavy footsteps lumbering up the top stairs and the door was flung wide.

She knew instantly, and a red flash of anger snuffed out her crushing fear. 'Where the hell have you been?' she attacked her father at once. 'Oh, there be no need to tell me! You reek of it! How many have you had?'

'Aw, don't be like that, princess!' Emmanuel slurred, staggering into the room. 'A man's got to 'ave a drink once in a while.'

'*A* drink, maybe! But not a day's wages, which is probably what *you*'ve spent! You just can't be trusted, can you? Oh, sometimes I really ... really...'

A squeal of desperation broke from her throat and she shot out of the door and careered down the stairs. Outside, the cold, damp air stung her cheeks. She wanted to scream, but instead stomped down the darkened street in an agony of frustration. She needed to turn to someone she knew, but she couldn't burden Assumpta, and she certainly couldn't go to Connor. He must never find out about her father's drunken tendencies, or he would sack him there and then.

She stumbled on halfway down Bannawell Street, slowing her pace as she finally came to a halt by one of a pair of grander, double-fronted houses on the right that almost seemed out of place among the other humbler dwellings. She stood in the circle of light beneath the lamp-post opposite and leant her face against its cold surface as the tears rolled down her cheeks.

She did not hear the front door open.

'Excuse me, miss, are you all right?'

The voice made her jump and she at once knuckled her eyes in embarrassment, lifting her head haughtily. 'Yes, I's proper clever, thank you.' And then, realizing it was quite obvious that she wasn't, added, 'A friend of mine buried her husband today and I were crying for her, that's all.'

'I'm mighty sorry to hear that. But, oh! Aren't you the girl who came in the shop looking for work? And then you were walking by the canal with Mr O'Mahoney the other Sunday. Won't you come inside for a minute, Miss ... er...'

'Ladycott,' she answered automatically, sniffing away her final tears. 'And you're Mr Trembath.'

'I am indeed. Our business is in West Street but we live here. So, would you care to come in?'

'Thank you very much, but no. I must be getting back.'

'Well, if you're sure–'

'Morgan, what in heaven's name are you doing out there in the street at this hour and letting all the cold air in?' A woman's imperious tone came from within. 'And who is that ragamuffin you're talking to?'

In the lamplight, Tresca saw Morgan Trembath roll his eyes skywards. 'I'd better go,' he sighed, turning away. 'Coming, Mother!' he called, and went inside, shutting the door quietly behind him.

Tresca stood in the street and drew a deep, calming draught of air into her lungs as the anger pulsed out of her. Parents! She set her jaw defiantly and began to climb back up the steep hill.

Eight

'Morning, Assumpta. How are you today? Oh, Vera! I didn't see you there.'

Tresca paused on the threshold. Her friends were folding the few spare clothes that the Driscoll family possessed into a neat pile, while the children played about their feet.

'What's happening?' Tresca frowned.

She saw a smile light Assumpta's thin face for the first time since Rory's death. 'We're going home, so we are. To me parents' in the Emerald Isle. Sure they're as poor as church mice, but we'll be happy together.'

'Oh, I'm so pleased for you. But will the compensation be enough to pay for your passage? I could give you a few shilling if it would help.'

Assumpta reached out and squeezed Tresca's arm. 'You're a good person, so you are, Tresca.

But there's no need. Vera's arranged it all for me.'

'Oh?'

Vera looked up from folding a child's undervest that was more hole than garment. 'Well, you know I work with the poor of the parish, and I have a lot of dealings with Dr Greenwood. Lovely man he is. I happened to mention how Assumpta longed to go home now she's, well, on her own. And Dr Greenwood said he knows someone, a Captain Bradley, who sometimes sails to Dublin for Irish whiskey. So he wrote to him, and he had a telegram back this morning. Captain Bradley is in Plymouth, and as luck would have it he's sailing to Ireland at the end of the week. He's promised to take Assumpta and the children for free. All she has to do is get to Plymouth by Friday.'

'How wonderful! Warms your heart, doesn't it, to know there are such good people in the world?'

'The good man even said we can have his cabin, so he did. It'll be cramped, but aren't we used to that. And he says he'll stop anywhere along the way, so I'm hoping he can take us to Rosslare.'

'That *is* good. But I'll miss you.' Tresca smiled, even though her heart had indeed saddened at the idea of losing her new friend.

'Won't I be missing you, too. We've only known each other a few weeks, but you've been so good to me.'

Tresca nodded, trying to hide her disappointment. She was glad for Assumpta. After all, what could be worse than losing your husband so tragically? But at the back of Tresca's mind niggled the frustration with her father on the night of the funeral. Although Emmanuel had not come home late or drunk again, she suspected that he had taken to having a swift beer on the way home each night. Could she trust him to keep to just the one?

The memory of that night, waiting for him up in their horrible little room, sliced into her brain – and suddenly clicked it into thought. If Assumpta was leaving, her room would be up for rent. Although cramped with a whole family living in it, it was twice the size of the attic lair she shared with her father. It was on the ground floor, so with the water closet being just across the yard it would be far more convenient – especially at night.

'This seems callous to ask you now,' she said, almost holding her breath with anticipation, 'but do you know if the room's been relet yet? It's so much nicer than ours.'

'Didn't the telegram only come this morning. So I'm sure the landlord would be delighted. Doesn't he live next door, so why don't you go straight round? Two and six a week the rent is, but he does like a month in advance to start, and then he collects it every fortnight after that.'

Tresca did a quick calculation. Emmanuel had been working for about six weeks. He had bought himself a waterproof and some new strong boots that were essential for his work. Tresca had sewn him a couple of shirts from material bought in the market and was now making herself a new winter dress. They were eating better quality food and they had treated themselves here and there; nothing extravagant, but enough to brighten their lives a little. Tresca had saved everything else, so they could easily afford the ten shilling advance on the rent, and her father would be paid again at the end of the week.

She did not hesitate. They had just paid another fortnight's rent to Mrs Mawes, which she doubted the woman would return, but no matter. If she didn't take up Assumpta's room straight away, she would lose it. There was no use waiting until Emmanuel returned from work and discussing the matter with him. Her mind was made up. Without further ado, Tresca went next door to the landlord.

'Well, I'll see you tonight, in our new home!' Tresca exclaimed the following morning.

'Aw, didn't I say I'd make a good life fer my little princess one day?' Emmanuel chortled back.

'It's just the beginning, mind. We can spend some money to make it nice, but after that we'll start saving again. And I'm certain to find a job eventually, and then, well, who knows?'

'So bein' dismissed from Tremaine Farm weren't so bad, arter all?' Emmanuel suggested, lifting a hopeful eyebrow. 'But I musts be off or the lord an' master won't like it.'

Tresca grinned back and shooed him out of the door. It was going to be a busy day. They might only be moving down the street, but everything had to be packed up, their few new clothes carefully folded and placed in Tresca's basket, and other items tied into a bundle. They had half a bucket of coal left, and she certainly wasn't leaving that behind. She hummed as she worked, for this was going to be the first day of a bright, new future!

She and Vera were shortly to see Assumpta and her family off from Tavistock's South Station – as it was to be called to differentiate it from the new station, when it eventually opened. She donned her coat and hat and stepped out on to the tiny landing, taking a deep breath to contain her jubilation. It wouldn't be right to appear so joyous when her happiness had come out of Assumpta's tragedy, and she would be sad to say goodbye to her new friend. Her heart darkened at the prospect, and she hesitated a moment before setting out.

It was then that she heard the muffled sobs coming from Bella's room. Poor Bella. What a hard life she had led, but Tresca had never heard her cry before. The sound tore at her heart and she tapped softly on the door.

There was no answer and the weeping ceased at once. But something was obviously wrong and Tresca opened the door and went inside. Bella looked up, her cheeks ravaged with tears.

'Bella, whatever's the matter?' Tresca sat down beside her on the bed and put her arm around the girl's trembling shoulders.

It was some moments before Bella was able to answer. 'Oh, Tresca,' she gulped between sobs. 'I's in terrible trouble. I's … I cas'n pay the rent,' she blurted out in a rush.

Tresca breathed a sigh of relief. 'Is that all? There's no need to worry about that. I'll pay it. And you can pay me back when you can.'

Bella instantly threw up her head. 'No, you

cas'n do that,' she protested.

'Yes, I can. There's no greater pleasure than helping a friend. Oh, there's your rent book.'

She picked up the dog-eared little book and opened it at the last page. Fury frothed up inside her as her eyes scanned the figures. 'She's put your rent up to two and three a week? The mean old cow! One and nine we've been paying. Well, we'll soon see about that!'

'Tresca, don't–'

But Tresca was already flying down the stairs and an instant later was banging loudly on the landlady's kitchen door. When Mrs Mawes opened it, her expression very clearly showed her displeasure at being so rudely disturbed. But Tresca was bursting with unleashed rage and thrust her finger at the entry in the rent book.

'How dare you put Bella's rent up like that? Two and three for that little hole, when we'm only paying one and nine. And it's not even worth that! Now here's one and nine, and you can make do with that, you avaricious old biddy!'

Her cheeks flamed scarlet as she glared at Mrs Mawes, but the woman lifted her nose and sneered. 'Just cuz you'm leaving, you cas'n tell me what to do. It's two and three fer that little strumpet, or she goes.'

'Fine. She can come with my father and me, then, and you'll have two empty rooms to find tenants for. Bella!' she called, making for the stairs.

'All right, then,' Mrs Mawes conceded grudgingly. 'One and nine.'

Tresca turned back in triumph. 'I want it written in the rent book. One and nine a week for the next year. And your signature against it.'

If looks could kill, Tresca would have been stone dead, but the woman did as she demanded. Tresca watched her, still fuming but pleased that she had achieved justice for her friend. 'Thank you,' she said with a forced smile. 'And here's this week's rent. Good day to you, Mrs Mawes.' And snatching the book from the woman's fingers, she walked with supreme dignity up the hallway.

Tresca and Vera waved a tearful, bitter-sweet farewell to Assumpta and her six children on the station platform. They all hugged, wishing each other luck and promising to write, and then the train lurched and began to chug forward, taking Assumpta Driscoll, her three sons and three daughters out of their lives for ever.

'Come along, we've work to do,' Vera said, wiping away a tear, and they made for the exit.

Vera helped Tresca to move her and Emmanuel's belongings, such as they were, into their new home. The landlord was able to swap the two double beds for two singles and Tresca set to, turning the room into a proper little home.

When Emmanuel returned at the end of the day, he was amazed. The two single beds were neatly made, leaving a good space in the middle. The little range, freshly blackleaded, was throwing out a glorious heat, and a frying pan, sizzling with two chops and a pile of onions, was filling the air with an appetizing aroma. If Tresca noticed a whiff of alcohol on her father's breath, in her cheeriness she chose to ignore it.

'Aw, this be all proper grand!' Emmanuel

declared, and Tresca agreed with him.

'Good morning, Mr Trembath.'

The young man poring over the pile of papers on the counter lifted his head, eyebrows raised in surprise. Then, as recognition dawned, he smiled broadly.

'No, it's all right, thank you, Mr Penwaite,' he said as the elderly assistant Tresca had seen before shuffled forward. 'I'll serve this customer.' He turned back to her, lowering his voice as the warm smile reached his cinnamon-coloured eyes. 'So, how is my young lady of the lamp-post? I do hope your friend is recovering from her loss.'

A shadow passed over Tresca's face. 'I don't suppose it's something you ever get over. But she's gone back to her family in Ireland and she were mortal pleased to be going home.'

'Of course. And really, how insensitive of me. I know how it was when my father died. He built up this business from scratch, you know. Now, how can I be of service?'

'I'd like to look at some saucepans, please,' Tresca announced, feeling proper grand that she could afford a new one for cooking on the range stove, which, though small, could fit two pans at the same time. 'And I'd like to choose an oil lamp, too.'

'Shall we see to that first?' Morgan Trembath came round to her side of the counter, pointing to a shelf displaying a range of lamps. 'Is it for indoor or outdoor use?'

She chose a prettily shaped one with a fluted glass globe for one shilling and ten pence, and a

91

small saucepan for cooking vegetables. Morgan would deliver them free of charge, and she paid the bill, smiling her thanks. As she turned away from the counter, a severe-looking woman she recognized as Mrs Trembath entered the shop. Tresca nodded briefly at her, but the woman seemed to stare right through her.

'What are you doing, serving customers?' Tresca heard her demand as she reached the door. 'That's what we pay assistants for. And especially not a little guttersnipe like that. Did you see her threadbare coat? And wasn't she fraternizing with that great Irish navvy chap recently? Really, Morgan, you should know better.'

Tresca's heart plummeted. She had been having such a wonderful time, buying things she had never thought they would be able to afford. She had found a thick rug to go over the floorboards, and some pretty gingham material to make two new bedspreads. The room would look so fresh and cosy by the time she had finished.

Now she felt ashamed and disillusioned, her happy mood chased away. How dare Mrs Trembath talk about her like that – especially when she had just spent a fair sum in her shop. Tresca set her jaw defiantly. Oh, damn her! What a hateful woman. And pity young Mr Trembath for having her as a mother.

'You've got this room looking really lovely,' Vera told her admiringly as she drank tea from one of the pair of fine china cups Tresca had bought in one of Tavistock's many little shops.

'Well, with just my father and me living on his

wage, I've been able to spend some money on it,' Tresca explained, a little bashful at Vera's praise. 'And it's all somewhat better than our room at Mrs Mawes's house. Oh, I'm sorry.' She pulled herself up short, blushing with remorse. 'I shouldn't have said that. Mrs Mawes is your friend, and we were mortal grateful when you sent us to her when we first arrived here.'

But Vera flapped her hand dismissively. 'I wouldn't exactly call Mrs Mawes a friend. She was very upset when her husband died. That's how I came to know her, through the vicar who conducted the funeral. I think the real reason, mind, was that she didn't know if she could afford the lease on the house.'

'She doesn't own it, then?'

'Good Lord, no. Virtually all the houses in Bannawell Street belong to the Duke of Bedford. But he doesn't mind people taking in lodgers, so that's what I suggested to Mrs Mawes. She didn't like the idea at first. Considered it beneath her. Though God knows why.'

Tresca blinked in astonishment. She could not have imagined the refined, benevolent Vera Miles either thinking or speaking like that. The surprise must have shown on her face as Vera laughed aloud.

'I'm not so naive as you may think,' she grinned. 'And I'm so looking forward to having you as a friend. But I must be off. Some unfortunates of the parish to call on. Thank you so much for the tea.'

'It's my pleasure, Vera. Do come again, whenever you want.'

'I should be delighted. Thank you.'

Tresca saw her out of the front door, feeling like a real lady. She had worked hard to have the room looking so fresh and pleasant, but now it was finished, she would spend no more time or money on it. And she would renew her search for work, for what was she to do all day with just the one room to keep clean and tidy? But first she would walk up the hill and call in to see Elijah Edwards's wife. A lovely woman she was, but her legs were playing her up in this bitterly cold weather and she couldn't get out, so Tresca was sure she could do with a little company.

She went out into the frosty December afternoon, grateful for her warm coat, and turned up the street. The coalman was coming down the hill, his massive carthorse blowing clouds of steam into the air, and Tresca stood back to let the wagon past. Beautiful animal, she sighed to herself, and just for a split second she saw herself back at Tremaine Farm. A pang of regret pricked her heart, and she forced it aside. No looking back, only forward.

Besides, Bannawell Street really was beginning to feel like home.

Nine

It was mid-afternoon and Tresca was preparing the vegetables for the evening meal when the door opened quietly. She glanced up, and there was Emmanuel on the threshold.

'What you'm doing here?' she asked in surprise. 'Has the tunnel collapsed and you've had to stop work again?' It had happened the previous week, a minor fall laying off a few labourers, including Emmanuel, for an afternoon while more skilled men shored it up.

Emmanuel rubbed his chin, his lips wrinkling into a sheepish knot. And slowly Tresca's heart sank as her father staggered into the room.

'That there bloody Irish Paddy 'as given me my marchin' orders,' he grumbled. 'Said as I were drunk. Only 'ad a sip. Fellow's got fer keep warm this snipey weather.'

Tresca stared at him, stunned and horrified. Surely she must have heard wrong. Yet she knew she hadn't. Black anger flared up inside her as she watched Emmanuel lumber past her and drop down on to his bed, her stomach sickening at the stench of alcohol on his breath. She could fly at him, yell out her frustration, but what was the point? After everything they had been through, all her hard work, the fight drained out of her, leaving her lost and fragile. Defeated.

Before the shock had properly taken hold, Emmanuel was fast asleep, snoring for England, drunk as a lord. It was no wonder Connor had dismissed him. But what were they to do? Tresca's eyes lingered over the room Vera had admired only the previous day and she could have wept.

Oh, what a fool she had been! She knew what her father was like, so why had she trusted him, even allowed him some pocket money? She had been so caught up in the euphoria of having a proper home of their own for the first time ever that her mind had blanked out all its doubts.

She sat, staring into space, for ten minutes as the veil of shock slowly lifted and her brain began to function again. They had food for the next few days, so she might as well continue preparing the evening meal, though she had such a sinking feeling in her stomach that she didn't think she could eat a morsel. Her mind searched for a solution as her fingers worked automatically. She had nearly nine shillings in her purse, five of which would be needed for the fortnight's rent due at the end of the following week. But they also had to eat. Oh, if only she hadn't spent all that money on those things to make their life more comfortable!

But crying over spilt milk wouldn't solve the problem. She supposed it would be too much to expect that Emmanuel might have some money left in his pockets. He didn't stir as she moved him around on the bed to get at them. A silver sixpence and a few coppers were all she could find. And an empty hip flask which he must have purchased at the same time as the brandy to put in it.

Tresca sat down again, clawing her way through the fog. One of them would have to find work, so the search would be on all over again. Unless... It came to her in a flash of inspiration. Connor liked her. Although she felt angry with him, she supposed she couldn't really blame him. But perhaps she could make use of their friendship, plead with him? It would mean swallowing her pride, but this was a fight for survival.

Darkness descended in a cold, raw curtain, but while Emmanuel slept on, Tresca was thinking about what she would say to Connor. As the time approached when she knew he would be home, her stomach began to churn with apprehension. Perhaps she should wait a little, give him time to eat his dinner and then maybe, on a full stomach, he might reconsider.

When she knocked on his front door, all the words she had planned disappeared from her head.

'Can I speak to Mr O'Mahoney, please?' she stammered at the landlord when he opened the door.

'Come in out of the cold,' the elderly man invited her at once. 'Wait here and I'll go up to his room. He'll be down directly for dinner anyway. Who shall I say be calling?'

Oh dear. She hadn't timed it right after all. Connor would be hungry and wanting his dinner. But it was too late now. 'Miss Ladycott,' she answered, trying to sound more confident than she felt.

'Wait here. I won't be a moment, young maid.' But the fellow's bandy legs took him up the stairs at an agonizingly slow pace, leaving Tresca alone in the hallway. The house smelt of good food and polish, there was an elegant hallstand, and carpet on the stairs, held in place by gleaming brass rods. Oh, it was so much nicer than even their own new home, and Tresca's heart pricked with envy.

'He'll be down directly,' the landlord told her, taking the stairs a step at a time, then he disappeared through a door at the far end of a narrow passage. Tresca heard footsteps on the floor above, and the tall, familiar figure of Connor O'Mahoney tripped down the stairs, remarkably light-footed for a man of his size. What startled her was that he was in his shirtsleeves, cuffs rolled up to the elbows and buttons undone showing the top of his chest. He had evidently been washing for there was a towel slung round his neck and shaving soap on his cheek where he had missed it in his haste. It made him look altogether quite attractive, and Tresca reared away from the thought.

'Ah, Tresca.' She noticed his eyes weren't bright and mischievous as they so often were. Rather he was looking at her cautiously. 'I think I know why you're here.'

'I'm sure you do. Please, Connor. Give my father another chance. Give him his job back. I don't know what we'm going to do, else.'

She gazed up at him, heart battering against her ribs, while he seemed to consider. But then his frown deepened. 'Sure I can't, little one.' He sucked in his lips, watching the distress on her face. 'You know how dangerous the work is. Blasting, using dynamite and gunpowder. The inevitable rockfalls no matter how careful we are. All the men need to be on their toes the whole time. Can't one drunken man put the whole team in danger. I just can't take that risk. And sure isn't it the company rule to dismiss anyone found drinking on the job.'

'And you'm worried about your own job, too, I suppose!' Tresca hissed, bitterness sharp on her tongue because she had convinced herself that his obvious affection for her would sway him.

'That, too, and why not? Why should I be risking me own job and the safety of others for one labourer who can't keep sober and isn't a great worker anyway? No, I'm sorry, Tresca, that I am. But I can't do what you're after asking of me.'

'And doesn't it matter to you that we've little money left? I were relying on my father's wages and I've spent so much on our new home on the strength of it.'

'Sure that's not my fault. But I–'

'You can't blame me for wanting a few nice things when it's the first time we've ever had any money to speak of,' Tresca blurted out, hot tears of humiliation pricking her eyes.

'Sure I didn't say that, child–'

'And now I don't know what'll happen to us. Jobs aren't easy to get, you know, if you're not working on the railway. But then you wouldn't know that, would you, with your nice safe position?'

Connor stared at her darkly and shook his head. 'Sure, child, I'll not see you starve–'

'And stop calling me a child!'

'Well, you are so.'

'No, I'm not.'

'Fifteen, isn't it?'

Tresca's eyes flashed. 'Sixteen the day after Boxing Day.'

'There you are then. A child. A bright and lovely one, but not so wise as you thought. I'll give you some money to tide you over, and then we'll talk in a few days, so we will, when you're feeling more grown-up.'

Anger had been fermenting inside Tresca's chest and now it burst out in a squall of rage. 'I wouldn't take anything from you! You think you can make everything right by throwing your money around? Well, there's–'

'Tresca, please–'

'No! Good night to you, Mr O'Mahoney. I hope you enjoy your dinner!'

She spun round, but as her fingers reached the door knob, Connor's big hand closed over them.

'No, Tresca, I won't–'

'Won't what?' She glared up at him, holding his gaze so intently that he was unaware of her boot flying out until it cracked against his shin. He hopped backwards, drawing a pained breath through his teeth and releasing his hold on her hand. She seized her chance and shot out through the door, running back up the street and driving her fury into the ground beneath her feet.

'Tresca!' Connor called after her through the harsh night air. But he made no attempt to follow and she didn't stop until she was back indoors, the door slammed shut behind her.

Ten

Tresca woke from a fitful, troubled sleep and peered into the hostile darkness. Her father was up again, his bare feet padding to the door. It was the same every night. Tresca slept so lightly these days, their worries creeping into her mind like a slithering evil, that the slightest sound woke her. Emmanuel seemed as disturbed as she was as he regularly got up several times in the night and went out across the yard to the water closet. It had turned bitterly cold and she couldn't understand why he needed to go outside so often. All she wanted was to snuggle down in bed and drift into a reviving sleep that wasn't invaded by nightmares.

A thousand thoughts chased each other round her head. The previous day they had paid the rent, which would take them up to just before Christmas, and she prayed to God that He would bring some miracle to save them from destitution. Neither of them had been able to find a job, nor had they been able to find anywhere cheaper to live. And there was no way she would ask Mrs Mawes if their old room was still available and beg her to let them have it back.

The coal had run out five days before, and when Tresca drew the curtains that morning, the windows were encrusted with ice on the inside. She had slept in her clothes to try to keep warm, and felt sticky and uncomfortable, but it was simply too cold to strip off and wash in water that would come straight from the near frozen standpipe in the yard.

A stale crust was all that remained in the food cupboard, and in her purse, one shilling and seven pence three farthings. She and Emmanuel sat in silence, chewing on the dry bread that stuck in their throats with only icy water to wash it down. Tresca's dull, vacant eyes were trained on the bare floorboards where once the lovely rug had been. It had gone back to the shop, reluctantly taken by the proprietor for a fraction of what she had paid for it.

Her thoughts stole unbidden to Tremaine Farm and the happy Christmas preparations that she imagined would be taking place in the warm kitchen. But her memories of the farm had long become a broken dream, faded and indistinct, melting into shadows. Now she must face reality.

'Good morning, Tresca, my lover,' Mrs Ellacott greeted her as she entered the dairy an hour later. 'I's not seen you in a while. Half a pint, is it?'

Tresca might have blushed with shame, but she had gone beyond that now. 'I'm afeared I can't afford it,' she admitted wearily. 'But I were wondering if you needed any help?'

'Still not found any work, then? Well as it happens, Sally's gone to visit her mother what's been took poorly, so you can help me making the butter. Give you sixpence if you works a few hours.'

Sixpence. It wouldn't go far, but it was better than nothing, and Tresca felt good doing something useful again. So she spent the morning

102

churning the cream into butter and squeezing out the excess whey until it was ready to pat into half-pound blocks. Mrs Ellacott watched her, nodding approvingly at her skill.

'If I ever wants a dairymaid, I'll have you, Tresca, cheel,' she smiled, round cheeks shining. 'But I cas'n see Sally leaving me for many a long year.'

With the sixpence safely in her purse and carrying the block of butter and pint jug of milk that Mrs Ellacott had given her, Tresca arrived home early in the afternoon. Emmanuel was supposed to be out looking for work, but at least Tresca now kept every penny in her purse so he couldn't take any to buy himself a drink. The sixpence would buy a loaf and a little ham and cheese, enough to feed them for a day, and made more palatable by the butter and the cold milk to drink. But what would happen the day after that – or when the rent was due again?

Tresca's shoulders slumped wearily. Why, oh why? Everything had been going so well, and now it had all fallen apart. She knew exactly how Bella must have felt all her life, and her heart wrenched with sympathy.

Bella. It would be good to talk to a friend and to see someone who was definitely worse off than she was. For surely there could be nothing worse than having been reduced to selling one's body for a living.

She hurried back up the street. Mrs Mawes only locked the front door at night so Tresca was able to go straight in. Coldness gripped her heart as she climbed the dark, familiar stairs. Perhaps it would have been better if they had stayed in the cramped little room under the eaves. At least they might have had enough savings to tide them over until spring when they could probably have found work on the land again.

She knocked on Bella's door and waited for an answer. None came. Her already dark mood sank with disappointment. It was unusual for Bella to be out during the day, unless she had secured a daytime 'client'. Tresca shuddered, but she had come to accept Bella's profession as part of life. She was sure Bella wouldn't mind if she waited for her, so she opened the door and let herself in.

She sensed instantly that something was horribly, unutterably wrong. The air was cold, as still as death, grey ashes in the grate. Tresca's eyes travelled over the room, and a gasp of shock scraped itself from her throat.

Bella was lying in bed, eyes closed in a marble white face. Her hair lay in a wild tangle, and Tresca followed her arm, which was hanging limply over the side of the bed. Then she noticed the burgundy puddle from the thick, dark liquid that was dripping from the middle of the mattress.

Every muscle in Tresca's body froze rigid. She stared in agonized horror for several seconds before she broke free from her shock. She threw back the covers and recoiled, hands over her mouth, at what she saw. Bella was lying in a pool of blood that seemed to be coming from the lower half of her body.

Oh, God.

In all her young life Tresca had never known the

panic that locked itself about her. She must *do* something, but her head was spinning, making thought impossible. And then somehow, through a blinding fog, she found herself careering down the stairs, screaming for Mrs Mawes. But the house was as quiet as a morgue and the hallway deserted when she reached it.

She hammered on the kitchen door, frantic with desperation, and almost fell in when it was finally opened. Mrs Mawes bore an expression like thunder, which exploded when she saw who it was.

'What the devil do *you* want, you–'

'Get a doctor! Quickly!' Tresca shrieked at her. 'It's Bella–'

'Oh, it is, is it?' Mrs Mawes replied with painful slowness. 'If you thinks–'

'Where can *I* find a doctor, then? Vera ... Vera mentioned a Dr Greenwood. Come on, *quickly!*'

Mrs Mawes screwed up her lips. 'There be a Dr Greenwood in Parkwood Road, so I believes–'

Tresca was already tearing out of the front door. Parkwood Road. She knew where that was. She raced down the hill, almost falling over her own feet in her headlong rush. Duke Street, then Brook Street, dodging in and out of people on foot, carts and carriages. Brook Street became Parkwood Road. There weren't many houses here on the edge of the town, but which one? She spun round in a frenzy of despair, ready to break. And there was a brass plate, shining out at her.

She shot up the garden path.

'One and thruppence!' Emmanuel crowed, burst-

ing in through the door. ''Elped clear out someone's attic. So I bought a bag o' coal cuz this
room's cold enough to freeze us to dead. An' don't
you be tellin' us off fer that! Oh...' He stopped
abruptly as Tresca lifted her tear-stained face to
him. 'Yere, princess, things bain't so bad.'

She blinked at him. Sniffed. 'Bella's dead,' she
croaked, her voice broken and empty.

'What?' he breathed incredulously. 'Surely...'

'The doctor said it must have been a backstreet
abortion. And it was all my fault,' Tresca moaned
wretchedly. 'She said ... a few weeks ago ... that
she were in trouble. But then she said it were
because she couldn't afford the rent. That
weren't it at all. If I hadn't gone rushing in, pok-
ing my nose in, she might have told me the truth
and we could ... we could have helped her.'

She dropped her head forward again, closing
her eyes against her tears. Emmanuel sat down
beside her and she wept against his shoulder as
he held her tightly.

'Aw, no, princess. You'm not to blame. A cheel
who lives like Bella did, well, no good ever comes
of it. I knows 'ow you 'as a practical 'ead on your
shoulders, but you cas'n solve everyone's problems all the time, you knows. Things isn't always
what us wants. Let me light this fire, an' us'll feel
better then?

Tresca nodded. She didn't mind one jot that he
had spent some of his precious earnings on coal.
She felt so numb that she really didn't care about
anything any more. But once they had the range
fire going and its warmth seeped into her frozen
bones, she began to feel the life returning to her

limbs. They boiled some water and made some tea with the few spoons of dried leaves that were left. They had been used twice before, but weak tea would be better than no tea at all.

Emmanuel sighed as they huddled in front of the open firebox. 'This be a terrible shock. Fer both of us, but mainly fer you. But there be some things us cas'n do nort about. Like me not gettin' no younger an' not 'avin' the strength I used to. Must be old age creepin' up on us.'

'More likely the cold and being hungry all the time,' Tresca murmured in reply.

'But summat'll 'appen for us, surely it will,' Emmanuel told her, putting his arm round her shoulder again. 'Just you sees.'

Yet at that moment, Tresca felt that their whole world was crumbling to dust.

Eleven

The bell on the shop door gave an ominous clang like a pauper's death knell as Tresca struggled inside with the heavy basket on her arm. The weather had changed overnight, less cold but bringing sheeting rain that skated down the steep surface of Bannawell Street in a torrent. Yet if they were to eat that day, Tresca needed to get some money from somewhere. And so she had trudged down the hill and then up West Street to Trembath's hardware shop, rain driving into her face. Not surprisingly, Tavistock was almost deserted.

Anyone with any sense would stay indoors, but needs must and so Tresca had battled miserably through the rain, her skirt soaking up water from the street so that it clung, cold and uncomfortable, about her knees.

'Miss Ladycott, let me help you!' Morgan Trembath sprang forward the instant he saw her. 'What made you come out on such a morning?'

He ushered her inside, holding the door for her and taking the basket, which surprised him with its weight. The forlorn expression on her lovely face made something happen to his heart. She looked thin and pale, the bloom gone from her cheeks, and it worried him.

But when she reached the counter, the fire came back into her eyes. Morgan heaved the basket on to the polished surface and was taken aback as she removed several bundles of rags and carefully began to unwrap them without uttering a word. And then he realized with astonishment that each parcel contained a part of the oil lamp he had sold to her a month previously.

'Oh dear, was there something wrong with it?' he asked apologetically.

'No,' she answered flatly, lifting her chin. 'But I were hoping you might buy it back from me. You can see it's in perfect condition.'

Morgan's eyes opened wide. He had never been asked such a thing before. It certainly looked brand new, as if it had never been used. Either that or she had given it a jolly good clean. He picked up each component in turn, inspecting it before he assembled it into the one item.

'Well,' he faltered, pursing his lips, 'I wouldn't

108

normally buy something back, but maybe, as it's you…'

Tresca held his gaze hopefully. Then the doorbell clanged again and there were footsteps behind her, but she didn't turn her head. She mustn't let him be distracted.

'We don't deal in second-hand goods,' a woman's high voice declared, and Tresca's courage shrank as Mrs Trembath appeared from the room, some sort of office she assumed, behind the counter. She had evidently heard the conversation and now she stood gloating, arms folded implacably across her mean bosom.

'B–but, Mother, it's like new,' Morgan stammered.

'Then she'll get a good price for it at the pawnbroker's.'

Tresca met the woman's steely eyes, hoping her own challenging expression might make her rethink. But Mrs Trembath threw her a withering glance and disappeared back into the room, closing the door with a deliberate flourish. A shattering silence echoed around the shop, broken only by Mr Penwaite clearing his throat as he pretended to tidy an already precise display of kitchen utensils.

'I'm so sorry, Miss Ladycott,' Morgan began sympathetically.

'That's perfectly all right. I understand.' Tresca wondered, though, how she had spoken with such clarity when she was almost choking on her humiliation.

'That's a mighty pretty lamp, so it is.'

The voice behind her made her jump. She

109

recognized it at once. She had not seen Connor since the night he had refused to give Emmanuel his job back, and now the hatred froze solid inside her. It somehow pleased her to see him dressed in his working clothes, his muddied waterproof as wet and dripping as she was.

'I've come to order some more casks of oil for the workmen's lamps,' he went on, 'but I were after buying another lamp for meself, and doesn't that one rather take me fancy. How much was it new?'

'I believe it was one shilling and ten pence, wasn't it, Miss Ladycott?'

'Then I'll give you one and six, if you think it's a fair price.'

He had already taken a handful of change from his pocket and was counting out the money. Tresca might have thrown the coins back in his face, but she couldn't do so in front of young Mr Trembath, and one and six would feed them for another few days. She managed to mumble her thanks and then escaped from the shop as quickly as she could.

'Tresca, wait, will you?'

She ignored the voice calling after her and hurried on down the street. Rain lashed into her face, mingling with the smarting tears of degradation Connor had caused her to suffer and running down her neck inside her clothes. She could have cursed, turning her head away as Connor's footsteps splashed up beside her.

'Sure you're wet through, child. What happened to your coat and that fancy umbrella I've seen you with?'

110

Oh, God. She couldn't admit to him that they were at the pawnbroker's, along with the pretty quilts she had made, her father's waterproofs and their spare clothes, the saucepan she had also bought from Trembath's but was sure they wouldn't take back, and anything else they could do without. As soon as night closed in, she and Emmanuel took to their beds to shiver through the hours of darkness as they couldn't afford a candle, let alone oil for the lamp. And it wasn't as if they hadn't tried like fury to find work. But times were hard and even the better-off were being careful with their money. And if shop-keepers were enjoying good business with the navvies in town, any extra jobs had long been taken up and the days had passed without a sniff of work.

'Here, have me coat, *acushla*.'

Before she knew it, Tresca felt the weight of Connor's waterproof on her shoulders as she scuttled along. Raging contempt swept her agony aside, and she flung the garment off. It landed in a puddle. She gave an ironic laugh and hurried on.

'Holy Mother of God, why won't you let me help you?'

She whipped round, a kind of madness seizing her as she watched him standing in the middle of the road, getting as wet as she was, his hands raised in incomprehension. Her heart filled with loathing. Everyone had let her down: Emmanuel, Mr Trembath, but most of all Connor O'Mahoney. And all her bitterness focused on him as they faced each other in the pouring rain.

'Cuz it's all your fault, that's why!' she screamed at him. 'Now go back and collect your precious lamp and leave me alone!'

She spun on her heel and broke into a run as she turned the corner and pounded up the hill towards Bannawell Street, blinding tears streaming down her cheeks. Back on West Street, Connor stood, arms hanging by his sides, oblivious to the rain and totally at a loss.

Tresca had never been to Vera's home in Paddon's Row. As she set out along Duke Street, a glacial wind struck through her shawl. But she was already so cold and miserable that she scarcely noticed. She had come to the end and her brain was numb.

The string of little shops on either side, once the source of delight – and the hope of employment – passed by unnoticed and anonymous. They were all busy, with Christmas being only three days away, but Tresca was oblivious to them since neither they nor all the wealthier households in the town had been able to offer the work which would have saved her and Emmanuel from the dire situation they now faced.

She ducked through the narrow passageway that brought her out into a little courtyard with quaint, rickety buildings on either side. One of them had a small sign in the window declaring it to be a dressmaker's establishment, and Tresca went inside. The small front room was empty but for a couple of velvet-covered chairs and a little table where a lamp, turned low, cast eerie shadows on the walls. But the doorbell had alerted someone in

112

the back room and a slim woman, herself smartly though simply dressed, appeared through the door.

'Can I help you, madam?' she asked pleasantly.

Madam? Tresca could have laughed. As if she had come to have some beautiful new gown created.

'I've come to see Miss Miles, if she'm at home. I'm Tresca Ladycott.'

The woman's face fell, though it was clear she tried not to let it show. 'Oh, yes. Vera's told me all about you. She's up in her room. Do come through.'

Tresca followed her into what was evidently the work-cum-fitting room. Beyond it was a small, plainly furnished kitchen. Another door revealed a tiny, narrow staircase that led up to two rooms above. The woman knocked gently on one of the doors.

'Vera, you has a visitor. Your friend Tresca.'

She left them to it, and Tresca stepped into a good-sized room. It was almost as spartan as her own, with bare floorboards, a plain washstand and a simple iron bedstead in one corner. The walls were painted white and were bare apart from a 'Home, Sweet Home' sampler over the tiny fireplace. But for all its puritanical sparseness, it appeared to Tresca like a haven of peace.

'Tresca!' Vera got up from the rustic chair by the fireside, and setting the bible she had been reading on the bed, she came forward with her hands outstretched in greeting. 'What a lovely surprise! Welcome to my humble abode. Oh, you're frozen!' she declared as she took Tresca's hands.

'Where's your coat and gloves? Oh, come and sit by the fire.'

Tresca obeyed meekly. Kneeling in front of the lively fire in the tiny grate, she could feel the heat penetrating her icy flesh. Vera knelt down beside her, her eyes deep with concern.

'Is something wrong? You look so pale. Oh, my, it's not your father, is it? Oh, good Lord, nothing's happened to him, has it?'

Tresca could have died from shame. The moment had come to admit it. She took in a deep breath, lifting her eyes to the ceiling as she wrung her hands.

'Not exactly. But... Oh, Vera. He were dismissed from work. About a month ago. He ... he has a drink problem, you see. He'd been drinking at work, and Connor – Mr O'Mahoney, his foreman – sent him packing. And we've tried everything to find work, but there's nothing. I've pawned everything we have, and there's simply nort left. We've had no coal for I don't know how long and we've been living on bread and water the last few days. And the rent's due again tomorrow and there's nort to pay it with. And ... and I don't want to end up like poor Bella.'

Her last words were blurted out on the brink of hysteria, and she turned to Vera's horrified face, her eyes brimming with tears of despair. The spirit had finally died inside her and a brutal sob broke from her lungs.

Vera pursed her lips and a curtain of silence shrouded the room. 'And there's no one else you can turn to?' she prompted at last.

'No,' Tresca answered, firm, defiant, empty.

Vera hesitated. 'Oh dear. This sounds awful but there's little I can do to help. As you see, I live very frugally myself. My allowance covers the rent and my day-to-day living, but it stretches no further than that. I'm sure Thirza wouldn't mind you sharing my room, but neither of us could afford to feed you. And if my uncle were suddenly to put in an appearance as he sometimes does without warning, and found you living here, he'd likely cut off my allowance altogether. And it wouldn't solve the problem of somewhere for your father to live.'

Her words cut into Tresca's brain like shards of glass. But what else had she expected? She already knew that Vera led a simple life, doing charitable work among the poor with no reward for her efforts. But to have it placed so starkly before her when she had hoped so desperately that Vera could help her was crucifying. The tiny flicker of hope that had struggled to keep aflame inside her was finally extinguished.

'There's only one thing I can do for you,' she realized Vera was saying, her voice low and cracked. 'There's a meeting of the Guardians tomorrow. I can have a word with the vicar. Get him to recommend your case to the Board. You ... you were both born in Tavistock, weren't you? Or in one of the parishes of the Union?'

Tresca slowly bowed her head. She knew what Vera meant, and the pain and misery tumbled down around her. The bleak, daunting edifice at the top of Bannawell Street, so cold and hostile. She had turned her head away on the few occasions she had walked past it, pitying the poor souls who were incarcerated within its heartless walls. And what was it Bella had said? That she would rather die then enter the 'institution'? Her wish had been granted.

'The master in charge is a good man. Mr Solloway his name is,' Vera went on, trying to make her own voice lighter, although Tresca could tell it was false. 'And Dr Greenwood, he keeps an eye on the ... on everyone's health matters. It usually falls to a far less senior physician, but he has such a care for the poor... Well, you know what I mean. So ... so what do you think?'

Tresca could not meet her friend's eyes. Her life had been crushed into a million pieces, but there was nothing else she could do. After all her efforts, the fight had finally gone out of her. And the spectre of Bella, who had died from poverty and neglect when all was said and done, haunted her day and night. Surely anything was better than that.

Slowly, she nodded her head, and beside her she heard Vera's soft sigh. She realized that Vera had not dared to utter the word that was imprinted on both their minds in heavy, black letters: workhouse.

Twelve

They dragged themselves to the top of Bannawell Street, carrying the few possessions they still had. The air was solid with the cold that sliced cruelly through their thin clothes, since all their warmer ones had been pawned. Dry snowflakes swirled on the frozen ground like white dust, but it was too cold for it to settle, and Tresca reflected dispassionately that it was unlikely to be a white Christmas.

The long climb up the steep hill did little to warm them, and Emmanuel coughed as the frosted air rasped in his lungs. As for Tresca, she felt her heart had turned to stone. She had sworn to make it impenetrable, and if the tears that ran down her cheeks were turning to tiny icicles on her skin, then they weren't tears at all but merely the result of the Arctic wind making her eyes water. A scraggy kitten, one of many feral cats that survived on the rubbish so often thrown into the gutter, tiptoed across the road, walking delicately to keep its paws off the icy surface as much as possible. Normally Tresca might have stopped to play with it for a minute or two, but today she ignored it, deliberately hardening her heart to all feeling.

And there it was, sitting at the top of the hill like a great vulture on its nest, waiting for its prey. The long, low building across the front with the great archway entrance was dwarfed by the three-storey soulless prison behind. Tresca realized that both she and Emmanuel had come to a halt, staring, every nerve stretched with tension. The moment had come. Their eyes met, and if Tresca had ever blamed her father, all the resentment fled at the anguish she read on his face now. He seemed slightly bent, suddenly old, and once more he coughed painfully. His fingers reached for hers, she returned his watery smile, and they walked up to the solid wooden gates hand in hand.

Emmanuel yanked on the bell pull and they heard its dull toll from somewhere inside. Tresca listened, the knot of apprehension tightening in her stomach as a heavy key turned. A door cut into one of the gates creaked open and a man, swathed in a heavy greatcoat, stuck his head out.

'Yes?' he barked.

Tresca saw her father swallow. 'Emmanuel Ladycott,' he barely whispered, 'an' my darter, Tresca.'

'Yes. Us was expectin' you.'

He jerked his head for them to come inside and they stepped across the threshold into a cold, empty world. Tresca shuddered as the door was locked behind them. It was like being buried alive.

'Wait yere,' they were ordered brusquely. And they did, silent and afraid.

'Anither one for you, Mrs Solloway,' they heard a distant voice. And then the man reappeared. 'This way. No, not you, you girt idjit,' he growled as Tresca went to step after her father. 'Men and women is separate in yere.'

Tresca stood, frozen in time, as Emmanuel was pulled away. Her arm was dragged forward, their hands clinging, fingertips touching until the very last second.

'Father!' Her vision misted with unshed tears so that the last she saw of him as he was marched away was his blurred face. She was sure he mouthed the words *I love you* over his shoulder. And then he was gone, swallowed up through a door that was shut firmly behind him.

'Now then, Tresca Ladycott, is it?'

She swiftly pressed the base of her thumbs against her eyes, and then wiped them on her skirt. She wasn't going to let them see her tears. She set her jaw defiantly and turned round. The woman she found standing there was far less formidable than she had expected. Round and plump as an apple, she was clad in a thick, woollen cloak with a black cap tied beneath her chin. She reminded Tresca of a fat crow. The only obvious sign of authority was the massive bunch of keys that hung from her belt.

'Bark's worse than his bite, that one.' She nodded so that the pleats on her cap flapped like a bird's wings. 'Be all right, your father will, if he does as he's told. Now then, come this way. I'm the Matron, Mrs Solloway. I'll take you through to the women's probationary ward and get you ready for the doctor. You're lucky he's due to come later this morning. Only comes once a week unless we need him urgently in the infirmary. And not the most pleasant place, the probationary ward. Got an imbecile in at the minute, we have, waiting for Dr Greenwood's assessment.'

Her words barely registered in Tresca's brain as she followed her across the extensive square formed by the building. At least it would have been extensive if it weren't divided into two by a high wall.

'Exercise yards,' Mrs Solloway explained, and then producing her bunch of keys she unlocked a door at the far side.

Dear God, it was just like a prison, Tresca thought miserably as she was led along a dark corridor. Or a morgue, silent as death itself. The only figures she saw in the distance were grey, floating like ghosts.

'In here,' the Matron instructed, and Tresca found herself in a large, high-ceilinged room with six iron bedsteads. The windows were tall, and high up in the bare walls so that you couldn't see out even if you stood on a chair. There were no curtains and the small hearth was empty and lifeless. An old woman, dressed in a gown that might once have been white, was sitting on one of the beds, rocking herself back and forth, her long, grey wispy hair wild about her face.

'Ah, Mrs Drake,' Mrs Solloway addressed a woman sitting at the desk. 'Take our new inmate along to the bath house and prepare her for the doctor. You can leave your little bundle here with me, Ladycott.'

Tresca obeyed, for what else was there to do? But she was determined not to let her fear show. The bath house smelt of damp and metal and the sharp, acrid odour of carbolic soap. Tresca stared at the row of tin baths propped against the wall and the army of large white enamel jugs standing to attention by a long sink with four taps coming off a rusty pipe. There was a huge boiler but it clearly wasn't lit as the room was as cold as the winter's day outside.

'Sit on that stool, Ladycott,' Mrs Drake commanded. 'Take the shawl off your head. I'll just get the scissors.'

'Scissors?'

Alarm swept through Tresca's body and she leapt up again, her heart trying to escape from her chest. But Mrs Drake nodded her head emphatically.

'Can't have hair as long and thick as yours in here. Lice, you see. Seems a pity to cut it off, mind, but we can sell it to the wig-maker and it'll help pay for your keep.'

'But I don't have lice!' Tresca protested, hands clamped protectively over her head in absolute horror.

'You soon will have in here with that mane. Besides, it's the rules.'

'B–but what about the old woman just now? You hadn't cut *her* hair off.'

'Oh, we will, cheel, we will. Just as soon as I can get Mr Blake to hold her down for me. Now come along, let's get it over with.'

Tresca gazed at the woman, her heart pounding. Good God, as if it wasn't soul-destroying enough, now she had to submit to this appalling degradation as well. Perhaps Bella had been right, after all. Tresca wanted to lash out, but if she wanted a roof over her head and food in her belly over the next days and weeks, what choice did she have? A thin, anguished sound gurgled in

121

her throat and she slowly lowered herself back on to the stool.

She stared at the wall ahead, unblinking, a study of composure. With each rasp of the scissor blades, a thread more of the spirit that had once been Tresca Ladycott was severed and fell to the floor with her silvery tawny hair. Within seconds, she was shorn like a sheep in springtime. And to add to the humiliation, Mrs Drake was retrieving the long, thick tresses and hanging them over her arm in admiration.

'Should get a good price for this at the wig-maker's,' she said approvingly.

A spasm of pain twitched at Tresca's face and her trembling hand travelled falteringly up to her head. Her fingers found a short cap of down. Not just chopped off on a level with her ears, but cropped almost to her scalp. Silent tears collected in her eyes, but she must not cry. Her heart closed into a hard knot somewhere deep inside her.

'Right now, help me with one of the baths and we'll put some water in it. Only cold today, mind. But you can be quick about it. Get your clothes off and I'll take them for fumigating. Then they'll be stored until you leave.'

'And how will I leave?' Tresca demanded with a momentary flash of her old spirit.

'You can leave any time you wish. But I suggest you wait till someone comes for you. A relative or a friend. Or until someone comes wanting a girl for work. In service or the like.'

'I'm a skilled dairymaid, but I'd do any work that's on offer,' Tresca informed her, her heart rising in reckless hope.

'Just as well, as you're going to have to work hard in here. So, give me your clothes and I'll fetch you a uniform.'

Tresca felt as if her soul had caved in as she took off her clothes and handed them to Mrs Drake. She cowered at her nakedness and stepped into the freezing water. Was her father suffering the same brutal indignity? She imagined so. Thank God Mrs Drake left her alone to bathe herself, and she scrubbed vigorously with the evil-smelling carbolic soap as if ridding herself of her shame. When the assistant returned, Tresca was wrapped, shivering, in a threadbare towel, her heart aching with emptiness.

'Here, get these on and quick about it.'

Tresca glared back at her. 'I'm going as fast as I can.'

'And you'd better watch your tongue or you'll be on the punishment diet before you even start.'

Punishment! Wasn't this punishment enough? Tresca threw her a dark look before pulling on the itchy woollen drawers and shift, and long grey stockings. The dress that went over the top was a shapeless sack in broad, washed-out blue and grey vertical stripes. A band with a large 'P' for pauper was sewn on to the sleeve. She pushed her feet into a pair of hard and uncomfortable hobnailed boots that were several sizes too large, and the crowning glory was a plain and unflattering mob cap. But at least it hid her mown head.

'The doctor's waiting for you. Follow me.'

Tresca did as she was instructed, since what else could she do? She could have hung around Dr Greenwood's neck when, a few minutes later, he gave her a warm, compassionate smile that eased her pain.

'Tresca Ladycott?' he asked. And then his forehead swooped into a frown. 'Aren't you the girl who came to me a couple of weeks ago, when your friend died in unfortunate circumstances?'

Tresca was surprised he had recognized her in the faceless uniform and with no hair. But she nodded, grief spearing beneath her ribs as she was reminded of Bella.

'I was so sorry. If she'd been found earlier, I might have had a chance of saving her. Such a waste of life. And I'm sorry to find you in here, too.'

'Not as sorry as I am. But my father and I tried everything to get work. But we just couldn't find ort.'

'Times are hard,' the doctor agreed. 'Building the railway has been a godsend to many businesses. Helped them to survive. But it's still a struggle for many.'

'Well, we're planning on leaving here in the spring and finding work on the land again,' Tresca told him confidently. 'This is only to tide us over.'

'Ah.' Dr Greenwood's tone dropped ominously and Tresca's heart lurched as he looked across at her. 'I'm not sure your father will be fit enough. He has given me permission to tell you as you won't be permitted to see him. I found that he has what we call an enlarged prostate. A slightly delicate subject, I know, but you may have noticed him relieving himself more often. Many older men have this without any problem, but your father is on the young side to have it, and the prostate feels very firm. Which makes me fear that it might be cancerous.'

'Cancerous?' Tresca croaked as the breath became trapped in her throat.

'I could be wrong, of course, and I hope I am. But I have seen it many times before. And it spreads, quite frequently to the bones. And your father has aches around his pelvis, which is often where it starts.'

'Oh, I see,' Tresca muttered. The blood rushed from her head and seemed to circle about her heart. What other cruel trick did fate have in store for her? 'He has been complaining of feeling, well, not unwell as such, but of losing his strength,' she answered, although her lips seemed to be moving of their own accord. 'And he has been coughing a little of late.'

'His chest *is* a little unsound. But perhaps he's merely developing a common cold. As to the other business, let's hope I'm wrong, but I felt I had to warn you. Now let's give you a quick check-over. First may I ask your age?'

'I'll be sixteen in three days' time. The day after Boxing Day,' she murmured.

Christmas, and her birthday. She had never felt so wretched in all her days, and this news about her father was the last straw. She was lost in a deep, dark ocean where threatening shadows writhed and from which she could see no escape. And who was to blame for it all?

The answer in her mind was quite clear. A tall Irishman by the name of Connor O'Mahoney.

Thirteen

'On this the day of Thy birth, Oh Lord, let us thank You for the food You have provided. May we do Your work this day, and we pray You will bring us all to Your Eternal Light at the end of our days. Amen.'

Mrs Solloway lifted her head and gave her little dumpling smile as she surveyed the women's refectory. 'As it's Christmas Day, we will allow you to talk at meal times,' she announced.

'Lucky us,' the girl sitting next to Tresca scoffed under her breath.

Tresca looked at her sideways. She had noticed the girl before but hadn't had a chance to speak to her. She walked with a pronounced limp and her left hand was badly twisted.

'Seems unnatural, this silence at meal times, doesn't it?' Tresca said, trying to strike up a conversation. The previous day she had been put to work in the laundry. The atmosphere was so thick with heat and steam that it was hard to breathe, let alone carry out the strenuous work. Her face was bright red within minutes, her body running with sweat as she plunged and twisted the washing dolly among the heavy sheets in the washtub. Twenty minutes of swishing and pounding them in the hot, soapy water before hauling them through the mangle. And the instant one load was finished and passed on to the rinsing tubs, she was given another, with not a second's rest in between.

They stopped work for an hour for dinner, most of which was taken up with queuing for the food and then swallowing the unpalatable, thin stew – all in silence. And then back to the gruelling work for another five hours. Then it had been another silent meal, this time a chunk of bread and a morsel of cheese. Tresca had been so exhausted that she had barely had the strength to force down the meagre meal. She certainly hadn't been in the mood for talking before they were ordered into bed. She felt so miserable and weary that she had almost forgotten that her mane of beautiful tresses was no longer attached to her head. And when all the other women in the dormitory removed their caps and they, too, were shorn of their hair, the pain seemed easier to bear. Anonymous. Just one of a forgotten crowd.

Tresca was accustomed to sleeping in the company of others, but in a barn there were always low whispers or muted chuckling. The workhouse rule of silence made the dormitory seem hostile and malevolent. Tresca felt trapped, sorrow and resentment brewing up inside her, but this morning the old flame was flickering and steadily growing. If she was to spend the next few months in here, she was going to make the best of it, and she might as well begin by making some friends.

'Nort natural in yere at all,' the girl grumbled, shovelling the lumpy, overcooked porridge into her mouth. 'Yere, doesn't you want yourn?'

'It's pretty disgusting, isn't it?'

127

'Huh, this be good, special fer Christmas Day. Usually it's made with water. Proper gruel wi' a lump o' carrot if you'm lucky enough fer find one. At least this be made wi' a drop o' milk an' a spoon or two o' sugar.'

Tresca had to suppress a groan of resignation. It was food of sorts, she supposed, and more than she would have been eating if Vera hadn't helped her to be admitted into the workhouse. And it was only until the spring, she kept telling herself, until they could find work on the land again. She pulled herself up short. What if her father wasn't fit enough to work? A desolate fist tightened inside her, and she pushed her dish towards her neighbour.

'You'm certain you doesn't want it? Lucy, by the way,' her new friend introduced herself, plunging her spoon into Tresca's bowl.

'Tresca. And yes,' she sighed disconsolately, 'I suppose I'll have to get used to everything. We only came in yesterday–'

'I knows. I sees everythin'. You does when you was born in yere like I were, an' no 'ope of ever gettin' out.'

'You were born in here?' Tresca was horrified. 'And you've never been outside?'

'Once.' Lucy smacked her lips and shrugged. 'Someone tried me out as a domestic, but wi' only one 'and what works proper like, I cud'n do everythin' they wanted so I were brought back. Born like this I were. Mrs Solloway, she's pretty good. 'Ad other matrons in yere what wasn't 'alf so kind.'

'But what about your parents? Couldn't they…'

128

Lucy wrinkled her nose casually. 'Me mother died givin' birth fer me, an' she didn't know 'oo me father were, they say. What 'bout you?'

Tresca was so flabbergasted by Lucy's story – and her stoical acceptance of her lot – that it took a moment or two for the question to filter into her brain. Compassion tugged at her heart, just as it had with poor Bella. The thought of her tragic end slashed across Tresca's memory and she had to drag herself back from her morose thoughts.

'My mother died when I were five,' she answered. 'I scarcely remember her. But my father came in here with me yesterday. And now the doctor's found something wrong with him. I don't really understand but I think he could be dying. Slowly.' She forced out the words that had wanted to stick in her throat, and felt her heart tear.

'Sorry ter 'ear that. But 'er's good is Dr Greenwood. 'Elped me a lot over the years. I means, no one can do ort fer change this.' She paused to jab her head towards her left side. 'But 'er's given me exercises fer strengthen me muscles. Used fer wear a leg iron when I were a tacker, but cuz o' Dr Greenwood, I doesn't no more.'

Tacker? Lucy looked no older than she was. 'How old are you now?'

'Me? Fourteen. You?'

'Sixteen. Day after tomorrow.'

'Put you straight on women's work, then? You gets school in yere up till twelve. Useless, mind. The old faggot what teaches us is an inmate 'ersel'. Eighty if she's a day. Deaf as a post an'

129

don't see too well, neither. 'Ardly larnt nort from 'er mesel'.'

Mrs Solloway ringing the bell brought their conversation to an abrupt end. 'Clear away,' she commanded. 'The vicar's coming to hold a service in here in half an hour, so I want the tables completely cleared and everyone back here and sitting quietly when he arrives.'

'No peace fer the wicked, eh?' Lucy winked at Tresca over her shoulder as she got awkwardly to her feet. 'You sticks by me, cheel, an' you'll be all right. An' mind that one over there,' she added, nodding towards the old woman with the vacant expression and the long, wispy grey hair – now shorn – who Tresca had seen in the probationary ward the previous day. 'Looks 'armless, but she'll suddenly attack you like a divil. 'Ave yer eyes out in no time, she wud. Don't go near 'er. An' niver talk fer 'er. I knows. Bin in an' out o' yere fer years, she 'as. More in than out. 'As a cousin what comes fer take 'er out every now an' then, but always brings 'er back agin. Better button me lip now.' And she limped off towards the door.

The service was only half an hour because the vicar had to deliver another sermon in the men's refectory before conducting the Parish Eucharist in Tavistock's magnificent old church. What a shame they couldn't be marched down there, Tresca sighed, so that she could enjoy a taste of freedom again – even if she had only been incarcerated the previous day! But she supposed she would then have to suffer the humiliation of being paraded before the whole town. She didn't want anybody to know of their disgrace, least of all Mrs

130

Mawes and that horrible Connor O'Mahoney whose fault it all was.

Later, they were handed out a motley collection of coats and shawls for going out into the exercise yard. Tresca counted over a dozen inmates under sixteen, and about forty women, some younger but others quite elderly. It was bitingly cold, and the younger ones were walking around in aimless circles in an attempt to keep warm, while those who could barely totter on their walking sticks were allowed to shiver on the one long, uncomfortable bench.

'Only got ten minutes, me.' Lucy suddenly appeared at Tresca's elbow. 'I works in the kitchen. You'm in fer a treat. Best meal o' the year, so you makes sure you eats it.'

'Yes, I will, if just to please you,' Tresca promised, glancing ruefully at the high wall. 'I suppose my father will be out in the other yard when the men's service is over. So near and yet he might as well be on the moon.'

'Listen.' Lucy beckoned her with a conspiratorial wiggle of her finger, and lowered her voice. 'You keeps on the right side o' Mrs Solloway an' in a few weeks she might ask the master if you can see each other. Bend the rules yere an' there, they does. 'As you noticed there's no boys over the age o' seven in wi' us?'

Tresca raised her eyebrows and glanced across at the group of younger children playing tag. 'Oh yes. I hadn't noticed before.'

'That's cuz when they gets fer seven, the boys 'ave fer go in wi' the men. Government rules.'

'What? They're dragged away from their

131

mothers at just seven years old?'

'Yes.' Lucy nodded at the horrified expression on Tresca's face. 'Families, 'usbands an' wives, all split up. But the Solloways, they takes 'em off fer little meetin's on the quiet, like. S'pposed fer keep our mouths shut 'bout it, an' us does. If they was found out an' dismissed, God knows 'oo us'd get instead. Bin some proper divils in the past, takin' loads o' food while us was 'alf starvin'. Doesn't want fer go back fer that, I can tell you. But I musts go now. Doesn't want fer get on the wrong side o' the head cook, I doesn't. Don't want fer lose 'er position, so she drives us 'ard ter make sure everything's just so. See you later.'

Tresca watched her walk back inside with her odd, listing gait. She somehow had the feeling that Lucy, with her funny little ways and wise philosophy, was going to prove a good friend. She was shrewd with a sharp wit, and under other circumstances might have made a good life for herself. But what chance did she have of that, poor soul?

A sudden loneliness took hold of Tresca's heart as Lucy disappeared indoors. So many times since they had arrived in Tavistock she had been obliged to brace herself to approach strangers, and now she was going to have to do so again. She gathered up her courage and walked over to a group of women wandering about together.

'Good day,' she said, nailing a broad smile on her face. 'And I suppose Happy Christmas. My name's Tresca. I'm new.'

'We knows that,' an older woman she recognized from the laundry snapped at her. 'An' one more mouth means less fer the rest of us.'

If the woman had slapped her face hard it couldn't have hurt more. Tresca was hoping to make some friends so that her stay was more bearable. She prayed her father was faring better.

'An' you works too 'ard,' another inmate put in. 'You'd best slow down or us'll all be expected to work 'arder, an all.'

'Us'll slow you down ourselves if *you* doesn't!' the first woman joined in, and they put their faces together in a malicious, impenetrable wall.

Tresca's eyes travelled over their threatening expressions. The words *'I'll work as hard as I please'* sizzled on the end of her tongue, but she bit them back. The pair looked vicious and until she knew how things worked, it was best to keep out of trouble.

'Take no notice of them.'

Tresca barely had time to turn her head before another inmate, a woman of about sixty, took her by the arm and whisked her away to the far side of the yard. Tresca was grateful, if a little bewildered, and turned to face her saviour when they came to a halt.

'Nasty pieces of work, those two. Matron knows and keeps an eye on them. As does Mrs Drake. Hard as nails, she is, but she knows who the troublemakers are, and she deals with them. Put you to work in the laundry, did she?'

Tresca nodded and went to open her mouth to speak, but the woman began again, 'I guessed so. If you've been a cook you go in the kitchen, if you've been in service it's either cleaning or the laundry, and if you've been a dressmaker or you're disabled in some way, you get put in the sewing room. Were you a domestic before?'

'No, a dairymaid. But unless it's a very big dairy we're working at, I usually work in the farmhouse as well. What about you?'

'Dressmaker, fortunately. We make all the uniforms, or mend them most of the time,' she added wryly. 'And we take in mending from outside, too. And anything that comes into the laundry and needs mending, as well.'

'So, it's not just the workhouse laundry we do, then?'

'Oh, no. Tuesday and Thursdays is outside laundry. All helps to earn our keep. Used to be picking oakum back along. You know, teasing out old tarred ships' ropes. Cut your fingers to shreds, apparently, so we should be thankful we women don't have to do that any more. The men still have to sometimes, though, I believe. In the vagrants' ward, anyway. Either that or they have to break a yard of stones into pieces small enough to go through holes in a mesh before they're allowed to stay the night.'

'Oh dear.' Tresca's strung-out nerves tightened further. 'My father were admitted yesterday as well. The doctor found something wrong with him. Thinks it could be some sort of cancer.'

'I'm sorry to hear that. But Dr Greenwood won't let them work him too hard if he's unwell.'

'You don't think so?'

'Oh, no. Definitely. So don't you fret none on that score. Enjoy what there is to enjoy on Christmas Day.' The woman beamed, though her

134

expression was tempered by an ironic lift of one eyebrow. 'I'm Susan Grey, by the way. Come and meet my other sewing ladies.'

Tresca felt as if she was at once accepted into the fold of this small group of women, who all seemed more refined than the two hostile laundry women. They related to her various tales of how they had been reduced to entering the workhouse. Susan herself had lived a good life, even travelling across Europe with her rich spinster mistress. They had grown older together, but the mistress had died suddenly without making a will. With no family who might have inherited and seen to it that her seamstress-cum-companion was comfortable, Susan had been left on the streets. Unable to find employment, she had come to the workhouse in desperation.

Tresca sat with them at dinner, which was, as Lucy had predicted, a reasonable meal – a good slice of beef with potatoes, carrots and cabbage, followed by a tiny portion of plum pudding. Quite a feast, although Lucy had confided that the diet would be poorer than ever for the rest of the week to make up for it! Tresca spent the remainder of the day with Lucy and Susan and her friends, and they enjoyed bread and jam for supper.

When she got into bed that night, Tresca considered that the day hadn't been so bad after all. If only she had been able to see her father. But Lucy's words had given her hope. She blessed the strange girl, wishing there was some miracle that would straighten her limbs. But as Emmanuel had said recently, you couldn't always put the world to rights. Sometimes you had to make the best of a situation, which was exactly what Tresca planned to do.

Fourteen

'Well done, Ladycott,' Mrs Drake pronounced over Tresca's shoulder. 'You work hard. Some of these other lazy sluts should take a leaf out of your book. I shall report your good conduct to Matron.'

Tresca wiped the sweat from her brow. 'Thank you, Mrs Drake,' she said briefly, and then returned to scrubbing a particularly stubborn stain on the wooden washboard. Her fingers were raw from being constantly immersed in soapy water, but it was worth it. The corners of her mouth lifted in a secret smile. The more she got into Mrs Solloway's good books, the more likely she was to be permitted to see her father. She had received no news of him since their admittance to the workhouse two weeks previously and yearned to find out how he was.

Her moment of optimism was shattered an instant later as a sharp pain seared into her shin, making her stifle a yelp. What on earth...? She turned her head and her nose almost touched that of the evil face of Enid Turnbull, the woman who had threatened her on Christmas Day.

'That be my last warnin'!' Enid hissed, and then hurried off before Mrs Drake noticed what had happened.

Tresca bent down to rub her shin. It was already tender to touch and would come up in a nasty bruise. Oh, damn Enid Turnbull. But nothing would stop her in her quest to see her father again.

'Phew, another day over.'

It was seven o'clock in the evening, and an hour before the inmates would be ordered into bed. Tresca sank on to the edge of the bed, since they were not permitted to lie down. Although every muscle in her body ached and she yearned to spread herself on the thin straw mattress, it was her favourite time of the day. Mrs Solloway had noticed the friendship that was developing between the hard-working new girl and the young cripple, and had rewarded the good behaviour of both parties by allowing them to occupy adjacent beds.

Opposite her, Lucy stretched wearily and pulled off her cap, shaking her spiky dome of dark hair. 'S'ppose I'd better brush out the lice,' she said glumly, having a good scratch. 'You got any o' they buggers yet?'

'Sh!' Tresca warned, although she wanted to laugh. 'Don't let Matron or Mrs Drake hear you using such language. You'll be punished.'

'I's not that daft!' Lucy grinned back. 'I looked fust. Neither o' them is yere.'

Tresca studied her friend's cheeky face and couldn't help a quiet chuckle. She really liked Susan Grey and was enthralled with her stories of her travels whenever they had a chance to chat. But it was with Lucy that she was able to snatch the odd moment of fun. It felt as if there was some intangible thread that linked them together. Lucy was like some little mascot weaving mysteriously in and out of every room in the vast, lugubrious building, accepted and invisible. She had a pert, pretty heart-shaped face, and Tresca contemplated her with a wistful sigh.

'Haven't you ever wondered what it's like to have hair?' Tresca took off her own cap and put her hand up to her cropped head to ensure that what she had left was still there. 'I feel naked and so degraded like this.'

Lucy merely shrugged. 'S'ppose I's used fer it. It grew a bit that time when I were in service, but it were niver long enough fer tie back or ort like that. An' I guesses it niver will.'

Gazing at her new friend, Tresca suddenly felt overtaken by some powerful force that was stronger than she was. 'Let's make a pact,' she whispered with such conviction that it astounded even herself. 'We'll always help each other, come what may.'

Lucy blinked at her in astonishment and then threw up her head with a roar of laughter. 'An' what 'elp does you think us can give each other in yere? An' don't let no one 'ear you talk like that. They'll put you in wi' the imbeciles!'

Tresca blushed to the roots of her shorn hair. 'No they won't. But I mean it. Help each other just in little ways. But *always*.'

Lucy screwed up her nose. 'Fine by me. But us doesn't need no pact fer that. Us'd do that anyways, wud'n us?'

138

Tresca smiled bashfully. 'Yes, we would.' She glanced around the room with an aimless sigh as sad figures moved about it like ghosts. It seemed so pointless. So *numbing*. 'I wish we could read books,' she complained listlessly.

'You can read the Bible,' Lucy pointed out, trying to be helpful.

'No, I mean people like Dickens and Hardy.'

Lucy's eyes widened in incomprehension. ''Oo?'

'Charles Dickens. You must have heard of him. His books are hard to read, but I understand most of it. He wrote *Oliver Twist,* about a little boy in the workhouse. And then there's Thomas Hardy. His stories are more romantic. I could tell you some of them if you like.'

'No, tell me the one 'bout the work'ouse.' Lucy bent forward, her eyes shining like stars.

'Well, I might not remember the details exactly, but it'll be near enough. It were one dark and raining night in the city of London. A young girl hammered on the door of the workhouse. She were all alone and nobody knew who she were. But she were in a terrible state and she were having a baby–'

'You means it were comin', like?' Lucy's eyes grew wider.

'Yes. She were in such a bad way that they took her in. And although the baby survived, she didn't.'

'You means she died, just like my mother?'

'I'm afeared she did,' Tresca said gently. 'But the baby were a boy, not a girl like you. They never discovered who the mother were, but she had a locket around her neck that the woman

139

who were looking after her stole. Remember that because it's important later on in the story. Anyway, the workhouse master, Mr Bumble he's called, he named the baby Oliver Twist. And Oliver grew up in the workhouse just like you. One day, the other boys dared him to ask for more gruel. Mr Bumble were furious and punished Oliver, and–'

She broke off as two other women sidled up to listen. Tresca felt oddly embarrassed, but she had started the tale for Lucy and felt she had to go on. She cleared her throat and began anew.

'So, Mr Bumble apprenticed Oliver to a horrible undertaker who treated him worse than ever. He were made to sleep–'

By the time they were ordered to ready themselves for bed, almost everyone in the dormitory had been listening, enthralled and mesmerized. Even Mrs Solloway was stood in the doorway, her face intrigued. She might even have let Tresca go on another five minutes, but rules were rules when she had so many inmates in her charge.

'You will go on wi' the story tomorrow?' someone asked.

'Of course I will if you want me to.'

'To think a famous book were written about people like us,' someone else muttered as they dispersed, their heads full of the kind Mr Brownlow, the scheming Mr Fagin and the innocent little Oliver. But as she began to undress, Tresca caught the menacing glower thrown at her by Enid Turnbull at the far end of the dormitory, and her pulse throbbed uneasily.

'You will finish off the story tonight, won't you?' Lucy asked, and several voices echoed her question.

'Of course. I'm enjoying remembering the story myself. I'm just going to use the closet and I'll be back.'

'Oh good,' the eager inmates chorused.

Tresca smiled at them and made for the door, her spirits revived by what had become an evening ritual over the last few days. It made the long hours of back-breaking toil more bearable and, what was more, Mrs Solloway seemed to approve wholeheartedly.

Lucy watched Tresca go, almost jumping up and down with excitement. What was to happen to little Oliver? She prayed he ended up having a better life than she had. She was so wrapped up in her expectation that she didn't see Enid Turnbull and her malicious crony follow Tresca outside.

When Tresca hadn't reappeared after ten minutes, Lucy couldn't contain herself any longer and limped out to the water closets. The unearthly scream that howled from her throat echoed eerily through the bare, hushed rooms of the building, so that Mrs Solloway and Mrs Drake had already come running by the time Lucy stumbled blindly back out into the corridor, jabbering incomprehensibly and gesticulating wildly towards the door to the conveniences.

'Aw, my little princess.'

Buried deep in some black, sepulchral fog, the familiar voice triggered a sweet, tender dream in

141

her sleeping brain. The memory of something good and strong made her mind claw its way through the darkness to the spangling light at the far end. Her eyelids flickered open and her eyes wandered, confused and uncertain, for a second or two before the beloved face wavered into focus.

'Father?'

Her voice sounded strange, weak. But there was Emmanuel, his craggy face taut with worry. She felt comforted, cradled in peace. Her father was there and nothing else mattered.

'Aw, Dr Greenwood, she'm comin' round.'

'Glad to see you back with us, young lady,' she heard another voice say. 'Now, this might seem silly to you, but can you tell me who you are and where you are? And who's this?'

'Tresca Ladycott,' she murmured, her lips feeling like rubber. 'I'm in the workhouse. I was about to go on with *Oliver Twist*. But I can't remember... And this is my dear father, Emmanuel. And ... oh, my head hurts.'

'And I'm afraid you're bruised all over as well,' the doctor informed her. Then his expression changed and he pulled in his chin. 'Do you know who did this to you?'

Tresca frowned, feeling an intense soreness high up on her forehead. 'No,' she answered falteringly. 'I really don't remember anything.'

'Well, something might come back to you. If it does, let us know. We need to find the culprits and call in the constable. Now, I'll leave you with your father, just for a few minutes, mind. The blow that knocked you out split the skin and

142

could do with a couple of stitches before it swells up too much. I'll give you a few drops of laudanum, and that will probably make you too drowsy to talk anyway.'

He must have moved away as Tresca wasn't aware of him any longer. All she could see was Emmanuel's softly smiling face illuminated in the sepia glimmer from an oil lamp placed close to the bed, and she felt his love flowing through her.

'What time is it?' she asked him.

''Bout nine o'clock, I reckons. Us'd just got into bed when I were sent for.'

'I've not been unconscious long, then.'

'An hour or so, I thinks. Aw, princess, I 'ates to see you like this. An' all your beautiful 'air all gone. An' all my fault.'

'No. No, don't you say that. You'm here, and that's all I care about. And now we know you'm not well, at least we know there's a reason why you've not been yourself of late. So ... how have you been?' she scarcely dared to ask.

'Aw, not so bad, cheel. A bit achy, but nort more than that. Put us on what they calls light duties, they 'as. Is larnin' to make boots. Fancy that. A new trade at my age. Better than bein' out in all weathers shiftin' muck, I can tell you. An' the doctor's ordered me the invalid diet, an' all, cuz o' what I's got. So altogether, I cas'n complain. Just misses my princess, that's all.'

A forlorn sigh breathed from Tresca's lungs. 'I miss you, too. But I've been working hard and being very good so as they might let us see each other.'

143

'So what work you bin doin'?'

'Laundry,' she grimaced. 'But I've made some friends. Particularly a crippled girl called Lucy. And in the evenings, I've been retelling the story of *Oliver Twist*. The book by Charles Dickens,' she explained as she saw Emmanuel's blank expression.

'Oh,' he nodded, then added brightly, 'Always said that cliver brain o' yourn'd come in useful one day. Gets that from your mother, you does, not me.'

Tresca smiled, her heart full. Such a good man was her father, despite his faults. But no one was perfect.

'Sorry to interrupt, but I must ask you to leave now, Mr Ladycott,' Dr Greenwood said as he reappeared carrying a little glass of liquid. 'I'll arrange for you to see your daughter each evening until she's better.'

'Wud you? Aw, thank you, Doctor,' Emmanuel replied, bending down to place a kiss on Tresca's cheek. 'I'll see you tomorrow, then.'

Tomorrow. Oh, yes. She couldn't wait.

'Tresca! Aw, I's proper pleased fer see you back! You looks so much better. Covered in blood your face were when I found you. Aw, bit of a mark there'll be, but it'll fade, I expects.'

'It's good to see you, too, Lucy,' Tresca grinned. 'But at least they let my father in to see me every night.'

'Aw, that's cuz you'm so good. But you still looks pale. Matron!' she called with a familiarity only she could get away with, catching Mrs Sol-

144

loway's eye as she passed by the open door of the dormitory.

'Yes, Lucy?'

'You'm not gwain fer put Tresca back fer work in the laundry, are you? She'm still not fully better.'

Mrs Solloway smiled with unusual indulgence. 'Mrs Drake is going to put her in the sewing room. You can sew, Ladycott?'

'Yes, I can, Matron.'

'But I's got a better idea. I 'ardly larnt nort from Miss Miller in the schoolroom. She's far too old fer teach. Cud'n Tresca take her place? I's sure she'd be much better.'

Mrs Solloway's face stilled in astonishment, but then she cocked an eyebrow. 'Do you know, that's not a bad idea. Do you think you could teach, Ladycott?'

Tresca was utterly taken aback, but the proposal was certainly appealing. 'Well, yes, I think so. I always loved school myself and I'm sure I could pass it on. Reading, writing and arithmetic, and a little history and geography. And I'd be good at nature, having worked on farms all my life.'

'Well, I don't know how much the little tackers would take in. Not very bright, some of them.'

'That's cuz they've not 'ad Tresca fer teach 'em!' Lucy declared emphatically.

Mrs Solloway failed to suppress a smile. 'Well, you can start tomorrow, and we can see how it goes.' And she left the two girls hugging each other.

'Told you us cud 'elp each other, didn't I?'

'Yes, but I never expected ort like that. You *are* clever, Lucy. I'll have to think of a way to pay you back one day.'

'You doesn't 'ave fer.' Lucy shrugged in her funny, unique way. 'We'm friends anyway.'

Lucy didn't realize how grateful she was, Tresca mused. She had been dreading going back to work in the laundry, not because of the gruelling labour, but because of Enid Turnbull. She had pretended she couldn't remember who had attacked her, but she knew all too well. Now she wouldn't be torn between working hard so that she might be allowed to see her father occasionally, and slacking off so that she wouldn't risk further reprisals.

Oh, Lucy, you're an angel!

Fifteen

'Once four is four, two fours are eight–'

'Ladycott?'

Mrs Drake came in through the schoolroom door, followed by the ancient Miss Miller tottering on her sticks. Tresca at once broke off from leading the chanting of the times tables, and the children's voices petered out in response. Oh, Lord, did they not approve of her classroom methods? In the few weeks she had been teaching, the children had come on in leaps and bounds. But now it looked as if it was all over.

'Yes, Mrs Drake?' she answered, her mouth

suddenly dry.

'You're wanted in Matron's office. Miss Miller will take over from you.'

Tresca's feet dragged as she walked down the corridor. Surely she wasn't going to be put back to work in the laundry – to face the wrath of Enid Turnbull again? Would she be forced to reveal the identity of her assailant after all? A vile, sinking feeling squeezed her stomach as she knocked on Matron's door.

'Come in.'

Tresca's heart rose to her mouth as she obeyed. But she was so astounded when she opened the door that for a full thirty seconds she stood dithering on the threshold. Mrs Ellacott was sat in a chair, grinning broadly at her.

'Aw, Tresca, Is that glad to have found you!'

'Mrs Ellacott's come to take you away, Ladycott. She has a job for you as a dairymaid. Pity, really. You were doing a sterling job as our school mistress. But if someone offers you work, you have to take it or leave. It's the rules.'

Tresca continued to stare at them. A job with the homely Mrs Ellacott. Leave the workhouse. It was almost too much to take in.

'Sally's mother died, so she's gone back to look after the family. An' I always said that if I ever needed a new dairymaid, it'd be you.'

'You are pleased, I take it, Ladycott? Not that you have any choice in the matter.'

Tresca had been too shocked to utter a word, but now her thoughts were beginning to click into place. 'Yes, of course,' she stammered. 'I'm delighted. It's just ... so unexpected. B-but what about my father? Will he be able to come, too?'

A nervous hope had spiralled up inside her, but the next instant it was dashed to smithereens. 'I's afeared I cas'n afford to offer him a home an' all, cheel,' Jane Ellacott replied, her voice portraying genuine regret.

'And don't forget your father is unwell. There could be medicines and doctors' fees to pay. If he stays here, such things will be free. And he isn't your dependant, strictly speaking, so he's not obliged to leave the workhouse if you do.'

Tresca lowered her eyes. 'Oh. Oh, I see.'

'Bearing in mind he is unwell, we might be able to stretch the rules and let you visit once in a while.'

'Would you? That's very kind.'

'You've worked hard, Ladycott. And we're not entirely without compassion, you know. Not Mr Solloway and me.'

'And can I say goodbye to Lucy, please?'

'If you're quick. We mustn't keep Mrs Ellacott waiting. I'll have your own clothes brought out of storage and you can change in the dormitory.'

Tresca hurried out of the door, her emotions turned upside down. To be freed from the workhouse when she had been there little over two months was wonderful news. But her elation was tainted with sadness. She had hoped to be leaving in the spring with her father, taking him out to the countryside again, which would surely cure him of his cancer. And she would miss Lucy so much, as well.

She found Lucy at her work in the kitchens, doing her best to wash up the huge pans with her crooked left hand. Tresca had to explain to the formidable head cook that she had Matron's permission, and met the woman's steely gaze with equal defiance.

'Aw, I's that 'appy fer you!' Lucy cried. 'Dream fer iver, I will, 'bout all they stories you've told us.'

'And I'll never forget you, I promise. And one day ... *one day...*' Tresca declared, her eyes gleaming with determination.

But Lucy shrugged. 'One day can be a long time comin'. You just make a good life fer yersel', Tresca Ladycott.'

They hugged, and Tresca dragged herself away, biting back her tears. She had never dreamed she would leave a little piece of herself behind in the workhouse. But when, within the hour, she found herself dressed in her own shabby clothes and walking down Bannawell Street's steep hill sharing Jane Ellacott's umbrella, her heart at last began to dance in her chest.

'How did you know where to find me?' she asked as they splashed along, trying to avoid the puddles.

'Well, it weren't easy, my lover. You suddenly disappeared off the face of the earth. No one knew where you'd gone. An' then I saw that nice Miss Miles in the town, an' I asked her, knowing you were friends. At first she said she didn't know, but when I says to her it were because I wanted to offer you a job, like, then she tells me.'

'That were my fault. I felt so ashamed, I told her I didn't want anyone to know.'

'Well, I can understand that, so no harm done.

But, oh, let's get in out of the rain. Not stopped for a couple of weeks, it hasn't.' She unlocked the door to the dairy and ushered Tresca inside. 'First thing we must do is get you some decent clothes an' a good coat if that's all you've got.' And she went behind the counter and was soon holding out a shiny florin she had taken from the till.

'Oh, I can't possibly–'

'Your first week's wages in advance. Get yersel' down to the Market House an' see what you can find. An' when you gets back, we can have a nice cup of tea afore we starts work. Off you go, now. An' take my umbrella, cheel.'

'Thank you. And I've still got the slips from the clothes we took to the pawnbroker's. They'll have run out, but you never know.'

She pulled her old, worn shawl back up over her head. She no longer possessed a hat and didn't want anyone to see her shorn head, even if her hair had grown back to a cap of silvery brown, inch-long curls. She had been due to be scalped again in a few days' time. Thank goodness Mrs Ellacott had come when she had, or it would have been even worse!

She hurried downhill, the euphoria of her release flowing through her and her head reeling with plans for the future. Yes, she needed a few items of clothing, but then she would save every penny she possibly could. And one day she would be able to take Emmanuel out of the workhouse, even if it took several years. He hadn't seemed *that* unwell, and surely kind Dr Greenwood would be able to give him something that would

150

make him better?

She was so lost in her spirited resolve, her vision obscured by the umbrella, that she collided with the figure that came round the corner of Market Street in the opposite direction. It was a man, and a very tall one at that, her umbrella only coming halfway up his chest. She felt horribly embarrassed and looked up, burning with apology.

'Oh, I'm *so* sorry,' she gasped. And then stopped abruptly.

Connor O'Mahoney's thick, auburn eyebrows shot up towards the brim of his hat. 'Tresca!' he exclaimed. *'Cunuss thuee?'* he asked, in his surprise reverting to his native tongue. 'How are you? And where have you and your father been hiding? Haven't I been asking for you all over, but nobody seemed to know where you'd gone.'

Tresca glowered up at him, her instantly re-ignited hatred simmering just beneath the surface of her self-control. 'None of your business where we've been. And why are you all dressed up in your Sunday best? Got a promotion on the back of other men's hard work?'

She caught the stab of hurt indignation on his face and felt pleased. Her remark had obviously hit exactly where it was intended. Or so she thought. She was intensely disappointed when his explanation wiped out her success.

'Sure it's been raining non-stop the last two weeks,' he told her, raising his eyes to his own umbrella. 'The ground's saturated and you can't dig tunnels when the whole lot is likely to fall down on you. And you can't build embankments

151

when there's a danger of mud slides. So we've all been laid off, so we have. And I don't see why I should wear me old muddy clothes if I'm not working. Now I've answered your question, but you've not answered mine.'

'Nor am I going to. Now will you kindly let me pass.'

She tried to dodge past him, slipping between him and the wall since there was a large puddle on his other side. But as she did so, he caught her by the elbow.

'Sure, why are you always so—?'

He got no further as he snatched in his breath. His sudden grasp on the shawl had pulled it clean from her head, exposing her shame to full view. The disgrace of it turned her to immovable stone and she stood, perfectly still, like a statue.

'Oh, *acushla,* what happened to your hair? Have you been ill? And ... what's that mark on your forehead? I'd swear to the Holy Mother it wasn't there before.'

Tresca felt something rupture inside her, and all the strain and resentment of the last months erupted like lava from a volcano. 'Well, if you really want to know,' she spat viciously, 'because of *you,* my father and I had to go into the workhouse.'

'The workhouse!'

'Yes. And they cut off your hair so that you don't get lice. Not that *you*'d care. Now kind Mrs Ellacott has just given me a job at the dairy, but my father's still inside because he's not well and might never be able to do manual labour again.'

Connor's eyebrows swooped into a frown. 'I'm

152

mighty sorry to hear that, but sure it's not my fault he's ill. If only you'd allowed me to help you when I wanted instead of letting that stubborn pride of yours get in the way.'

'Help? Oh, as if you cared…'

'But I do. I care for all my men and their families.'

'But not my father and me, or you wouldn't have dismissed him.'

'You know I had to, *acushla*. Wasn't it his own–'

'And stop calling me that! I know what it means, and I'm no sweetheart of yours. So,' she snapped, moving her eyes with caustic disdain to where his hand was still on her arm, 'if you'd kindly let go of me, I'll be on my way.'

Connor's arm at once dropped to his side, and with supreme dignity Tresca pulled the shawl back up over her head and walked majestically away. But inwardly she was cursing the fact that Connor O'Mahoney lived on the same street as the dairy and so it would by no means be the last she would see of him.

Her lips compressed into a rebellious line and she marched off towards the pawnbroker's. She was seething after her meeting with Mr High and Mighty O'Mahoney, and was just in the mood to confront the nasty little money-dealer. She pushed open the door of the dark, musty shop so hard that it nearly came off its hinges.

'Half a crown to redeem,' the fellow demanded when he found Tresca's old coat still hanging on the rack.

'What! A shilling you gave me for it, and I only paid two shillings for it in the first place.'

153

The pawnbroker shrugged. 'Three months' interest charge,' he slurred slyly. 'And it's a nice piece. Did well to get it for two shilling, you did.'

'Well, I'll give you one and six, and that's a good return. Better than nothing at all.'

She held his gaze defiantly while he sniffed extra loudly and turned the coat over in his greedy hands. 'All right,' he finally agreed. 'But don't expect to do business with me ever again.'

'Don't worry. I've no intention of doing so.'

She paid the money and at once slipped into the coat, but kept the shawl tightly over her head. She only had sixpence left, but she simply *must* have a hat. She crossed hurriedly to the Market House and searched out the second-hand stall where she had originally bought the coat. She found a somewhat plain black bonnet and managed to knock the price down to fourpence, declaring that it was rather old-fashioned and nobody else would want to buy it. She kept very quiet about the fact that it was exactly what she wanted as it would hide her shorn hair. That left tuppence. All she could afford on the material stall was a poor-quality calico, but it would have to do. She was able to buy just enough to sew herself a spare blouse, and then she would save up to buy something better at a later date.

'That's better, my lover!' Mrs Ellacott beamed when she walked back into the dairy ten minutes later. 'Now I've had the kettle on the go, but first, come an' see your room.'

'Thank you.'

She followed Jane Ellacott through the side door, which led down a couple of steps into the working part of the dairy, and then into a narrow scullery where a staircase took them directly upstairs. On the right on a tiny inner landing was a room the size and shape of a corridor, so narrow that there was just room for a single bedstead at one end and a chest of drawers at the other. But it looked so cosy with rose-patterned curtains at the window that, after the austerity of the workhouse, to Tresca it was pure heaven.

'Is that all right for you, cheel? My own room's just here,' Jane said, indicating a door at the top of another few stairs, 'an' Mr Preedy, my lodger, has the other two rooms. Grumpy old so-and-so, he is, but he pays his rent regular enough. Summat to do with the highways, he is. Takes his meals up here, so I hardly ever sees him, an' that's how I likes it,' she winked.

Tresca wondered what Mr Preedy was like, but at that moment she didn't really care. 'Oh, it's a lovely room, Mrs Ellacott! Thank you so much!'

'Well, I could see you knows what you'm doing, an' I reckons you'll work hard. I's not a slave-driver, but I does expect a good day's work.'

'And you'll get it. I can't tell you how grateful I am. And for the loan of the money.'

'Well, no good me lendin' you any of my clothes!' Jane wobbled with laughter. 'Wouldn't see you inside them, would we? But what I can lend you,' she went on, her face more serious now, 'is an apron. An' a cap to hide your hair. Beautiful, it was. But it'll soon grow, an' that little scar's not goin' to spoil your good looks. Proper asset you'm goin' to be. Sally were a lovely girl, but she weren't as bright as you. Goin' to be proper friends, us. I can feel it in my bones.'

'Oh, yes, so can I!' Tresca cried, and she could have wept with joy.

Sixteen

'Vera!' Tresca cried as the tall figure came in out of the rain, shaking the water from her umbrella.

'Tresca, my dear! How good to see you! And first of all, I must apologize for breaking your confidence, but I thought, under the circumstances–'

'Oh, no, not at all. I'm so grateful, really I am. I couldn't be happier than working here.'

'Good! I'm only sorry there's nothing I can do for your father at present, but if I hear of any work–'

'He's learning to make boots,' Tresca informed her, 'now that he may not be able to do labouring any more.'

'Oh, dear, is he unwell?'

'Did you not know? Didn't Dr Greenwood tell you?'

'Not allowed to. Well, I'm sorry to hear that. What's wrong, if you don't mind my asking?'

'Dr Greenwood thinks he may have some sort of cancer. I don't really understand. At first I had the impression it were something serious, but Father seems fine. A little tired, perhaps. But I'm going to save up and in a few years' time, I'll take him out of the workhouse. I'm sure he'll get better then.'

156

Her voice had been light and full of confidence, her happiness at living and working at the dairy filling her mind and pushing aside all other doubts. But now she saw Vera purse her lips pensively.

'Cancer is very serious,' Vera said hesitantly. 'It drains people's strength as much as anything. I know – it's what my mother died from. But hopefully your father will have many a long year in front of him yet.' She had deliberately made her tone brighter, not wanting to spoil Tresca's obvious delight at her new situation. 'Now then, I was wondering what free time you have? It would be lovely if we could go for a walk if this dreadful weather ever stops. It's been raining stair rods for nearly three weeks now. All work on the railway's been suspended, and the men don't get paid, you know.'

'I hadn't thought of that,' Tresca confessed, remembering her altercation with Connor O'Mahoney. 'So *none* of them get paid?'

'Not a penny. We've set up a soup kitchen for them. A penny for a quart of good, thick broth. Just about keeping some families alive. And Mr Massey, the navvy missionary, wants to set up a sick club for them. Did you hear about that dreadful accident a few weeks back? A young navvy tripped on the rails and was run over by a cart. Crushed both his legs. They tried to save his life by amputating them, but he died an hour or so later. Terrible,' she said, shaking her head. 'Dreadfully hard lives these navvies lead, all of them. And such dangerous work.'

Tresca sucked in her cheeks. Perhaps she had

been a little hard on Connor. Emmanuel *had* deserved to lose his job. It wasn't right that he should have been drunk at his work. It was irresponsible and dangerous. It was just that their lives had blossomed because of his job, and she was sure that given a second chance...

'Yes. Look at poor Assumpta,' she sighed, driving Connor O'Mahoney from her mind. 'Have you heard from her at all? She said she'd write.'

'But she hasn't. And to be honest, I'm not sure she could write. Anyway, when are you likely to have some time off?'

'I don't really know. Maybe on Sundays. We still have to see to the cows, of course, but Mrs Ellacott doesn't open the shop. I might be needed to help cook dinner, but it certainly would be lovely to have some time with you. I'll ask Mrs Ellacott.'

'Excellent! Well, while I'm here, I'll have half a pound of butter, please. And then I must hurry home before I have to swim for it!'

'Just a gill o' milk, if you please,' the customer asked. 'All I can afford just now.'

'Does your man work on the railway, then?' Tresca enquired sympathetically as she took the old jug the woman offered her and went to measure a quarter pint of milk into it.

'Rather he's *not* workin' on it. Been nearly a month now an' no wages comin' in. Supposed to survive on thin air, are we? If it weren't for Mr O'Mahoney, we'd be starvin' by now.'

At the mention of Connor's name, Tresca gave an involuntary jerk and spilt a drop of the creamy milk. 'Mr O'Mahoney?' she repeated cautiously.

158

'He's the ganger for my Herbie's part o' the line. You must know him. Big Irish chap lodgin' almost opposite yere.'

'Yes, I do,' Tresca admitted reluctantly.

'A grand man. Subbin' those of us with families out o' his own pocket when he won't be gettin' paid, either. There's not many would do that for you. You'm new in yere, bain't you, but haven't I seen you afore?'

'Yes. I were living further up the hill,' Tresca answered somewhat absently. For a moment her mind was distracted from her wonderful new life, and was instead invaded by a vision of a thatch of red hair and a pair of deep-set blue eyes. She didn't want Connor to spoil her present contentment and she didn't want to hear what a kind man he was. Angrily she pushed any thought of him aside.

'Will that be all?' she asked instead.

Tresca stepped into the street and took a deep breath of the fresh spring air. After nearly a month of continuous rain, the sky was clear. It was Sunday. Having brought the cows down for milking and stored the rich white liquid ready to make butter the next day, she had herded them back up to their field and was now free until evening milking. She had washed, changed into the plain white blouse she had sewn from the calico, and donned her coat and hat. It was three months since her head had been shorn and her hair was growing so that she wasn't quite so self-conscious about it. But it would be a long time before she could feel anything like a young woman again.

She was in buoyant mood today, if only because it had finally stopped raining. Mrs Ellacott was chapel, but Tresca was going to St Eustachius's Church with Vera and afterwards they would spend a little time together. And that afternoon she was going to visit her father. On the first Sunday of each month, the Solloways had said, and she was bursting with anticipation.

There were still puddles on the pavement and Tresca lifted the hem of her skirt to avoid getting it wet. The inhabitants of Bannawell Street were setting out to their various forms of worship – those that had one – and after all the weeks of being deserted as people cowered from the rain, the street seemed to have exploded into life. Familiar faces nodded a greeting at Tresca, and she smiled back.

Oh, Lord. She stopped in her tracks when she reached the point where Bannawell Street became King Street. The little houses facing each other on either side had been stripped of their roofs and the windows removed, as if they were being demolished. They looked sad and forlorn, and Tresca felt a cold shock slithering down her spine.

'Pity, isn't it?' a voice said at her shoulder. 'But sure, they've got to come down for the viaduct.'

Tresca turned, all her animosity towards Connor O'Mahoney snapping back into place. 'And I suppose you'll be in charge of building it?' she said icily.

'Me? Oh, Jesus, no. Sure, I'm not an engineer. Would have loved to have studied engineering at college or university, so I would. But what chance

160

would a lad brought up in a backwater of Tipperary have of that? No, I might be senior among the gangers, but I'm only fit for digging cuttings and tunnels and laying track. Have to leave viaducts and bridges to the experts. Sure, it'd fall down if I built it,' he concluded, tipping his head upwards, 'and we wouldn't want that, would we?'

His generous mouth moved into a tentative smile, his eyebrows arched questioningly. But if he thought an attempt at friendly banter was going to soften her after what she had suffered in the workhouse because of him, then he would have to think again. She stared back at him, her expression implacable, and felt pleased at the awkwardness that came over his face.

'Going to cross right up there, so it is,' he went on, gesturing towards the sky. 'Wonderful feat of engineering. And built from your Dartmoor granite, so it'll not look out of place.'

Despite herself, Tresca found her eyes following his heavenwards. When she considered the steepness and height of the hills the viaduct was to bridge, it would certainly be a thing to behold. For a moment, she was swept up in the same awe as Connor, but then reality overtook her again and she spun irritatedly on her heel.

'Well, I'm afeared I don't have time to stand about considering some monstrosity that's putting people out of their homes,' she announced acidly. 'I'm going to church with a friend.'

'Aren't I going that way meself.' To her annoyance, Connor fell into step beside her. 'Wish there were a Catholic church here, but the nearest one I know of is in Plymouth. So I have to confess me

161

sins straight to God and hope He's listening, and give meself me own penances.'

'That must keep you very busy, then,' she retorted. Oh, why wouldn't he leave her alone?

'Well, I've had time enough on me hands with no work over the past month,' he went on, replying blithely to her scathing remark. 'But hopefully the ground will start drying out and we'll be back to work in a week or so. Need to if some of these poor families are to survive.'

Tresca waited for him to boast about helping them, but he didn't. So at least he possessed a shred of humility, she thought grudgingly. 'Yes, it's been hard for some of them. And I know what that's like.'

'Yes, I know.' Connor's voice was grave now. 'And I really am sorry for what happened to you. But you know it really wasn't my fault.' He had caught her arm and his eyes, a dark sapphire in their intensity, bore into hers. 'All the same, I beg your forgiveness. You know I'd have done something to stop you going in the workhouse if I'd known.'

Tresca knotted her lips. He was offering her an olive branch, but it was one she couldn't possibly accept. 'So where are you going now?' she asked in an attempt at civility, although heaven knew she didn't care *where* he was going – unless it was back to Ireland, in which case she would have rejoiced.

'Thought I'd take meself up on the moor. There are no trains up there on a Sunday, of course, so I'll have to walk. Which is why you might have noticed I'm not in me *Sunday best*,' he told her,

162

emphasizing the words to remind her, she considered heatedly, of their conversation the day Mrs Ellacott had rescued her from the workhouse. 'Pity I won't see the railway running. Wouldn't it be nice to see it when I spent a couple of years of me life building the thing. Loved working on the moor, so I did. But I've a notion I told you that before. Haven't you worked up on the moor yourself, being a farm girl?'

'Dairymaid,' she corrected him, but felt obliged to answer his question. 'So I've never worked up on the high moorland. You don't get dairy cows on the moor, unless it's a house cow just for a farmer's own use. And hilltop farmers don't need casual labourers. But my father and I have worked on farms on the *edge* of Dartmoor often enough. Farms that grow fodder crops and the like on the lower slopes.' They had reached the bottom of Market Street and Tresca wondered quite how she had become engaged in conversation with this man she loathed. 'Now, if you'd excuse me, Mr O'Mahoney, I can see my friend waiting for me.'

'But of course. And remember, it's *Connor*, not O'Mahoney.'

He raised his hat from his mop of bright hair and then strode off across the town's main square. Tresca breathed a sigh of relief and scampered over to where Vera was waiting, the interlude with Connor discarded to the depths of her memory.

'Good morning, Tresca!' Vera greeted her. 'And a fine one it is, too.'

'It certainly is. Makes you feel better, doesn't it? Shall we go in?'

The old church was hushed and reverent, the sun shining through the beautiful stained-glass windows, as the congregation assembled in the pews. Tresca's experience of religion was scanty and intermittent, but the service gave her a sense of peace. When they came back out into the sunlight, she felt happy and refreshed.

'Miss Ladycott, isn't it?'

The man's voice behind her made Tresca turn round. She recognized the young fellow at once and returned his open smile. 'Mr Trembath, how are you this lovely morning?'

'Very well, thank you. I haven't seen you for some while, since you ... well, when you came into the shop,' he concluded diplomatically. 'That was before Christmas. Have you been unwell?'

Tresca tipped her head. 'You could say that, but I'm much recovered now and feel so much better now that spring has finally arrived.'

'April,' Morgan Trembath sighed pleasurably. 'Such a wonderful month. Daffodils in bloom, and the air so full of expectation. I was about to take a little wander along the canal. Would you and your friend care to join me?'

'I'm sure we'd both be delighted. Mr Trembath, this is my good friend, Miss Vera Miles.'

'Pleased to meet you, Miss Miles.'

'Likewise. I have seen you so often in church with an older lady.'

'My mother,' Morgan informed her as they made their way towards the area known as the Meadows. 'She is in bed with a head cold, otherwise she wouldn't have missed the church service.'

'I'm sorry to hear that.'

'To be honest, I'm rather glad to have a little time to myself,' Morgan confessed, 'and I'm sure my mother will recover quite soon. She relies on me a great deal since my father died and it's sometimes a little tiring.'

'I'm sure you are always the dutiful son, but it is nice to enjoy a little freedom on one's own at times,' Vera nodded knowingly.

'Indeed it is. We live in the same house and we run the shop together. Trembath's ironmonger's in West Street, if you know it. So it does get a little claustrophobic at times.'

Claustrophobic, Tresca scoffed to herself. Poor Morgan Trembath seemed to her totally dominated by his mother. She was glad the woman was ill so that the poor fellow could enjoy himself a little.

'Miss Ladycott,' he said, suddenly addressing her, 'I'm afraid I don't have any crusts as Mr O'Mahoney usually does. I remember watching you feeding the ducks with him some while ago, and you really seemed to enjoy it.'

Tresca felt a twinge of resentment. She really didn't want to be reminded of Connor O'Mahoney again! She hoped he would get lost on the moor and never come back.

'Never mind. I'm in such good company, and on such a wonderful morning as this, it's just so marvellous to be out of doors.'

She noticed a pink hue blush into Morgan's cheeks. He really was such a pleasant young man and didn't deserve his haranguing mother. She didn't know how he put up with her. He must have the patience of a saint.

165

They ambled along the path as far as the road-bridge over the canal. The sun warmed their backs, the trees were coming into leaf, and Tresca felt that all was well with the world. If it hadn't been for her father...

'I'm afraid I must return now,' Morgan announced, 'if you ladies will excuse me. I'm sure you'll be perfectly safe here together.'

Tresca had to suppress a chuckle. If only he knew the situations she had faced in her life! But it was all part of the young man's kind-hearted-ness – so different from Connor O'Mahoney's attitude towards her.

'Yes, thank you, I'm sure we will,' Vera assured him. 'Unless you wish to return now, Tresca?'

'Oh, no. I feel quite exhilarated and I'd like to walk a little further.'

'Good day to you, then, ladies, and I'm sure I'll see you both again.' And so saying, he gave a short bow and walked briskly back the way they had come.

'What a pleasant young man,' Vera commented as they crossed over the road and began to follow the tow path on the opposite side of the bridge.

'Yes, but I've met his mother. Proper old harridan, she is.' Tresca pulled an ugly face, twisting her mouth so that she looked like a gargoyle. Vera at once broke into a fit of laughter, and Tresca giggled back. Oh, she was so lucky to have found such a good friend!

'How you'm feeling, Father?' she asked that afternoon when she was allowed in to see Emmanuel. An icy, nervous sweat had slicked her skin as she approached the workhouse gates, the horrible memories beating down on her. Mr Solloway, whom she had scarcely glimpsed when she had been an inmate, had hurried her along to a small, dark and heartless room, more like a cupboard, where her father was waiting for her.

'Aw, fair to middlin',' Emmanuel answered. 'Made my fust pair o' boots all by mysel' this week.'

'Really? Oh, well done!' Tresca's lively mind sprang into action. 'Maybe when I get you out of here, you can set up a little business. There's three bootmakers in Bannawell Street, so you could do the same. Or you could supply them to German's, you know, that huge footwear shop on the corner–'

'Aw, cheel, it took us the 'ole week to make one pair. And they'm not very good. Takes years it does to larn proper like. They'm only fit fer the work'ouse inmates. But mortal 'appy I am to see you'm making plans, as usual,' he chuckled. 'Now tell me, 'as my princess got 'er eye on a young man yet?'

Tresca tossed a light laugh in the air. 'No, I haven't. Mrs Ellacott's treating me so well, and just now that's all I care about,' she declared adamantly. And it was quite true!

Seventeen

'Tresca, dear,' Mrs Ellacott said to her one day at the beginning of May when she was vigorously turning the handle of the butter-churn. 'We'm goin' to need the services of Farmer Hiscock's bull afore too long. I wants you to save my poor old legs an' walk out to his farm this afternoon an' arrange summat with him. I'll give you directions. You can't get lost.'

And so after lunch, Tresca set out on her mission. She enjoyed her work immensely, but it was always pleasant to be out and about as well. As she walked briskly down the hill, she passed the point where nothing remained of the little houses that had been demolished to make way for the railway viaduct. Now it was a hive of activity with navvies digging deep to create the foundations for the giant pillars, and three men in bowler hats, the engineers presumably, consulting pages of plans. Tresca fleetingly recalled her conversation with Connor about the demolition of the houses. Did he really have some sense of regret? She had heard that the tenants had been given assistance to find new homes, so she had to admit that was something.

'Good day to you, Miss Ladycott.'

'Mr Trembath. How nice to see you.'

Tresca was supremely relieved to see that Morgan's hard-faced mother wasn't with him. She and Vera had kept their distance on subsequent Sundays when he had been accompanied by Mrs Trembath, but he was a friendly, amiable fellow and Tresca was always happy to speak to him provided he was on his own.

'On your way back to the shop?' she asked affably.

'I am indeed. And where are you off to, may I ask?' When she told him, he nodded his head thoughtfully. 'Well, I'd hurry if I were you. Looks like rain later.'

'You might be right,' she agreed. 'Have a good afternoon, then,' she said as Morgan went to turn up West Street.

'You, too. Take care now.'

Tresca bade him farewell and set out across the little passage in front of St Eustachius's Church. She turned right and followed along Plymouth Road, crossed over West Bridge, and shortly afterwards struck out along Crowndale Road. The long, lonely lane led out to Shillamill. The navvies who laboured on that part of the line and who were lodging in the town used it to get to and from work, but now, in the early afternoon, it was deserted.

Farmer Hiscock and Crowndale Farm were to be found a mile or so down the lane, and Tresca couldn't miss it, so Mrs Ellacott had said. The air was turning cooler and Tresca shivered as her eyes moved skywards. Oyster-grey clouds were piling up ominously, and yet it was uncannily still. Tresca hoped there wasn't a storm brewing, but she had a horrible feeling there was.

She had spoken with Farmer Hiscock and was

169

making her way back along the lonely lane when the first raindrops began to fall in fat, heavy spheres. The wind suddenly whipped up in a squall, whistling through the hedgerows. The trees, their leaves unfurling in bright, verdant green, started to sway and bend, and in a matter of moments everywhere was plunged back into winter. The sky darkened to a swirling, ashy pewter, and all at once a torrent of hailstones the size of peas was battering down from above.

Tresca hunched her shoulders and scurried along, searching for somewhere to shelter as the hail drove into her face. She had never been along the lane before so had no idea where she might take refuge. The pearls of ice were turning into sharp, stinging sleet, the angry wind howling with rage. It tore at the towering trees, ripping off a dead branch that crashed to the ground, just missing Tresca's head. A frightened scream escaped her lips but was lost in a reverberating roar as a thunderclap broke overhead. She wasn't one to be perturbed by the average storm, but this was something evil and dangerous and she knew she must take shelter.

The sleet had turned to torrential rain, blinding, an impenetrable wall, and Tresca could hardly see where she was going as she battled against the gusting wind. There was no sign of it abating, rather it was worsening, with flashes of dazzling light ripping into the now charcoal dome of the sky and followed instantaneously by a crack of thunder. The storm must be overhead, and Tresca rejoiced when a small stone barn loomed out of the murk just beyond an open field gate at the side of the road. The door was rotten and hung from its hinges, swinging perilously back and forth with each blast of the wind.

Tresca dodged thankfully inside. The rain had soaked down inside her neck and she was cold and shivering, but at least she was safe from the fury of the storm. She wondered how long it would last, but she would just have to wait it out. She peered into the darkness, searching for somewhere to sit down and her wildly beating heart began to slow.

'What 'ave we yere, then?'

A terrified squeal lodged in Tresca's throat. The featureless form of a man was silhouetted against the dank gloom inside the barn. And, dear God, a second faceless figure appeared at his shoulder.

'Summat fer while away the time, I reckons.'

Tresca's heart bucked painfully in her chest. For a split second, she was paralysed with panic, but she flung it out of her head and catapulted towards the door as it banged dangerously in the gale. But it was too late. A pair of hands grabbed her arm. She tried to wrench them off, but her other arm, too, was locked in a strong hold and she was dragged deeper into the barn. She wriggled like a thing possessed, heaving her shoulders, kicking. She managed to crack her boot against the first man's shin and he released his hold with a yelp. Tresca lashed out with her free arm, aiming her clenched fist at the other man's head. She missed. An instant later, the first brute had hold of her again, cursing and swearing.

'Pay fer that, you will, you little minx!' he hissed, and between them they hauled her, screaming and struggling, to the back of the barn and flung her on to the ground.

She landed with a thud on the damp, compacted earth, the wind knocked out of her so that she could hardly breathe, let alone move. Terror clenched about her heart, every nerve of her body on fire and ready to strike out if only she could catch her breath. And just when she felt she might be able to retaliate, she felt a heavy weight on her chest as one of the attackers straddled her, his teeth gleaming out of the darkness. He grinned down at her, laughing, as he yanked off the buttons of her coat and then ripped open her blouse and the camisole beneath. The cold air on her naked flesh stung her body alive again, and she found the breath to release an ear-splitting shriek.

'Scream away, my lovely. No one's goin' fer hear you out yere!'

'You can 'ave that end. It's this end I wants!'

She felt the other demon at her flailing legs. She tried desperately to kick out, but with the weight pinning her down, her crazed, valiant efforts were futile. She knew he had lifted her skirt, was trying to force her knees apart. Oh, no, please, God, NO! And as her lungs heaved with air, she let out another deafening screech...

'Holy Mother–'

She was hardly aware of what happened next, her mind shutting down in its abject horror. The outline of a third massive form towered over the other two. Oh, Lord, let me die first...

She heard the roar of anger, then a muted cry cut short. She dared to open her eyes and saw the dark bulk of a man sweep another off his feet and hurl him aside. A second later, the weight miraculously lifted from her chest and the other savage received the same fate. Tresca somehow managed to crawl backwards into a corner, curling up into a defensive ball and scarcely daring to peer out at the fierce fight that had broken out between the three men. Shouts and grunts, thuds as fists found flesh, crashes as bodies were flung against walls or on to the floor. Dear God, they were fighting over *her*. Over which one should have her. She should make her escape, but she couldn't, simply couldn't move.

The third intruder was being beaten down by the other two, but he fought back, kicking, punching, his superior strength and size slowly gaining the upper hand. What chance would she have... Then she saw clearly his big fist strike the face of the first man, who let out an almighty scream and collapsed on to his knees with his hands over his mouth. His companion whipped round, and Tresca saw the whites of his eyes, wide and fearful, in his lurid face. He had obviously had enough and slunk off, followed a few moments later by his evil companion, who was still moaning in pain and clutching at his face. The tall shadow of the third man stood for a moment or two, staggering slightly, breathing hard, wiping the back of his hand across his mouth. Then he turned to Tresca, and she tried to dig her way into the wall.

'Tresca? Oh, *acushla*.'

She was nearly sick as he came towards her. Oh, sweet Jesus. But then he flopped down on the floor next to her, his back against the wall as his heavy panting gradually lessened.

'Oh, *acushla*, my little love,' he breathed, gulping, and scooped her into his arms. 'Thank Holy Mary I were passing just then and thought to take shelter in here. What in the name of the Father were you doing in here with those monsters? Sure weren't they the devil incarnate. Oh, and just look at you.'

He delicately pulled the ripped edges of her blouse together and she stared up at him, her gaze frozen. But deep within her, a feeling of gratitude, of peace and safety, was gathering itself together. And tears of relief trickled unheeded down her cheeks.

'C–Connor?' she barely croaked.

'Who else?' His arms tightened around her, but she was happy to lean against him. Could hear his heart pounding strongly. 'We'll get you home as soon as the storm's over. Do you know who those two blackguards were?'

'N–no. W–were they navvies?'

'I don't know. I certainly didn't recognize them. But aren't there over two thousand of us in the area and I can't know them all. I don't know what I did to that fellow just now, but sure me hand knows I hit him hard. And won't the other one have a black eye to prove who he was.'

'Oh, Connor, th–thank you,' Tresca stammered. 'I ... I came in here to get out of the storm. I didn't ... know they were ... in here.'

'Well, you're safe now, little one. You know I wouldn't harm a hair on your head.' Connor exhaled sharply and dropped back against the wall.

Neither of them spoke again as they waited for the rain to stop battering on the tin roof, for the door to stop banging in the wind. All Tresca was aware of was her whole body still shaking uncontrollably but curled in the protection of Connor's arms of steel. Connor O'Mahoney who she hated.

'I think we can go now,' he said at length as light began to glimmer through the broken slats of the door. He tried to stand up with her still gathered in his arms, but drew the breath through his teeth in a wince, resting her back on the ground. 'Are you all right to walk? I think one of them got me ribs.'

'Yes,' she whispered hoarsely, though she was feeling stronger now. 'I wasn't hurt.'

'Good. Come on then.'

He helped her to her feet and together they stumbled outside. The sky was still a slate grey, but the wind was dying down and the rain had stopped. Evidence of the storm, though, was all around, with leafy twigs and lengths of broken branches strewn everywhere in the muddy lane. They stood looking all around them, and when their eyes met, Tresca's opened wide. Blood from a badly split lip had dried on Connor's chin and one of her attackers wasn't the only person who was going to have a black eye. He saw her looking, and put a tentative finger up to his mouth.

'We're going to look a right pair,' he said wryly, 'and I only went into town to have a word with Mr Szlumper about the scaffolding in the tunnel. Hold your coat about you, now. Will you be able to sew on some new buttons, d'you think?'

Tresca almost smiled. It seemed such a minor

thing to worry about when Connor had bravely saved her from being ... well, she couldn't even think the word. How could she ever...? 'I can't thank you enough, Connor,' she murmured.

'Sure, wouldn't anyone have done the same. I'm just glad I were a match for them. And you calling me Connor is thanks enough. I hope you can forgive me for what's gone before. You know I'd have helped you if you'd let me.'

A watery smile lifted the corners of Tresca's mouth. 'Yes, I'm sorry I should have trusted you. I were just so angry about what happened and I suppose I wanted someone to blame.'

'Sure, I can understand that. But let's forget about all that now. How is your father? You told me he were quite poorly.'

'Well, they say he is, but I find it hard to believe.' She was amazed at herself, talking openly to Connor O'Mahoney like this. And when her nerves were all so taut and ready to snap. But perhaps that was precisely why. 'The doctor reckons he has a type of cancer, but I just can't ... can't comprehend it.'

'Ah,' Connor grunted. 'Sure that's hard for anyone to comprehend. That can go on for years, or it can be mighty quick. Let's hope it'll be the former case with your daddy.'

Tresca sucked in her cheeks as she walked along beside him. Yes, she hoped the same. It struck her then how odd it was to hear Connor using that particular form of endearment: 'Daddy'. Connor O'Mahoney, who she always thought of as so self-assured and confident. And then she remembered how he had been with the ducks. Perhaps she had misjudged him entirely.

'We should be going to the police about this, I'm thinking,' he said softly. 'That's if you feel up to it. It could be difficult for you, going over exactly what happened. Trying to describe those devils.'

Tresca shook her head as the horror rushed at her again. 'It were so dark, I'm not sure as I'd ever recognize them. All I remember is that they were in working men's clothes. But, yes,' she answered, determination strengthening in her breast, 'I should report it. Some other girl mightn't be so lucky as I were. But … you will come with me?'

'Of course. And don't be forgetting they'll be bearing evidence of what happened on their faces,' he added, flexing his hand again.

'Oh, Connor, your poor hand, it's swelling up. And it's covered in blood.'

'Cut it on his teeth, I shouldn't wonder. I'm not sure if it's all his blood or mine.'

'Well, after we've been to the police, you must come with me and I'll patch you up. It's the least I can do.'

'So,' he faltered, his eyebrows dipped, 'we can be friends from now on?'

She looked up at him and nodded. And something in her heart softened.

Eighteen

'Aw, my little princess, tell me tidd'n true.'

Tresca blinked at her father. His forehead was pleated, his tall frame stooped, and he somehow seemed to have grown older since she had seen him the previous month. She gazed at him through liquid eyes and took him in her arms, aware for the first time of his frailty.

'I read 'bout it in the paper,' Emmanuel groaned. 'Lets us 'ave the *Gazette,* they does. An' when I saw it were you, aw, I were mortal crazed, I were.'

Tresca drew back and looked into his beloved, anguished face. She was so overcome at seeing the change in him that at first she couldn't think what he was talking about. It was three weeks since the vile incident in the barn and she had been trying desperately to forget about it. Now the horrific memory seared into her once more.

'Yes, it were me,' she admitted, trying to make light of it. 'But nothing actually happened and I weren't hurt at all. Just very frightened.'

'But I should've been there to protect you,' Emmanuel complained miserably, 'instead o' bein' cooped up in yere. An' 'ave they caught they buggers yet?'

Tresca shook her head. 'No, they haven't. But sit down afore you get too upset,' she encouraged, directing him to the hard, straight-backed chair

178

he nevertheless slumped into like a puppet whose strings had been suddenly cut. Tresca squatted down in front of him and took his gnarled hands. 'They tried, but I think it's all forgotten about now. I don't suppose we'll ever know if they were navvies or not. There are so many of them working all along the line at the same time. And Connor reckons they'll be long gone, whoever they were.'

'Connor?' Emmanuel's voice was sharp as he almost spat the name, his strength suddenly returning. 'So, it be *Connor* now, is it, not Mr O'Mahoney? That divil what put us in yere.'

Tresca felt a deep sigh in her chest. 'He'm really not so bad, you know. He took quite a beating when he rescued me, and he's never complained. And he didn't know it were me. Not at first. So it isn't as if he were trying to get in my good books or anything. And, you know,' she ventured, summoning her courage, 'he *was* right to dismiss you. It really is dangerous work. There have been so many accidents and he really couldn't take the risk of having someone ... well, you know, among his men. You know that, don't you, Father?'

Emmanuel's mouth wilted at the corners. 'I supposes so,' he muttered grudgingly.

'And it isn't his fault you've got this ... this cancer thing.' Swiftly changing the subject, she asked, 'How have you been?'

'All the better fer seein' you. An' I swears you've grown since you got out o' this place.'

Tresca smiled back. 'Do you know, I think I have! I've had to let down the hem of my skirt.

179

And I've bought some material to make myself a new summer dress.'

'Pretty as a picture you'll be. My princess be turnin' into a proper young woman. An' I sees your lovely 'air be growin' back an' all. Every young rascal in town'll be arter you. So you be careful. Don't want ort like *that* 'appening to you again.'

'Oh, don't you fret none. Connor's hardly let me out of his sight. Except when he'm at work, of course…'

She broke off abruptly. What would Emmanuel have to say if he knew of the attention Connor had been showing her? The attack and his valiant rescue had caused a seed of understanding to germinate between them. Tresca had even found herself enjoying his company, eagerly awaiting each evening when Connor would call into the dairy on his return from work to make sure she was still all right. At first she had wanted to know how he was, too, seeing the way his eye had swollen up and then turned every colour of the rainbow. The injuries he had collected in his defence of her had now healed and Tresca herself was more or less over the horror of the attack, but they had slipped into a daily routine that she sincerely hoped he was not about to break.

'O'Mahoney?'

'*Please*, Father,' Tresca begged. 'Connor's really very kind. You know how he helped Assumpta, and there's been other folk, too, but he never says a word about it. I think we misjudged him, you know.'

'That's as maybe,' Emmanuel mumbled. But

180

then his eyes snapped with animosity. 'But that don't mean 'er can go thinkin' 'er can get 'is mucky 'ands on you instead. Old enough to be your father, he be.'

'He'm thirty-one,' Tresca informed him, astounded at the way the skin around her neck was prickling defensively. 'And he'm always the perfect gentleman, so you've no worries on that score, I assure you.'

But later, as she walked back down Bannawell Street, she found, quite curiously, that she was thinking not of her father, but of the man he clearly still held a grudge against. It was as if a faint light was dawning deep inside her, growing stronger and brighter with each day that passed. And soon, perhaps, that glimmer would erupt in a glorious explosion of brilliance. She couldn't wait to find out...

'Connor!' Tresca's heart waltzed with delight as he appeared on the threshold. 'I thought perhaps you weren't coming today.'

She had tried to convince herself that there was good reason for his not turning up at the normal time, and that, having both recovered from the incident two months ago now, it wasn't because Connor hoped their relationship would peter out. And what relationship would that be, exactly, she dared to ask herself? One of two friends who happened to be of the opposite sex.

Yet she was intrigued by the tormented, delicious emotion that churned in her breast. She had come to realize that whenever she thought of Connor, her heart began to beat in the most alarming but exquisite way. Now it was summer, he no longer wore a neckerchief, the top buttons of his shirt unfastened and revealing the brown skin at his throat. Tresca wanted to touch it, feel its warmth beneath her fingers. His jacket was usually slung carelessly over his shoulder, his waistcoat accentuating his trim waist. He would saunter into the dairy, often whistling, and then smile at her with those twinkling, peacock-blue eyes that made her heart race.

And then a horrible fear had taken hold of her. Perhaps … oh, dear Lord, she prayed not … but perhaps there had been another accident. Only the previous week, a minor explosion had occurred when a lighted candle had inadvertently been dropped into a box of cartridges. And a few days earlier, a navvy had been killed when a charge had gone off prematurely. If anything happened to Connor after the way she felt about him now, Tresca would be devastated. Her mind had conjured up a terrible picture of him lying injured among a crater of mud and twisted iron rails, or perhaps buried in the Shillamill Tunnel as Rory Driscoll had been. So when Connor suddenly materialized in front of her, relief and excitement tingled through to her fingertips.

'I went home first to clean meself up a bit,' he explained, his generous mouth breaking into that mesmerizing smile. 'And to collect this. A present for you.'

'A present?' Tresca realized now that he was carrying a large wooden box. 'For me?'

'Sure, I don't see anyone else in here,' he teased.

'Well, you'd better come through.'

182

'Won't Mrs Ellacott mind? Won't she be objecting to a stranger coming into her home?'

'You'm hardly a stranger, Connor,' Tresca grinned back, and she led him through to the kitchen.

Jane Ellacott greeted them with her usual cheery smile. 'Mr O'Mahoney, how nice to see you. Will you have some dinner with us? There be plenty in the pot.'

'Isn't that so kind of you, but I've me own dinner waiting for me. I just wanted to give this to Tresca.'

His eyes glinted mischievously as he set the box on the floor, since the table was taken up with the two place settings and a tray ready laid to be taken upstairs to Mr Preedy. Tresca frowned inquisitively as she knelt down and began to remove crunched up balls of newspaper from the top of the box.

'I'll just take Mr Preedy's meal up to him,' Jane announced as she ladled a large portion of delicious stew into the bowl on the tray and then carried it out of the room.

'Go on then, *acushla*,' Connor encouraged. 'But be careful for aren't parts of it breakable.'

Tresca's curious eyes met his mildly teasing ones. Goodness, he seemed so attractive to her in his own unique way. She gulped, turning her attention back to the box and hoping he didn't notice the crimson in her cheeks.

She carefully unwrapped the base of a pretty china lamp, and her hands began to tremble as she stood it on the table. She stared at it, and then back up at Connor whose face was aglow. Perhaps

183

she was mistaken. But when she took out the fluted glass globe with its delicate pink hue, she knew she wasn't. And a surge of anger whipped through her.

'It's the lamp you bought from me when Mrs Trembath wouldn't take it back,' she said, her voice flat and expressionless.

'It is so. What would I be doing with such a feminine thing? Fit only for a lady, so it is.'

'And you want to humiliate me by *giving* it back? To remind me of your so-called act of charity towards me?' she accused, springing to her feet.

Connor's jaw slackened. 'No. I thought you'd be pleased to have it back. Didn't I want to make a present of it to you. To show you how much–'

'No, don't tell me! How superior you are to me! How much I needed your help and you–'

'No, woman! How much I–'

His tone was gruff, harsher than she had ever known it. She went to turn her back on him, but he caught her arm, roughly pulling her towards him. She glared up at him, her eyes narrowed challengingly, seeing the rebellious reply in his. Before she knew it, his mouth came down on hers, hard and demanding.

'Oh, *acushla*,' his lips murmured.

She tried to struggle, pummelling her small fists against his chest, but there was no escape. His hands were in the small of her back, and one of them moved into her hair so that it fell from the little knot she had begun to be able to pin it into. Their bodies were rigid, pressed against each other. But then she felt him relax, his hold

184

soften. His lips withdrew from hers, then returned, searching, gentle, brushing against hers in teasing little kisses before he drew away and gazed down at her, his mouth in a soft curve.

'There, that wasn't so bad, was it? I was going to say how much I love you. Didn't you stir me heart the very first time I saw you. Sure I know I'm a lot older than you, but ... you think you might come to like me one day?'

Her eyes glinted like the flash of the sun on polished steel. '*Like* you?' she grated. And then her hand shot out and slammed across his cheek. He stared at her for a moment, his expectant expression fading, and then he lowered his head.

'Please forgive me,' he mumbled, not daring to look at her again. 'We were getting on so well, I thought... Just the foolish hopes of a stupid eejit. I think, perhaps, I'd best be leaving you.'

He turned swiftly and left the room, closing the door quietly behind him. Tresca stood, staring after him. How dare he? She glanced at the lamp, the lovely object that she had chosen for its beauty and elegance. And she had to fight her hand that wanted to hurl it across the room.

'Oh, has Mr O'Mahoney gone?' Jane asked, her rosy cheeks flushed from the exertion of going up and down the stairs. 'What a kind man he is. Oh, an' what a pretty lamp! It'll look proper classy in your room. A handsome gift from a handsome fellow. Wouldn't surprise me if 'er isn't soft on you.'

'No, it wouldn't surprise me, either,' Tresca muttered back. And lifting her trembling hand, she gently fingered her lips.

'Oh, Vera, I don't know what I should do,' Tresca moaned, wringing her hands in her lap. 'I feel knotted up inside whenever I think about it.'

'And you say he's not been back to the dairy since?'

'No. And when I happened to see him in the street, he just lifted his hat in that infuriatingly polite way of his. He didn't say a word, not even good day, and his face were, I don't know, cold.'

'Well, it would be, wouldn't it?' Vera reasoned. 'He declared his feelings for you, and you rejected him. He must feel hurt and embarrassed. It would take any man a while to recover from that, especially someone who's as sincere as Mr O'Mahoney. Some fly-by-night wouldn't have taken it so hard.'

Tresca's eyebrows arched. 'I know. And I feel so guilty. I want us to be friends and I miss him. I mean, he really overstepped the mark, kissing me like that. But I overreacted about the lamp. It just brought everything flooding back. All the humiliation. How everything went wrong and we ended up in the workhouse. And how my father still blames Connor for it all.'

'Ah.' Vera's voice was low and wise. There was silence for a few moments, during which Tresca prayed that her dear friend could help her untangle the twisted thread of her emotions. 'And,' she was relieved when Vera continued at last, 'do *you* still blame Mr O'Mahoney?'

'No. No I don't.' Her answer came swiftly and with conviction. 'Not for dismissing my father. I understand now that he had no choice.'

'But, out of loyalty to your father, you still feel you should dislike him?'

Tresca's pretty mouth twisted. 'Yes, I suppose so,' she faltered.

'Then don't. Don't live your life as others want you to. Do what *you* want to. Don't be like me.'

'Like *you?* B–but you always seem so strong and self-assured. If you don't mind me saying so.'

Vera gave a wistful smile. 'Perhaps I give that impression. And I do enjoy helping people less fortunate than myself. But whatever I do, I'm governed by my uncle. If I were to do anything he disapproved of, he'd withdraw my allowance. And since I have no money of my own, the idea of having no income at all frightens me. But you, Tresca, if you were in my position, I could just see you telling him to keep his money if there was something you really wanted to do. So you see,' she said, staring intently into Tresca's eyes, 'you're stronger than I am, despite what you might think. So, if you want to be friends with Mr O'Mahoney, *Connor,* go and make it up with him. He clearly didn't want to upset you over the lamp. His intentions were just the opposite.'

Tresca blinked at her, considering her words. 'But ... what if he won't listen? What if he'm so angry with me–?'

'He won't be. And I think you could eat humble pie most beautifully.'

'Do you really think so?'

'I do indeed. And I suggest you go straight round there now. Strike while the iron is hot.'

Tresca drew in a deep breath. 'Yes, I suppose I

187

could. He should be home now.'

'Go on, then. And good luck.'

'Thank you,' Tresca nodded as she made for the door. 'I'm going to need it.'

As she made her way back through the town, she felt her insides screw into a tangled knot. Vera's words had given her strength and there was a joy bubbling up within her at the idea that she could set things right again. But on the other hand, she was dreading Connor's reaction. He would have every right to reject her apologies, and her heart was thumping as she knocked on the door.

Once again she was left to wait in the hallway while the elderly landlord made his way upstairs, but this time the house somehow seemed different. And then she realized what it was. Drifting from upstairs was the dulcet tone of some sort of flute playing a bright and lively rhythmical melody, and yet there was a bewitching quality to it. Tresca was intrigued, forgetting the daunting task ahead, and she was disappointed when the playing stopped abruptly mid-tune. She heard men's voices then, one of which was unmistakably Connor's, and she felt herself trembling.

She looked up. Connor was standing at the top of the stairs and she saw his face harden. He waited, not moving a muscle, while the old man slowly descended the steps and disappeared into one of the other rooms. Still Connor stood, and Tresca wanted to be swallowed up into a big black hole as, finally, he came down to her, his eyes harsh as they bore into hers.

'Yes?'

Tresca nearly choked. 'Connor, please,' she managed to croak. 'I'm sorry. It were really kind of you to give me the lamp. It just reminded me of everything. And I do want to be friends. Will you forgive me? Please?'

The silence that followed seemed interminable, strangling. She hardly dared to meet Connor's eyes, almost feeling faint. *Say something. Please.*

'Forgive you?' His voice, when he finally spoke, was almost inaudible. 'No, me sweet little colleen. Isn't it *you* who should be forgiving *me?* Wasn't it the most abominable thing I did. You were right to be angry, whereas my only excuse is that you really have taken the heart from me.'

Tresca stared at him, feeling something she couldn't quite identify settle in her breast. 'Still friends, then?' she whispered.

'If ... you really want to,' he answered guardedly.

'Yes, I do.'

She heard Connor let out a sharp sigh and she saw his eyes change from a muddied hue to their normal intense aquamarine. 'Sure that's a relief. I've been cursing meself ever since. Complete eejit it is I've been.'

'Well, let's say no more about it.'

'*Feignites,* then?'

She gave a grunt of amusement. 'Whatever that means, yes. And was that you playing just now?'

'What, me tin whistle? Not the greatest player in the world, me, but it reminds me of home.'

'I thought it were lovely. Was it an Irish tune?'

'It surely was. "The Black Velvet Band". About a fellow who falls for a beautiful young lady who turns out to be a pickpocket and tricks him into

189

taking the can for her. And doesn't he get transported to Van Diemen's Land for his troubles.'

'Oh dear. It sounded too happy a tune for that!' she laughed, and then a great flood of relief washed through her as Connor threw up his head with a roar of mirth.

'We've a lot to learn about each other,' he chuckled as his merry eyes came to rest on her face, and something inside her rejoiced.

Nineteen

'Good mornin', young maid,' Elijah Edwards beamed at Tresca one Sunday in August. 'Where you'm goin' wi' such a smile on your face? An' mighty fetchin' you looks in that there outfit, if I may say so.'

Tresca flushed with embarrassment. It was the first time she had worn the dress she had made herself, and she did indeed feel the cat's whiskers. It was a pity she had to wear her old, oft-mended boots, but they didn't really show beneath the full-length skirt. Besides, they were the only footwear she possessed.

'I'm meeting a friend,' she answered, trying to tamp down the excitement that threatened to burst out of her. 'We'm going for a walk up on to the moor.'

'Ha!' Elijah winked knowingly. 'An' wud that 'appen fer be a *male* friend?' he asked with a teasing light in his eyes.

190

Tresca felt the colour in her cheeks deepen. 'Yes,' she admitted in a tiny voice.

'The big Irish chap I've seen you with afore, I'll be bound. O'Mahoney, isn't it? Pleasant fellow from what I've seen. You 'ave a good day, then, cheel. Lovely weather you've got fer it.'

'Certainly have. Good day to you, then.'

Tresca smiled and watched Elijah stomp off up the hill on his crutches. Kind and cheerful he was, and so was his wife; Tresca had grown fond of them both. But not as fond as she had of Connor in the weeks since their argument. They had spent many hours together, and Tresca couldn't wait for this, their first major outing. She had woken at dawn, too excited to go back to sleep. So, while the rest of Bannawell Street still slumbered, she had brought the cows down early from their field for milking. And now her heart was dancing a polka as she stepped into the street at the appointed hour.

Connor was emerging from his front door. His tall, broad yet trim figure paused as he looked approvingly at the clear blue sky. His head was lifted in that proud manner Tresca recognized so well, and she could scarcely contain her elation as she ran across to him.

His eyes crinkled at the corners as he smiled at her. 'Morning to you, *acushla*,' he grinned. 'And my, don't we look stunning today.'

'Thank you,' she blushed, a spark of pleasure sizzling down her spine. 'And how are you today?'

'Sure, I'm great altogether, and looking forward to our little expedition,' he answered, swinging a full knapsack on to his back.

191

'Goodness, it certainly *looks* like an expedition! What on earth have you got there?'

'Didn't I tell you I'd be bringing a picnic? And by the looks of things we're going to have a grand day for it, so we'll be needing plenty to drink. So, shall we?'

He offered her his arm with a jaunty tip of his head, and with a light giggle, Tresca laced her fingers in the crook of his elbow, feeling just like the princess Emmanuel always called her. For a fleeting moment, doubt clouded her happiness at the thought that her father didn't know how close she was growing to Connor. But it was instantly gone as they made their way across the main town square.

'Connor, your hair looks a little wet,' Tresca observed as she frowned up at him.

'Sure, I've been swimming at the pool this morning,' he explained. 'It's open for an early men's session on Sundays. It's open three evenings, too, but it's too late by the time I get home.'

'Oh, I see.' Tresca bobbed her head. Mention of the open-air swimming pool at the top of Bannawell Street reminded her too much of when she had been an inmate at the workhouse. The baths nestled virtually at the foot of the inhospitable building that had incarcerated her, and she had glimpsed the large, rectangular pool from one of the windows. It had been closed for the winter then, and looked cold and uninviting. How anyone could *like* swimming, and why it was considered so remarkable that the town was one of the first in the West Country to boast such a facility, she really couldn't comprehend.

192

'So, you *like* swimming, do you?' she ventured as they walked briskly along Dolvin Road and then began the long, steady climb up Mount Tavy towards the moor.

'I do so. Nothing more refreshing. Learnt to swim in the river back home as a boy, so I did. So I was delighted to find there's a pool here. Have you never tried it?'

'Can't say as I fancy it myself,' she answered, a touch reluctantly as she didn't want to say anything that might make Connor think the less of her.

'Is that so? I'd've seen you as a bit of a tomboy.'

'I suppose I am in some ways. But the thought of all that cold water—'

'Once you get in and start moving around, it warms you up.' He glanced at her sideways and a hesitant smile spread over his face. 'And can't anyone learn to swim. I'd love to teach you meself, but sadly the men's and women's bathing is strictly separate. How ridiculous is that?'

'I suppose it's because those bathing suit things are too revealing,' Tresca answered coyly, imagining nevertheless what Connor's strong physique would look like in one of the said costumes. And perhaps, if he was there to support her, she might find the courage to try it out. In fact, it would be rather fun to be in the water, held safe in his arms.

'Well, it'd be a poor man who couldn't contain himself when he saw a lady in one of those suits. Cover every inch of the body, so they do. Pity. But perhaps you and Miss Miles should have a go together.'

'Vera? Yes, I suppose she might. I'll have to ask her.'

They fell into a comfortable silence, Tresca thinking that perhaps she would try and persuade Vera to sample the delights of the swimming pool with her – especially if it would please Connor. But for now she was happy to trot along beside him, hurrying as she tried to keep up with his long, vigorous stride.

'Am I going too fast for you?' he asked when they had been walking uphill for about a mile.

'Ooph, well, just a little. My legs are shorter than yours.'

'Oh, I'm sorry, *acushla. You* should've said. Let's rest for a while. I'll take off me coat and you can sit on it–'

'No, don't worry. Just a few seconds standing still will do nicely. I think I must have become out of condition living in the town. I used to walk for miles without ever thinking about it.'

'Used to walk from farm to farm looking for work, didn't you say?'

'Yes. If we couldn't find jobs, we could walk for days. But then one of us would get taken on, and we mightn't need to move on for weeks. Months sometimes. Like the last place we were. It were really good there, and we might've stayed on permanent, like. Only...'

They were moving on again, more slowly this time and talking as they went. Tresca hesitated. Should she tell Connor about the disastrous event – and her father's part in it – that had led to their dismissal from Tremaine Farm? Given the present circumstances, what harm could it do? And as the coolness of the early morning was quickly being burnt away by the warmth of the sun as it rose ever higher in the sky, she felt at once relaxed and inspired, caught by an overwhelming desire to tell Connor everything about herself.

'That's a sorry story, so it is.' He shook his head when she had finished. 'No wonder you were so cross with me when I gave your father the push as well. But, you know I had to. You do understand, don't you?'

He glanced down at her with such concern etched on his features that she suddenly wanted to melt against him.

'Yes, of course I understand,' she assured him. 'And it wouldn't have made much difference in the long run. If my father hadn't gone into the workhouse, it wouldn't have been discovered that he'm ill. He might have gone on working, pushing himself, and he might have got very sick very quickly. But as it is, he's quite comfortable, doing his shoemaking and being looked after. The workhouse mightn't be the most pleasant place to be, but until I can afford to support him, it's the best place for him, really.'

'So he's not going on so bad, then?'

'He seemed quite well last time I saw him. But I do wish I could look after him properly.'

'Ah, they can be a responsibility, parents, so they can. Being the eldest, I didn't like leaving me mammy all those years back, her being a widow and all. But it was the best thing to do, for couldn't I earn far more than anyone else and send it home every month. I keep some of me wages for meself now. The next one down, me sister Siobhan, she married a fairly rich man. A hotelier. And me mammy lives with them now. And me next two sisters are married and all now, and the three younger laddies are all at work, so things are not so bad.'

'So ... you'm the eldest of seven, then?'

'I surely am. There were two more as well that died as babbies.'

Tresca noticed Connor cross himself as they walked along. Yes, he was very Irish, she considered. But everything about him endeared him to her, and she could sense her feelings deepening with every step she took. They had been walking steeply uphill for about three miles, she reckoned, when they came to a natural halt, breathing heavily and drawing in the pure air of the moor. A small flock of Dartmoor sheep was cropping the grass not far away, calm and peaceful in the warm sunshine, and Tresca felt herself spill over with contentment.

'Shall we be leaving the road now, d'you think?' Connor asked, pointing up to the left. 'That great outcrop of rock is where I usually take a break. Sure, there's an amazing view from it.'

Tresca followed his pointing finger to where the ground rose up to the dramatic tor on the horizon, silhouetted clear and stark against the gentian sky. Not a cloud drifted overhead. It really was the most perfect day.

'Yes, that's Cox Tor. We worked at a farm over the other side once, Higher Godsworthy. Come on, I'll race you!' she cried over her shoulder, laughing with glee since she had already run away from him and he had the heavy haversack on his back. The tor was half a mile away, and the nearer they came, the steeper the uneven ground became. At last, the exertion and her teasing mirth as she glanced back at Connor robbed her of her breath and she came to a standstill. She turned, watching him catch her up, his stride nonetheless strong and sure.

'Bold strap, so you are!' he pronounced, his face split in a wide grin.

'A what?' she giggled breathlessly.

'A little strumpet, if you like!' he chuckled in return, and then the merriment slid from his face. 'Not that I was insinuating–'

'No, I know you weren't,' she told him, still laughing. She stood for a moment, her chest rising and falling in a deep sigh of contentment as she gazed all around. Connor, too, had taken the opportunity to catch his breath, drinking in the savage beauty of the moor.

'*Thaw shay guh hawling unsuh,*' he mumbled to himself, caught up, it would seem, in the intriguing mystery of the wild landscape.

'Pardon?'

'I'm sorry, *acushla*. Forgetting me manners. Doesn't it mean it's so beautiful here.'

'Yes. It's a feeling of, I don't know, timelessness, isn't it? Of eternity. We'll come and go, and yet the moor will always be here.'

'Sure, let's not get too philosophical about it. And let's get to the top and have a drink. Me mouth's as dry as a bone.'

Tresca fell into step beside him. When they finally reached the tor and scrambled to the top, Connor helping her as her long skirt got in the way, they found a suitable rock to use as a seat. Connor opened the haversack and took out two bottles, one of ginger beer and the other of lemonade. Tresca chose the lemonade and they sat, admiring the view, for half an hour. Neither of them spoke, wrapped in the enchantment of nature's spell. Not a sound intruded, just the sighing of the slightest breeze and the muted mewing of a pair of buzzards high overhead.

'That's the sea,' Tresca whispered, not wanting to break the silence as she nodded down over the folds of hills to the flat, silvery line in the far distance. 'And that's the Tamar estuary. And then, look.' She swivelled round so that she was facing in the opposite direction. 'Over there, on that pinnacle in the distance, that's St Michael's, a tiny church set all alone. I've been there. It's a real scramble. Like doing a penance afore you get there.'

'I thought you Protestants didn't do penances.'

'Well, *if* we did.'

Connor gave the light chuckle she was growing to love. 'Have you finished your drink? I usually walk down the dip and up the other side to the next tor.'

'Great Staple Tor, you mean? Yes, good idea.'

'And we can have our picnic there. Me stomach's rumbling already.'

He packed the empty bottles away and then helped Tresca to her feet. Her fingers quivered in his warm, strong palm as they clambered down over the rocks and crossed the long sweep over to the next soaring heights. They didn't walk a straight line but made a slight deviation down to a spring that fed a small natural pool. A group of wild Dartmoor ponies was grazing beside it, their teeth rasping as they munched the summer grass while others ambled to the water's edge to drink, their long tails wafting in the balmy air. The young couple paused to observe them for a while, and Tresca felt her heart overflow with the new and blithe sensation of being in love. For she was sure of it now. She loved Connor O'Mahoney.

They left the idyllic scene with the ponies and continued towards Great Staple Tor. Connor found a spot between two boulders where the springing grass was flat and dry, and yet they could still watch the glorious landscape. He spread his coat on it, glad to be rid of the garment it was so hot, and Tresca sat down, hugging her knees in pleasant expectation. Connor hadn't worn a waistcoat and Tresca's pulse skipped along as she secretly admired his powerful body through the thin material of his shirt. It made her knees turn weak and peculiar.

She could see, then, why the knapsack had appeared so heavy. Connor had brought along a veritable feast! Tresca marvelled at his appetite, but he was a big man and his abundant energy needed fuelling. It was all being washed down with a couple of bottles of cider that Connor persuaded her was not enough to make her drunk. Finally he produced fresh strawberries by way of dessert.

Afterwards, Tresca lay back, utterly content. The sun was so hot and strong it seemed to nail her to the ground. She shut her eyes, but the light was still so dazzling, she placed her hat over her face. Beside her, Connor did the same, and they lay, side by side, holding hands, in joyous silence. Tresca drifted asleep, her head whirling with the cider, the heat and the closeness of the man she knew she loved.

When she awoke, she instantly sought Connor's hand, but it was gone. She sat up abruptly, suddenly bereft. The picnic was all packed away, the haversack propped neatly against one of the rocks. And then she caught faintly on the air the haunting, wistful notes of a tune being played not far away. She followed the sound, and navigating some stones, found Connor leaning nonchalantly against the wall of rock behind him as he played on the instrument he called his tin whistle.

'Did Sleeping Beauty enjoy her little nap?' he asked, straightening up.'

'Don't stop playing. That were lovely. What were it?'

'A farewell song, called "The Parting Glass". But wouldn't you be after hearing something more lively now? To wake you up for the walk home.'

'Yes, if you like.'

'How about this? Rather appropriate as it happens. "Poor Paddy Working on the Railway".'

Tresca tossed up her head with a laugh as Connor began to play again, slow and rueful at first, followed by a fast and rhythmical section. Each alternate verse was either fast or slow, and Tresca couldn't believe how nimbly Connor's fingers played the fast ones, as he tapped his foot on the ground. She was disappointed when it came to the end.

'I'll sing you the words as we walk home,' he promised. 'At least I should have the breath for it going downhill.'

Ten minutes later, they were heading down towards the road that would take them home, with the moor rolling down to the Tamar Valley spread out before them. Connor sang on the top of his voice:

Oh, in Eighteen Hundred and Forty-One,
Me corduroy breeches I put on,
Me corduroy breeches I put on,
To work upon the railway,
The rai-ailway,
I'm weary of the rai-ailway,
Poor Paddy works on the railway.

Tresca was giggling as she hopped along beside him. She didn't think she had ever been so happy in her entire life. And when Connor grinned down at her, her heart soared to heaven.

Twenty

Hoots of laughter and the strains of a flute-like instrument playing a distinctive Irish jig drifted into the darkened street from inside Mrs Ellacott's dairy. Morgan Trembath halted in his tracks and his heart dragged in sadness. It was no good. In his hand he held the bunch of autumn flowers he had purchased at the florist's and kept

201

hidden from his mother. He had actually told her a lie, saying that he was going out to check on the shop as there had recently been a spate of burglaries in the town.

But it was too late, wasn't it? The girl who had stolen his heart was already in love with another. And who could blame her? The devil had rescued her from that abominable attack back in May and must appear as a hero in her eyes. To add to it, he was tall, exciting, handsome in a strange sort of way, and blessed with that lilting, romantic accent. How could he, Morgan Trembath, a dull shopkeeper under the thumb of his mother, ever compare? He had prayed the new railway would not take too long to build and that the navvies would soon be on their way, Connor O'Mahoney with them. But the route of the line demanded stunning feats of engineering that would take time to achieve, and Shillamill Tunnel, which Morgan understood O'Mahoney was working on, was only half-finished. So the big Irishman would be around for some time yet. Time for him to cement his relationship with Tresca Ladycott – if he hadn't done so already.

Morgan sighed dejectedly and turned away, his shoulders slumped. He just hoped the fellow wouldn't break Tresca's heart, for what would happen when the railway was finally completed? But he would be ready and waiting to pick up the pieces for her. His mother wouldn't approve, so it wouldn't be easy. And if he were honest, he wondered if he would have the strength to face up to her over it...

What should he do with the flowers? He

202

supposed he would give them to his mother since there was no other woman in his life. Perhaps it would assuage his guilt over the blatant lie he had told her.

While Morgan shambled back home, up in his room over the dairy, Ebeneezer Preedy's lips were drawn back over his teeth at the racket that was going on downstairs. He had lodged with Mrs Ellacott for nearly three years, paying his rent bang on the dot. He kept himself to himself, taking his meals alone and having a jug of hot water brought up to him each morning and evening, so that he was no trouble whatsoever to his landlady. It had all worked perfectly – until young workhouse had taken Sally's place. A pretty child and a good worker, he could see that, and she was always polite whenever he saw her. He didn't begrudge her having friends, or even a sweetheart. But why did she have to choose a navvy, and a *Paddy* at that?

No, this really would not do. He was a respectable gentleman, and he should not be subjected to such raucous behaviour as was going on downstairs. And what was worse was that homely Mrs Ellacott, whom he secretly admired, seemed to be encouraging the revelries. He would have to have a quiet word with the good lady, for he did not think he could remain in the house if such frivolity was to continue.

Downstairs in the kitchen, the table had been moved to one side and the rug rolled back from the flagstones. The four occupants of the room, three women and one strong young male waving a primitive wind instrument in his hand, were

203

falling about with laughter. Jane Ellacott flung herself down in one of the chairs, wobbling with mirth.

'Oh, my goodness, I doesn't think I can dance another step!'

'Sure you've done very well, Mrs Ellacott. It mightn't look it, but Irish dancing's mighty strenuous.'

'Let's have a rest,' Tresca spluttered, gasping for breath, 'and then let's have another go, shall we, Vera?'

'Wearing me out, you are!' Vera declared good-naturedly. 'I don't know. Had me swimming all summer long, and now I'm prancing about like a butterfly!'

'And a very pretty one, too, if I can make so bold.'

Connor met Tresca's sparkling eyes and grinned. She was a dark horse, was Vera. Although as nervous as Tresca on their first visit to the Bannawell Street Baths, they had both so enjoyed the experience that they had gone there twice a week until the place had closed at the end of the season. Tresca had initially gone there to please Connor, but had found the activity much to her liking. It was one of many things he had opened her eyes to, including the lively jigs that were, quite strangely, danced with your arms pinned to your sides while your feet and legs needed to be made of springing rubber!

'You will play us another tune, won't you, Connor?' she begged.

'Just one more, and then I must be going. Haven't some of us got work in the morning?' he chided, his eyes shining with mischief.

'I've got to be up early, too, you know, you old rogue!' she chortled back, pushing him playfully. 'So what'll it be?'

'How about "The Cork Hornpipe"?' he suggested with a smile that melted her heart.

Tresca gazed in fearful wonderment at the massive structures that were growing daily on either side of the street. Huge, solid cranes were hoisting gigantic boulders of squared-off Dartmoor granite towards the bright spring sky, settling them on top of what had already been built of the colossal piers of the Bannawell Street viaduct. Men were standing fearlessly atop the already lofty pillars, guiding in the next mammoth stone, while down below, huge carthorses, harnessed to stout ropes radiating from the cranes, were being encouraged to step forwards or stand still while straining into their mighty collars. And all was under the close direction of Mr Szlumper, the chief engineer, looking important and formidable as he stood in the middle of the road sporting a fine top hat.

Very soon, the joining arches would start to take shape in such a way as to give the viaduct the Herculean strength needed to support the monstrous steam engines that would thunder overhead. Tresca was, quite frankly, terrified at the prospect, but supposed that these expert men knew what they were doing. After all, Britain had led the world in engineering feats throughout the century. Nevertheless, she was sure she would always scuttle hell-for-leather beneath the viaduct when it was finished, just in case it suddenly crashed to the ground. Now she was obliged to wait for ten minutes while some activity was taking place which necessitated the public being held back while it was carried out.

Tresca's lungs collapsed in a wistful sigh as she waited. She wasn't just a dairymaid with Jane Ellacott. She had become the daughter the kind, jolly widow had never had, and while Jane had, in return, become like a mother to her, Emmanuel's health also seemed to have stabilized. There was only one problem to mar Tresca's supreme happiness, and that was Connor.

She loved him, as sure as night followed day. Her heart leapt for joy every morning when she awoke, knowing that she would see him for at least some part of the evening. The moment he walked in the door, her pulse galloped with expectation. If no one else was present, she would spring into his arms and he would envelop her in a ring of warm, strong flesh, protecting her, loving her, kissing her lips so softly, smiling down into her face, his eyes radiating with his own passion. And she would nestle against him, drowning in his presence and feeling so vital and alive.

All through the winter, their love had grown and expanded, filling every fibre of her soul, and she was sure it was the same for him. But now, as the days had lengthened into spring once again, the doubt that she had buried in the darkest recesses of her mind was creeping stealthily forward. There was no question about the elated rapture that existed between them. But as Tresca stared up at the growing structure before her – or rather above her – it symbolized her fears all too starkly.

For how long would it be before Connor's work took him away? The Shillamill Tunnel was well on the way to completion, and work was just beginning on the cleared site for the new station. It would be some time before the entire new line from Plymouth to Lydford – and eventually to London's Waterloo via Exeter – would be opened ... perhaps another year. But Connor's part in it would finish long before then. Yes, he could oversee the laying of track over ready-prepared ground at any point along the route, but his expertise was in digging tunnels. And Tresca was sure her heart would break when he had to move on.

Oh, why was life so complicated? The small crowd was waved on now, the possible danger over, and Tresca continued down the hill. But her mind wasn't only preoccupied with thoughts of her dearest Connor. She had gradually introduced her father to the fact that she was walking out with the man he still loathed. She had dropped hints for months, finally admitting that she had a strong affection for her saviour from the horrific assault almost a year ago now, and that her feelings were returned.

'I'll not see my princess consorting wi' that divil!' Emmanuel had expressed his passionate disapproval, and Tresca had attempted to plead and reason with him.

'But you don't know what he'm really like,' she had protested, and had gone on to reiterate the times when Connor had, like a silent hero, helped so many people less fortunate than himself. With his position on the railway, he had responsibilities which could make him appear a hard taskmaster. But underneath it he was kindness itself, sensitive and caring. And when you got to know him, she had insisted, you would learn that he was actually an incurable romantic. He was utterly trustworthy and now that winter was over, they had resumed their lonely rambles on Dartmoor. Tresca felt completely safe with him. They held hands, kissed tenderly, cuddled a little, but never had Connor overstepped the bounds of propriety. On the odd occasion when Tresca sensed his desires were about to get the better of him, he would abruptly pull his treasured tin whistle from his jacket pocket and start playing an Irish air instead.

'Doesn't it make me dream of home,' he would say, his eyes a faraway blue as he stared out across the dramatic landscape of the moor. 'Makes me think of me mammy in the little cottage we had when I was a lad. Take you there one day, so I will. Me mammy'll love you as much as I do.' And he would regale her with tales of his poverty stricken boyhood. A little monkey he had been, so he had, he would say, and Tresca would end up with tears of mirth trickling down her cheeks from his accounts of his childhood antics. Blessed with the gift of the gab, he was. Had kissed the Blarney Stone apparently, whatever that meant; it was an Irish expression she had often heard among the other Irish navvy families who lodged in Bannawell Street. Tresca didn't really understand, but somehow it fitted Connor perfectly. When she timidly asked him what it meant, he had roared with laughter.

'Sure, it's in an old castle a few miles outside Cork,' he explained, still grinning. 'Legend has it if you kiss the stone, it'll give you a gilded tongue. It's way up high below a parapet and the only way you can get to kiss it is to have someone you trust hold your legs and dangle you over the side and you pray they won't let go.'

Tresca had gasped in horror. 'That must be really dangerous!'

'Well, you wouldn't let your worst enemy do the honours, that's for sure! I did it as a lad, but it'd need a carthorse to hold me weight now and you can't get them to climb up the steps.'

His eyes had glinted in that rakish way of his, and Tresca had at last seen the funny side of his teasing and given a light laugh. But she wasn't laughing now. A horrible darkness churned in her belly and was beginning to temper the joyous enchantment she enjoyed in Connor's arms. For what did the future truly hold?

'Oh, *acushla,* what's the matter with you today?'

Tresca caught her breath, trying to quell the festering sadness that was eating into her enjoyment of the glorious summer's day. She glanced at Connor, noting the concerned, questioning expression on his strong, beloved face, and she had to avert her eyes.

'Nothing,' she muttered, failing miserably to put some brightness into her voice.

'Sure, don't I know when something's wrong,' Connor persisted. 'I bring you out for the day, all the way to Plymouth on the rival railway line which offends me conscience greatly,' he half-teased, his eyebrows arched cajolingly, 'and you've a face on you like a wet lettuce. Have I done something to upset you? Or ... you don't want to end our relationship, do you?'

His voice had suddenly slowed as he spoke, the animation on his face slipping away as his own words penetrated his thoughts. He looked so crestfallen, so very hurt, and Tresca at once turned to him, guilt ripping through her. How ever could she have made him think that? But the moment she had dreaded had arrived; the moment when she must voice her fears. When they would become real.

'Oh, no! Not at all! Just the opposite. In fact... Oh, Connor, I can see the end of the building of the railway looming fast. And ... and you won't be needed any more and you'll go away and I'll never see you again!' she blurted out in desperation. She was staring up at him, her forehead squeezed painfully, and watched as his wide mouth first dropped open and then curled up into a grin.

'Oh, would that be all?' He shrugged casually as if they were merely discussing the weather. 'And you think I'll be going away from you? And well I might if I can drag meself from the most lovely creature I've ever met. But if I do, it'll only be for a short while to earn enough money to put a ring on your finger. It won't be an expensive one because don't we need the money for other things. I've already saved a pretty penny in me bank account, and when there's enough, we'll take your daddy out of the workhouse and we'll all go and live back in Ireland with me family. You never know, your daddy and me mammy might like each other, too, and wouldn't that be grand?'

Tresca's eyes were glued to his face. They were standing on the green lawns of the Hoe, overlooking the unruffled water of Plymouth Sound and the sea beyond, which spangled with diamonds of light from the dazzling sunshine. Hundreds of people were dotted about the grass, all enjoying the warm Sunday afternoon. Some were taking a constitutional stroll and others were seated while children played with balls or chased each other round in games of tag. As always, a breeze was blowing in off the sea, adding to the cacophony of sound, but suddenly all the noise dropped away as the meaning of Connor's words percolated into Tresca's brain.

'You ... are you asking me to marry you?' she stammered, hardly able to breathe.

He frowned at her quizzically. 'Isn't that what I was after saying?' he said, nonplussed. 'Of course, strictly speaking, I'm not supposed to marry out of me own faith without dispensation from the Holy Pope himself, but sure I'm not that fussed meself. If I have to say a hundred *Hail Marys* a day for the rest of me life as penance, it'll be worth it to have the girl of me dreams as me wife. So, will you be accepting me proposal, or shall I be throwing meself in the sea there and praying that I drown?'

Tresca was still staring at him, studying his face which seemed to twitch with a mixture of anticipation and dread. He was clearly trying to make light of what he knew would be a huge step for the both of them. Trying to make it easier for her, she supposed, if she wanted to turn him

211

down. She loved him even more because of it.

A warm gladness seeped into the very core of her, and all the fears of the last months melted into nothingness. Without another thought, she stepped up to Connor. To his delight and relief, she cupped his face in her hands and, raising herself on tiptoe, placed her mouth over his. She kissed him passionately, not caring who might be watching. She entwined her fingers into his hair, drawing him closer, and he responded, his hands pressing into the small of her back.

When they finally drew apart, she gazed up at him, breathless and alight with joy, and he was grinning down, his eyes bright and piercing. 'Am I to be taking that as a yes?' he asked, blinking in amazement.

Laughter tripped off her tongue. 'I sincerely hope so!' she chuckled in reply.

At once, his arms locked about her and he lifted her clean off her feet, spinning her round in circles until she felt giddy. When he finally stood her down again, she had to cling to him until she could get her balance.

'Hasn't she just agreed to be me wife!' he crowed at the top of his voice to anyone who might be listening.

Then, taking her hand, he charged with her across the grass towards the main promenade. Through their own laughter, Tresca heard one or two bemused strangers call out their congratulations.

The rest of the afternoon passed in a joyous haze. Tresca thought the smile would never leave her face as she watched the pride and elation dancing in Connor's eyes. They ambled arm in arm the length and breadth of the Hoe, finally sitting on a bench and watching the sun sink over the horizon as it painted streaks of coral across the dimming sky and turned the flat surface of the sea to flame.

'Won't I be remembering this day for the rest of me life,' Connor sighed as they eventually made their way towards the station. 'The day me little *acushla* agreed to marry me.'

Tresca's heart was overflowing. That morning, a huge grey cloud had been pressing down on her. But now the sun had broken through, and she thought it would shine for ever. She clung on to Connor's arm, drunk with joy, for she was sure nothing could ever spoil her life again.

'We'll buy a small cottage with some land,' Connor told her dreamily a little later as she leant against his shoulder, gazing out of the compartment window as the train skirted the edge of Dartmoor on the return journey to Tavistock. Dusk was floating down and Tresca listened sleepily to Connor's low and happy voice. 'You can keep a couple of cows and your daddy can grow vegetables and live out his life in peace. And I'll find whatever manual work I can, and won't we be as happy as the stars in the sky.'

And Tresca agreed that they most certainly would!

Twenty-One

'What the devil do *'er* be doing yere?'

Tresca felt herself shudder. Under any other circumstances, she would have been pleased to see the animated response on her father's face. On her previous visit he had appeared weaker and more fragile, so she was delighted to see him stronger again. She only wished the reason for his sparking vitality wasn't that, after some gentle persuasion, Mr Solloway had allowed Connor to accompany her.

'Father, please don't be like that,' she begged. 'Connor wanted to come and see how you are.'

'Well, I don't want to see *'en!'* Emmanuel insisted.

'Wasn't I truly sorry to hear you'd been taken unwell,' Connor broke in, unperturbed. 'And if I'd known you were coming to the workhouse, I'd have done something to prevent it. But since you're the one who still holds it against me, I must be honest that I couldn't have given you back your job. Company rules, so it is. You can be as drunk as you like in your own time, but every man must be sober at his work, so it was nobody's fault but your own.'

Tresca cringed. This was exactly what she had dreaded, her father continuing to be unreasonable and Connor defending his decision. Oh, God, could Connor possibly ask for her hand if

214

they started off on the wrong foot?

'Father, let's put all that behind us,' she pleaded, but then she realized that Emmanuel was muttering something grudgingly under his breath. Could it possibly be…?

'I s'pposes it were,' Emmanuel conceded, glancing at his unwelcome visitor. 'And I agree it weren't your fault I've got this disease inside me. So maybies we can be civil to each other. I's too damned tired to argue.'

Tresca at once felt a flame of dread burning in her chest. 'You're not feeling worse again, are you?'

'Aw, cheel, it comes an' goes,' he sighed wearily. 'That good Doctor Greenwood leaves laudanum for me to take if I'm aching. Spreading all over, it is. But the medicine makes me want to sleep and I get all befuddled in my head.'

'Oh, Father.' Tresca dropped on her knees beside him, all thoughts of her betrothal swept from her mind. 'Is it really that bad?'

'Not with the laudanum, but it's in my bones all right. But I wants to know what my princess 'as bin up to this last month.'

He smiled, patting her hand fondly. She looked up at Connor, so tall and erect beside her. His presence seemed to instil strength and determination into her once more.

'Well, you know how lovely the weather's been,' she began, drawing up her courage. 'Connor and I have been out together every Sunday, and, well,' she hesitated, 'you know how I've told you how we've grown so fond of each other. We think the same about so many things, and we love being

215

together so much. So, well, we've come to be more than just friends.'

She paused, sweat oozing from her skin as Emmanuel turned his head upwards, his eyes narrowed. Oh, please, surely…

'An' now I s'pposes you'm come to ask for my princess's 'and in marriage, 'ave you? An' you needs my consent, else you'll 'ave to wait till she's twenty-one.' His tone was sharp and accusing, and Tresca saw Connor purse his lips as Emmanuel's gaze locked on to his. But then her father gave a grunt. 'Well, she'm a sensible maid, an' if she thinks you'm the one fer 'er, then I's sure she'm right. You've known each other some time, so you'm not rushin' into it. An' if it'll make you 'appy, that's all I wants.'

Tresca felt giddy with relief. She threw her arms around Emmanuel's neck. 'Oh, thank you, Father! You don't know how happy you've made me!'

'But if you lets her down in any way, I'll personally wring your neck,' Emmanuel growled over her shoulder.

'I'll not be letting her down, sir, I can promise you. Doesn't my every day start and finish with thoughts of her. And I can provide well for her, too. See, this is my bank book.' Connor withdrew it from his breast pocket and opened it for Emmanuel's perusal. 'That's a tidy sum, and sure it's my intention to add to it. But the life of a navvy's wife, even a ganger's, is no life for a lady. As soon as I've saved enough, I want all three of us to go back to County Tipperary. We'll have a little place of our own and I'll take care of the both of you.'

216

'Oh, you will, will you?' Tresca recoiled slightly at Emmanuel's wryness. 'Well, I appreciates the thought, but I doesn't think I'll be seein' the outside o' these walls agin.'

Tresca stifled a gasp. 'Father, don't say that. We'll look after you, and you'll get well again.'

'Well, we can try,' Emmanuel smiled at last. 'But now you must tell me what you'm been up to since I saw you last.'

An hour or so later, Mr Solloway came to tell them it was time for them to leave. The two men had gradually come to speak easily to each other, and when Connor offered Emmanuel his hand, he shook it warmly. Tresca's heart gladdened. That was one hurdle over, but she wasn't at all happy about what her father had implied about his health.

'Can't Miss Ladycott see her friend Lucy now?' Connor asked the workhouse master, drawing himself up to his own considerable height.

'No, she can't,' Mr Solloway said gruffly. 'It's enough that I let you in to see her father. Don't expect to come again. Lucy's well, that's all I can say.'

Connor raised an eyebrow. 'Sorry, I did try,' he bent to whisper in Tresca's ear as they were shown out of the main gate.

Tresca smiled wistfully at him. 'Yes, and thank you. At least we have my father's permission now.'

'Yes, and I'm mighty pleased. We can start making plans now, so we can.'

They began walking down Bannawell Street, hand in hand. There were still a couple of hours

217

of the afternoon left, time for a long walk together. And then Tresca noticed another couple
coming towards them, the elderly woman leaning
on the younger man's arm.

'Good afternoon to you, Mrs Trembath, Mr
Trembath.' Connor raised his hat politely. 'Sure
it's been another fine day. And even better, for
hasn't Mr Ladycott just given me permission to
wed his daughter,' he added, pride radiating from
his jubilant face.

Charity Trembath lifted her head haughtily.
What did she care? The little trollop deserved the
rough and ready Irishman. Beside her, Morgan
nodded his head and nailed a smile on his face.
But inside, his heart was bleeding.

'I can't believe what a good summer we've had,
so I can't,' Connor declared a few weeks later.

'I know. And this were a wonderful idea of
yourn to hire a couple of horses so we could go
further out on the moor than usual.'

'Isn't it just for the once,' Connor reminded her,
urging on the somewhat lazy giant of a beast he
was riding. 'Cost a small fortune, and aren't we
supposed to be saving up? But it's a sorry thing if
I work so hard and can't treat me little *acushla*
once in a while. Not ridden since I was a lad back
home, so I haven't, and I'll be as stiff as a poker
come morning. It'll have been worth it, though,
just to have seen their faces when you insisted
they changed the side-saddle for a man's one!'

'Well, I'm only used to riding carthorses bare-
back back and forth from a field, and always
astride, so I'm sure I couldn't have managed a

218

side-saddle.'

'And sure I don't mind if it makes your skirt ride up a little so I can see a few inches of those perfect ankles. Not that I'm after looking at them at all, of course.'

'Well, I'm certain my ankles are no different from anyone else's.'

'They are so!' Connor protested. 'And as your intended, I don't want any other man to see them, so shall we turn off this main highway somewhere soon and have us some privacy?'

'Of course. See the inn at the bottom of the hill and the bridge? Then the small farm just afterwards? There's a bridle path starts there that leads along the Walkham Valley. Then there's another farm further along the track. We rarely worked so far out on the moor, but my father helped with the lambing there once. Back along when I were a tacker.'

She led the way across the sweeping bridge and up the steep hill on the far side before turning off to the right by the first farmhouse. The track here was totally open, exposing them to the fierce August sunshine. The horses maintained a slow, steady walk and Tresca breathed in deeply the smell of hot grass and baked earth, and the animals' warm, hairy flesh. She was utterly content living with Jane Ellacott in Bannawell Street, especially with Connor lodging almost opposite. But she did miss the countryside, and her soul drifted off into a blithe reverie whenever Connor described the life he had planned for them back in his homeland.

They plodded onwards, the dull clip-clop of the

horses' hooves mesmerizing on the hard-packed ground. A boulder-strewn upward slope obliterated the view of the moor to their left, but on the right, the land dropped away steeply to the river whose rushing waters they could hear but not see. The view over the valley was, however, quite breathtaking and they ambled on in silence, drinking in the peace and tranquillity. Some sheep scattered nervously on their approach, while a herd of ponies further along went on calmly tearing at the grass and munching contentedly.

Tresca vaguely remembered the farm where Emmanuel had once worked. A dog ran out and gave a token growl before slinking off disinterestedly as the strangers allowed their mounts to pick their way down the uneven path to a little bridge over a stream. Water gushed noisily over algae-covered boulders that formed a pretty waterfall, and they paused for a minute or two to admire the charming spot before entering the dappled shade of an ancient wood.

'The path gets really stony from now on,' Tresca warned Connor, 'so let the horses find their own way.'

The rocky bridleway took them through the edge of the wood, and they were at once enveloped in a strange stillness of deep green shadows and creaking branches. Over hundreds of years, weirdly shaped trees had grown up through a tumble of boulders piled along a ridge possibly half a mile long. Beneath the canopy of leaves, emerald moss cascaded, undisturbed by time, over the damp rocks, and the trees themselves were patterned with lichen. The mystery of the place wreathed itself around the riders, and even the horses seemed to have slowed their pace more than was necessary over the difficult terrain.

They passed a spot where a huge rock bordered the way. Soon afterwards an even greater outcrop of granite jutted into the path, which made a small deviation round it. Several flat stones, thirty or so foot long, were piled on top of each other, looking as if they might at any moment slide down the hillside, even though they had lain there for thousands of years. They were crowned by a colossal triangular rock, just as long but about fifteen foot high, and the whole thing was enshrouded in the shadow of trees that had somehow taken root in the tiny crevices between the gigantic boulders.

'Isn't it like passing beneath the bow of a great ship,' Connor dared to breathe.

'Yes, I suppose it is,' Tresca agreed, her own voice little more than a whisper.

'Shall we stop here for our picnic? We can tether the horses in the shade and give them a rest.'

They took off the saddles and exchanged the bridles for the halters they had been given so that the animals could chew more comfortably the feed that had also been supplied. A small bucket had been tied to the saddle of Connor's horse, which he now filled with water from two leather bottles. Wherever possible, they had let the animals drink from streams along the way, but the creatures were still thirsty on such a scorchingly hot day.

'I reckon it's our turn now,' Connor announced, patting his mount's hairy neck.

They found a spot among the rocks where they could keep an eye on the horses and yet have some privacy in the unlikely event that anyone else would pass that way. They ate in easy silence, absorbing the mystic atmosphere of the wood. Tresca leant her head against Connor's shoulder, her eyes shut. She heard him grunt with relaxed pleasure, felt him stroke her cheek. Then he shifted position to kiss her mouth softly and then gently laid her back on the carpet of bouncing moss. His lips brushed hers again, light as gossamer, and a tingling excitement shot down to her loins. She glanced up at him for a moment, drowning in the intensity of his eyes, and then sank back into a private world that was filled with nothing but Connor's presence.

He kissed her again, her nose, her chin, her throat. And when he began to unbutton her blouse, she didn't stop him. His fingers slipped beneath her camisole, caressing the soft mound of her breast. She gave a tiny gasp, but it was instantly forgotten. She knew that this was what she wanted. What she craved. And she trusted Connor with every fibre of her being.

His hand moved so delicately, sending an entrancing thrill down to her belly. He was still kissing her, his breath fanning her cheek, and when his other hand reached to the hem of her skirt and began feeling its way up the inside of her thigh, every inch of her body was alight to his touch. An overwhelming force swept through her, a bewitching enchantment plunging down to that secret place that was only hers, but yearned to be Connor's as well.

Only for a split second did the vile memory of the attack on her in the barn flit across her mind. The men had been strangers, out for what they could get, ready to force her. But she loved Connor. He had won her heart against all odds, respecting her, proving himself, restraining himself. Until now...

When he touched the soft, sweet core of her, shock waves rippled outwards and she snatched in her breath. But he was so deft, drawing her on, enticing her, so that she gloried in every sensation that fizzled through her body. Connor was muttering some words she didn't understand against her cheek, but among them she recognized *acushla,* and all her fears vanished. Connor was doing something to his own attire, and when he gently slid into her, she felt no pain at all. But a feeling she had never known was in her exploded like a burst of stars, and she clung to Connor as, to her astonishment, he groaned and juddered before becoming totally stilled.

'Did I do summat to hurt you?' she asked, dizzy and confused.

'Oh, me little darling,' he murmured, and she felt him begin to shake with laughter. 'Aren't *I* the one who should be asking *you* that?' He propped himself up on one elbow, gazing down at her as he fingered her tousled hair. 'And *are* you all right?' he asked, concern taking the place of the merriment on his face. 'Sure I shouldn't have done that, but don't I love you so much. And I've not had a woman in years. In fact, not so many times in me life at all. Just once or twice with a girl I once loved who then went off with someone else.'

'You never told me that afore.'

'Sure, she wasn't a patch on you, so she wasn't. But now I've made you mine and we'll be together for ever and ever.' He paused again, his eyes like soft velvet. 'And I promise I'll not do that again until we're properly married.'

Tresca blinked up at him, her eyebrows mildly raised. For, in truth, she rather wished he would…

It dawned upon her slowly.

It was November, and the Shillamill Tunnel had long been completed. But in order to stay near Tresca, Connor was working on the Watts Road cutting. The hardness of the rock was proving a major obstacle and many tons of gunpowder were being used on it. The obstinacy of the cutting was even threatening to delay the opening of the entire line. The Bannawell Street Viaduct was nearing completion, as was the even larger one at Shillamill. Even the station buildings had now been constructed and were being fitted out ready for the opening, so the cutting was proving a real problem.

For Tresca, though, it was a Godsend, for what would happen when the line was entirely finished? Would Connor go to work elsewhere on another railway line? Should she go with him? Or would he consider that he had saved enough for them to return to Ireland and take Emmanuel with them?

In the meantime, they spent every minute they possibly could together. Connor kept to his promise. Tresca loved to cuddle up to his strong chest and breathe in the gentle, masculine scent of him, but never did he make any further attempt to take her. It wouldn't have been against her will, but she understood that it was his way of showing his respect for her, even though they both had to endure the frustration of it.

But Tresca was slowly beginning to realize that something was different within her. Her monthlies weren't always regular, but she hadn't had a show since before their heady love-making in the wood. Her breasts were becoming swollen and sore, and she was beginning to feel queasy in the mornings. She hardly needed telling that she was expecting Connor's child.

She had tried forcing it to the back of her mind, praying she was simply late. But she knew she wasn't, and her heart kicked out when she finally made herself admit it. She had to tell Connor, and she could hear her pulse crashing wildly as she waited for a moment when they were alone together.

They had eaten a meal in the kitchen at the dairy, and Tresca had arranged her face into a smile at Jane's usual merry chatter. But all the while she was inwardly trembling, glancing at Connor to judge what mood he was in. It was very rare that he was anything but kind and buoyant, but occasionally after an extra hard day, he could be weary and less willing to talk.

This evening, though, he seemed his normal self, and Tresca took courage. The instant Jane left the room to go and fetch Mr Preedy's tray, she turned round to face Connor, shivering with nerves. But she must be quick. They would only

225

have a few moments in private.

'I've got something to tell you,' she murmured, and then blurted out before her courage failed, 'I'm pregnant.'

Silence descended like a lead weight. Tresca waited, willing Connor to speak. His facial muscles seemed paralysed as he stared at her, and it seemed an eternity before his lips finally moved.

'Are you sure?' His voice was low, like gravel, and Tresca felt herself sway as she nodded. But then his mouth curved at the edges and a slow, wondrous smile crept over his face, lighting his eyes like beacons.

'Oh, my clever girl!' And she at once found herself wrapped in his strong embrace.

Tresca swooned against him, almost faint with relief. 'I thought you'd be cross,' she mumbled into his chest.

'Sure, why should I be cross? A child's the greatest blessing anyone can have. It just means we'll have to be married sooner rather than later. Me, a daddy already! Me mammy's the one who'll be counting the months, but no one else back home'll know any different, so she'll be happy enough. Now, will you be going to see the vicar tomorrow to make the arrangements?'

Tresca blinked up at his beaming face. 'But ... what about the dispensation from the Pope?'

'Aren't *you* more important than a piece of paper. No, we'll be married as soon as we can in the church here in Tavvy. I'll pretend to be an Irish Protestant and do me penance later. Oh, you've made me so happy, so you have,' he

226

crowed, holding her at arm's length and grinning.

Tresca burst into tears of joyous relief.

Twenty-Two

'I'll be seeing you tomorrow, then, me little love. And make sure you see the vicar in the morning. Oh, you've made me the happiest man alive,' Connor enthused, crushing Tresca to him. 'Now you be sure to look after our little one there.'

He bent his head, his lips brushing tenderly against hers, and she melted against him. In one way or another, everything was going to be all right. She watched him cross the deserted street. He obviously couldn't contain himself and gave a little skip of elation, making Tresca chuckle as she closed the front door.

The air was sharp with the tang of a heavy frost, and Connor drew in a lungful of its clarity. A daddy! Sure he couldn't believe it after just that one time, and his chest filled with pride. He'd have preferred to have waited for a family until they were properly wed and had saved more money, but wouldn't they manage somehow.

He felt so excited he was sure he wouldn't sleep, and sitting in bed reading wouldn't be the thing. He needed to expend his pent-up energy. Almost without thought, he found himself crossing beneath the towering viaduct and then turning right up the steep alleyway of Madge Lane.

He thrived on the challenge of his work, and his instincts were leading him to the Watts Road cutting.

Because of the delays, it had been decided that very day to hire over a hundred extra hands at fourpence halfpenny an hour, an additional penny on the normal rate. With the end of the project in sight, many navvies had already left to search for longer term prospects elsewhere, and it was hoped this offer might attract them to return, or encourage more men to take their place. The company was going to bring in gas lamps so that shifts could go on twenty-four hours a day.

Connor found himself at the top of the cutting. Down below he could see in the moonlight the smoke wafting up from the chimney of the night-watchman's hut. It was a raw night and the watch-man would be inside, huddled beside the little stove. Connor saw no reason to disturb him. For tonight, all was well with the world and Connor was floating on a cloud.

First thing in the morning he was going to check on the progress of the boreholes under his supervision. He wasn't classed as an explosives expert, although he knew almost as much as those who were, but certain members of the gang of men under him were skilled in drilling the holes deep into the rock. It crossed his mind that if he checked on those boreholes now, work could begin immediately in the morning.

He shared a shed at the top of the cutting with a couple of other gangers. The key was on a fob in his pocket together with that of his boarding house and room, so he let himself in and lit a storm lamp, which gave him enough light to scramble down the side and into the cutting. He went carefully, not wanting to spoil his best boots, or even to fall. An injury that meant no work also meant no pay, just a paltry sum from the sick fund, and he had responsibilities now. A family man. An irrepressible grin split his face again.

He climbed up the ladders on the scaffolding with the agility of a cat, despite holding the lamp in one hand. The hollow silence in a place that normally seethed with activity and echoed with men's shouting – often using quite unsavoury language – seemed unutterably strange. But Connor was soon making noise of his own, picking up a measuring probe and pushing it into the half-drilled holes. He replaced it on the planks across the scaffolding and then picked up the lamp again to inspect the surface of the rock more closely. It was proving so dense they would need more explosive and more boreholes than normal. It was only in the quiet as he searched out more natural fissures to use that he heard footsteps along the bottom of the man-made gorge.

'Sure, it's only me, Mr Hargreaves,' he called, leaning out and swinging the lamp so that the nightwatchman could identify him more easily.

But when he peered down, Mr Hargreaves wasn't alone. And on closer inspection it wasn't Mr Hargreaves at all. Two men were skulking in the shadows, pressed up against the rock face now they knew they'd been seen. Alarm bells began to toll in Connor's head. They must be up to no good – intent on breaking into the storage sheds, no doubt, and stealing equipment, maybe even dynamite.

'What d'you think you're doing down there!' he shouted fearlessly.

For several seconds, the men froze, but then amazingly one of them swaggered out into the pool of light that shone down from Connor's lamp.

'Look who uth've got yere, then!' he sneered in a lisping voice. 'If it ithn't the bathtard that knocked my bloody teeth out!'

The other fellow stepped forward now, encouraged by his companion's bravado. 'An' stopped us 'avin' that pretty young maid. Just ripe for the takin' she were!'

'Well now, you'm trapped up there, bain't you? An' at our merthy, it'd theem. Thee what thort of 'ero you be now, thall uth?'

Something like ice streamed through Connor's veins, followed immediately by a raging explosion of white hot anger. The two blackguards who had very nearly violated his darling little love. His *acushla*. Where had the devils been all this time? Well, he'd damned well catch them now, so he would, and bring them to justice.

With a roar like a demented lion, he slithered down the top ladder. In the darkness, the two villains exchanged fearful glances, but then the toothless one dug his buddy in the ribs. Nipping up the bottom two ladders of the scaffolding, he began pulling at the ropes that held the one above. His crony was instantly helping him and within seconds the ladder was dangerously loose.

'That'll do,' one of them hissed. ''Er won't have

bin able fer see what us was doin'.'

The other ruffian's mouth spread in a gummy, vicious grin and they slid back down to the ground. With one venomous mind, they put their weight against the scaffolding and started to rock it perilously back and forth.

'Get 'en back fer my teeth,' the savage brute chortled, and the pair of them laughed maliciously.

Halfway down, Connor felt the gantry lurch beneath him and he pulled himself up short. So that was their game, was it? Well, there was always some movement in scaffolding and you couldn't do his sort of work if you were afraid of it. So if they thought they could scare him like that, they would have to think again. He would just have to be careful, but he was determined to catch the buggers, so he was! As the black fog of fury engulfed him again, he swung himself on to the next ladder.

All too late, he realized it wasn't properly secured. As the whole structure swayed to one side, the ladder slipped along the crossbar it was resting on. The darkness of the night flashed across Connor's brain as he tried to grab on to anything he could to save himself. His fingers touched something hard and solid, but he couldn't get a hold, and as the ladder toppled over, it took him with it.

The two monsters below looked up at his cry. They watched, stunned, as the figure tumbled downwards, bounced off the edge of the stage below and was thrown outwards into mid-air.

Inside his warm hut, Mr Hargreaves dozed by

the stove.

'Connor not coming again tonight?'

Tresca lowered her eyes as she took the washed saucepan from Jane's wet hands. She had been asking herself the very same question. It wasn't that Connor called in every evening, but it was strange that he had decided not to come for two consecutive days after she had told him she was carrying his child. A quiet dread was trundling in her breast, and she tried to block it from her mind. Surely that wasn't the reason he hadn't appeared at the door with his cheery smile, his arms ready to enfold her in a warm, loving embrace? He had seemed genuinely delighted at the idea of becoming a father, and Tresca really couldn't believe he would abandon her because of it. She had even done as he had urged and gone to see the vicar to make the necessary arrangements for their marriage.

She hurled the thought aside. She really shouldn't be so silly. They said that pregnant women were apt to be emotional. Nevertheless, she tossed and turned in bed, and when she finally drifted off, it was into a restless and fitful sleep.

It was still pitch dark when she awoke and snapped at once into full wakefulness. She fumbled for the small box and struck a match to light the lamp, which, when all was said and done, Connor had given her and over which they had argued so long ago. Now the sight of it made her stomach churn.

She turned up the wick. The clock told her it was five o'clock. With winter coming on, the hours of daylight were shorter and work on the railway couldn't begin until there was at least a glimmer in the sky. That was why, as Connor had explained, the company were bringing in gas lamps so that work could go on round the clock.

Oh, she simply had to see Connor before he left for work! She threw on her clothes and let herself out into the dark street, feeling cold and uneasy. She crossed over to rap sharply on the door of Connor's boarding house and waited impatiently, cursing the slowness of the elderly landlord she could hear pottering along the hallway. When the door finally opened, the fellow was bleary-eyed and his thin, grey hair was all awry, as if he had just got out of bed.

'I'm sorry to disturb you so early, but is Connor up yet?' she asked politely as she tamped down her frustration.

'I'm afraid Mr O'Mahoney isn't here, maid. Hasn't been back for two nights. We were wondering if *you* might know where he be.'

Tresca frowned at him, disbelieving. 'N–no,' she stuttered, panic taking root inside her. 'I haven't seen him, either.'

'Well, he must be coming back. His things are still in his room and he's not the sort to go off without leaving word. Go up and have a look if you like. Your young legs'll be quicker than mine.'

Tresca didn't need asking twice. She shot up the stairs to the room she had seen only a few times, and then only for a matter of minutes as it was considered improper to be alone with Connor even if they were betrothed. But she had to wait

233

for the landlord to come up with the spare key to let her in anyway, and every second seemed an hour as he laboured up the creaking steps.

The room was in perfect order, Connor's working boots standing neatly on newspaper by the door.

So where was he?

Tresca's heart began to race even faster and she pushed past the elderly man and ran down the stairs again.

'Let us know if you find him,' she heard him call after her.

She didn't reply. Her brain couldn't find any words. Only Connor's name screamed in her head. Something was wrong. Unimaginably wrong. It wasn't that Connor didn't want to come to her. For some reason, he *couldn't*.

Tresca stood, staring up at the massive viaduct that loomed over her, a dark silhouette against the faintly lightening sky. She spun round, head back, giddy as she whirled in a circle. Oh, God. A black fear crashed down on her as surely as if a block of granite had fallen from the arch above.

Almost without thought, she catapulted into Madge Lane and raced up the hill. Only halfway up, a stitch seared into her side and she angrily slowed to a walk. When she came eventually to the cutting, in the darkness it was like looking down into the mouth of hell. Nobody was there yet, and it wasn't sufficiently light for her to climb down in safety. She would have to wait, frustration clawing at her as she paced back and forth.

At last, men started arriving, some making

ribald comments at the sight of the young girl waiting alone in the gloom. But Tresca ignored their lewd remarks.

'Have any of you seen Connor O'Mahoney?' she demanded instead.

So many shaking heads. After all, Connor was one ganger among many. And then, finally, a voice as concerned as hers.

'O'Mahoney? 'Er'm our ganger but 'er's not bin seen fer two days.'

'That's right, so it is,' another voice, this time Irish, agreed. 'Didn't we wonder if he were ill, for sure it's not like him.'

Taken ill? No, that was impossible. But ... what if he hadn't gone straight home that night? Perhaps he'd had an accident. Somehow. *Somewhere*. And he'd been taken either to the workhouse or the cottage hospital in West Street. The latter was more likely. Sick or injured navvies had been taken there before. By the time she had raced up to it, Tresca could hardly catch her breath. The sympathetic nurse there made her sit down with a glass of water until she could splutter her request. But there had been no one admitted answering Connor's description, and she had heard of nobody being treated for a serious accident by any of the town's physicians – for if Connor had had an accident, Tresca reasoned wildly, it must be serious for him not to have been able to have a message sent to her.

The workhouse, then. She banged on the gate until her fists were sore, her lungs collapsing from running up the long, steep hill. Mr Blake, the dour workhouse porter, opened the little door, his voluminous black coat making him appear like some demon from hell.

'No one like that's bin admitted,' he barked. 'An' don't you come yere agin wi'out permission.'

Tresca froze, rooted to the spot. Connor couldn't have just disappeared into thin air – he must be *somewhere!* Even if he hadn't wanted to face up to his responsibilities as the father of their child – which Tresca was convinced wasn't the case – he wouldn't have just gone off, leaving everything behind.

Everything. Not just his clothes and personal possessions, but his money.

A few minutes later, Tresca was back at his house, demanding to be let into his room again. And there it was, hidden in a tiny gap at the side of the wardrobe just as he had described to her. His bank book. What more proof did she need?

She stared out of the window down on to Bannawell Street. Dear God, what should she do now? Her eyes locked on to a familiar figure: Mr Szlumper, frowning up at the viaduct from beneath his black top hat.

Tresca hurried out into the street again before he strode off to inspect somewhere else, her heart hammering. For if anyone knew where Connor might be – if he had been sent on an urgent errand for the railway, for instance – it was the chief engineer. But when she gabbled out her question, his brow pleated into deep folds.

'No, I don't know where he is. And I'm surprised at him, a good worker like that. And usually so reliable. I had him in mind for a sort of promotion. But I can't give it to him if he's not here.'

Tresca's face was ashen, and a great, wrenching squeal escaped her lips. 'Something's happened to him, I'm sure!'

William Szlumper's heart softened at the young girl's obvious distress. 'Something strange happened down at the cutting the other night,' he told her. 'The nightwatchman didn't see or hear anything, but a ladder from high up on a particular part of the scaffolding was found on the ground in the morning, and there was a puddle of something that looked like blood. And I found this.'

He withdrew something from the breast pocket of his coat, and Tresca instantly recognized Connor's beloved tin whistle.

Mr Szlumper caught her as her knees buckled beneath her. 'Can someone help me?' he called out. And when two passers-by rushed up to him, he muttered under his breath, 'I need to get to the police station.'

'Vera?'

The older girl looked up as the door opened. Tresca's voice was so quiet, Vera wasn't entirely sure she had spoken at all. She looked like a little ghost, shrivelled and unreal, as she stood uncertainly on the threshold.

Vera flew over to lead her into the room and sit her down in the chair. A small fire flickered in the grate and Vera heaped on more coal, heedless of the cost. Tresca was as pale as death itself, her lips tinged with blue, and Vera felt she must do something to warm her.

'You look frozen to the marrow. Let me get you a cup of tea from the kitchen.'

To her surprise and relief, Tresca's voice was a little stronger this time. 'No. No, thank you. Tea's ... tea's making me feel sick,' she explained, trailing off into reverie again.

'Is it?' Vera sympathized, for once at a loss for any words of comfort, since what could get through Tresca's shell of grief? As Vera searched her mind frantically, it struck her like a thunder-bolt. Tea. Sickness. 'Oh my God,' she breathed. 'You ... you don't mean ... you're expecting Connor's child?'

Tresca raised her head and a sudden spark of life shone in her eyes. 'Yes. And I thank God I am. I don't care what people say. I don't know what's happened to Connor, but it's all I have left of him. Only ... I don't know what to do. I just know I'm not going to end up like poor Bella did.'

'No. No, of course not,' Vera murmured, her brain whirling in circles. 'What she did was illegal as well as, well, as killing her.'

'But I'm not going back to the workhouse either.' Again, that flash of determination for which Vera rejoiced. 'I won't have Connor's child ending up like Lucy.'

'So, what *are* you going to do?'

'I ... I thought *you* might tell me.'

Vera met Tresca's open, trusting gaze. Oh, Lord. 'I don't have all the answers, you know, Tresca. Have you ... do you have any money?'

'A little. Connor...' Her voice cracked and she paused to gather herself together again. 'Connor

238

had money. Money he'd saved for our future. But the police say the bank must keep the money until ... until we know for sure what's happened to him. Whether he's ... whether he's alive or ... or dead.'

She stared at Vera, dry-eyed. Her tears just wouldn't come. She wanted them to. She wanted them to come and fill up the dreadful, aching emptiness inside her and wash away her tormented grief. But so far, her heart had been like arid desert sand.

Mr Solloway frowned when Tresca arrived at the workhouse for her monthly visit. 'Er, not that way. I'm afraid you need to come to the infirmary. Your father's health has deteriorated since you were here last.'

Tresca's pupils dilated as she blinked at him, the only indication of the emotion that seared into her soul. She was already so overflowing with sorrow that she simply couldn't absorb any more, and so she followed the workhouse master in silence to the men's infirmary. The long, gloomy room was so depressing, with patients rasping and coughing from the austere rows of beds, or lying inert, toothless mouths open and eyes shut in grey faces, waiting to draw their last breath.

When she saw Emmanuel, Tresca's already deadened heart fragmented into dust. The change in him was shocking. She had yearned to seek some comfort in her father's arms, but he looked so pale, so withered, that she knew she would have to be the one to be strong for him. Her heart was savage with fear as she searched inside herself for something that wasn't there.

'Aw, my little princess,' he managed to smile as she approached, though he didn't lift his head from the pillow. 'I feels better already fer seein' you.'

'Oh, Father,' she said, forcing the corners of her mouth upwards. 'How long have you been in here?'

'Aw, just a week or so, till I picks up again. Reckons I'll be back at my workbench next week, I does. Now tell me,' he went on, forcing some life into his tone, although Tresca could see his eyes were pale and faded, ''ow be that young fellow o' yourn?'

His words were like a dagger in Tresca's side. Connor's disappearance had made the front page of the *Tavistock Gazette*. '*Have you seen this man?*' it had asked the good folk of the town. So, Emmanuel hadn't even been well enough to read the newspaper for a couple of weeks. He didn't know. Her thoughts spun in a tortured dance. Should she tell him, relieve some of her strangling anguish? But surely she couldn't burden him with her own devastating misery?

'I's bin thinkin' 'bout this move to Ireland,' Emmanuel went on before she had the heart to reply. To lie to him. 'It'll be a proper adventure, won't it? We'll all be mortal happy together, like.'

He was smiling at her, but she knew it wasn't real. Just a front. He wanted her to know that he approved. That when he was gone, she should go and live out her dream with the man she loved. And she must let him go, not knowing the brutal truth.

'Yes, of course we will,' she agreed softly, but her heart lay dying in her breast.

Dr Greenwood sent for her a few days before Christmas. She held Emmanuel's limp hand, the skin like paper to her touch. She watched his shallow breathing, heard the rattle in his chest. His eyes were closed in his cadaverous face, and when at last he did open them, they were glazed and wandering.

'Is that my princess?' he scarcely whispered, and then his lips began to move in low mutterings which made no sense, even though Tresca leant over to try and listen.

He went quiet again, almost as if asleep. The doctor came, took Emmanuel's pulse. 'Not long now,' he warned, and tiptoed silently away.

Tresca sat, cloaked in a black shroud, for two or three hours, not moving. Evening closed in, the ward was in darkness broken only by the mournful glimmer from the few lamps. And around midnight, Emmanuel slipped away.

Twenty-Three

'Oh, my poor little lamb.'

The usual rosy hue in Jane Ellacott's round cheeks had drained away. It was two months since Connor's disappearance and no clues yet as to what had happened to him, despite the local constabulary's extensive enquiries. And, of

241

course, Tresca's beloved father had passed away just before Christmas, so the poor cheel was going through unutterable devastation. Her face had faded to alabaster, her eyes the colour of mud in their dark sockets. She scarcely spoke a word, lost in a desert of emptiness that even the warm and compassionate Jane could not penetrate. The girl picked at her food, her already slender form becoming stick thin. Her clothes hung from her in folds, except that just now Jane had caught her sideways as she reached up for something on the shelf. And she had noticed for the first time the small but distinctive bump beneath her skirt.

'You'm expectin' Connor's babby, bain't you?'

The words were out before she could stop them, her jaw dangling open in shock. She watched as Tresca's face turned rigid, a determined light coming into her dulled eyes and her chin lifting defiantly. But she said nothing and returned to what she was doing, enshrouded in her own silent world again.

'Well, I's surprised at you,' Jane went on as her dismay subsided. 'But I supposes he were ... he *be,*' she corrected herself, 'a handsome fellow. An' you two so in love, the pair on you, an' you *was* promised to each other. An' now all this.' She waved her hand vaguely in the air, her way of indicating the desperate situation Tresca was facing. 'Well, you'm still the same person,' Jane declared fiercely as her natural instincts took over again. 'An' you've been dealt a rough hand. This is still your home, an' if anyone says ort, well, they knows what they can do. You'll hardly be the first to have a babby out o' wedlock in Bannawell Street, an' at least you didn't come by it the way some o' them has.'

'I'm not sure that makes any difference.' Ebeneezer Preedy's curt voice from the doorway startled them both. 'I had to put up with all that frivolity and music despite my protestations, and I have to say I've enjoyed the peace and quiet since that Irish chap left. Ran off when he knew the girl was pregnant, no doubt. And now you propose that I have to put up with a screaming child day and night. Well, I'm sorry, Mrs Ellacott. I believe I've been a good tenant to you these past years, but I cannot withstand the ignominy of living under the same roof as a trollop with an illegitimate brat. So, either you dismiss her within the week, or I shall be obliged to seek alternative lodgings. Now, where is my jug of hot water? And I no longer want *her* bringing anything up to my room.'

He turned back into the scullery and a few seconds later they heard him stomp up the stairs. Jane's face had inflated like a balloon, so scalding was her indignation, and she stood with her hands on her hips, lips bunched into a knot.

'Well, if he thinks he can tell me what to do in my own house, he can jolly well take hissel' elsewhere! I'll not have my little Tresca put out on the street. Where be his human compassion? Always been a miserable devil, he has, an' I'll be glad to be rid of him. Soon get another lodger, I will, with all the railway folk in town. An' one that's not so cold as a wet fish. Now then, my lover, we needs to look after you,' she nodded as her natural kindness drove out her fury. 'It'll be lovely to have a babby in the house. So come here an' give me a hug,' she invited, wrapping her plump arms about the young girl, who still stood like a statue, her face a blank mask.

But as she responded to Jane's warm embrace, Tresca's mind was far from inert. Jane was benevolence itself, and if Tresca's emotions hadn't already been numbed into sterility, she might have wept in her arms. But fate had destroyed any feeling in her heart. Find another lodger? One who was no trouble and paid his rent on the dot each week? And when the railway was nearing completion and workers already leaving the town? Jane *needed* that money to survive and pay her own rent to the Duke of Bedford. The kindly widow wasn't getting any younger, and her lodger and the little profit the dairy produced were her only pension.

No, Tresca couldn't do that to her. Connor's disappearance had gouged a void out of her soul, but there was still an innate sense of justice lurking somewhere in its depths, and she couldn't repay Jane's habitual generosity in this way. She would move out, no matter how Jane might protest. After all, what did it matter what happened to her now that Connor was gone? At first, she had clung to the existence of the child growing inside her, but as time had gone by, the emptiness had grown and obliterated all else. It was the not knowing that was slowly killing her. Connor was dead, she was sure of it. But without proof, a tiny, desperate flicker of hope refused to let her accept it and grieve as she should.

244

'We'm proper sorry, maid.' Elijah Edwards shook his head sadly as he glanced across at his wife, whose face had also moved into deep lines of sympathy. 'Us only 'as the one room as you knows. If us 'ad two, you'd be more than welcome. An' wi' a babby as well... Mortal shocked us was to 'ear what'd 'appened to Mr O'Mahoney. Nice fellow he were. An' you two seemed so much in love–'

'Course they was,' Mrs Edwards whispered. 'Else a nice cheel like 'er wouldn't be expectin', would she, like? Well, maybe Mr O'Mahoney'll turn up,' she said, addressing Tresca in a raised voice. 'Maybe 'er's 'ad an accident an' lost 'is memory, like. An' when 'er's better, 'er'll come runnin' 'ome.'

The elderly woman's well-meant words stung into Tresca's brain. Hadn't she tried to tell herself the same thing so many times? But as the days and weeks passed, that vain hope had been sliding away. If such a thing had happened, surely someone would have recognized Connor from his description that had been circulated far and wide? He had a pretty distinctive appearance, even if Tresca didn't have a photograph of him.

Not even a photograph. And what was breaking her was that it was becoming harder to conjure up a vision of him in her mind, to hear his lilting voice in her head. As if he was slipping away from her. As if she didn't care any more.

She nodded, knowing that Mrs Edwards was only trying to be kind. She muttered her thanks and felt their pitying eyes on her as she went out

245

into the raw January morning. Elijah would soon be leaving for work, which was why she had gone there so early. But how stupid could she have been? She knew that they could only afford to rent one room and couldn't possibly take her in. And it would be the same for everyone she knew. Even Vera couldn't help her.

One foot placed itself in front of the other entirely of its own accord since her brain had no idea where she was going. So cold, although she was only aware of the numbness that enshrouded her. The colossal viaduct was a mere blur as she passed beneath it, a forbidding spectre from her old life.

'Miss Ladycott.'

Her name scarcely registered in her mind as Morgan Trembath ran up behind her, and she continued on down the hill without paying him any heed. Morgan stood for a moment, his arms hopelessly by his sides as he watched her, a desolate, wretched figure. A ghost.

May God forgive him, but he had almost rejoiced at the news of O'Mahoney's disappearance. No ... rejoice was hardly the word. He had *liked* the man, for God's sake, even if he had been so jealous of his relationship with Tresca Ladycott. He had prayed they would have some violent disagreement that would destroy their love for one another. But never in a million years would he have wished the Irishman dead, which in all probability he was. And seeing the effigy of desolation Tresca had become, he would gladly have brought O'Mahoney back to life for her, were it within his power.

'Miss Ladycott, wait, please!' he called, springing after her. 'I just wanted to say again how sorry I am for your misfortune.'

The girl blinked up at him, a slow swoop and lift of her lashes, as if she was waking from a deep trance that was filled only with sorrow and despair. Morgan Trembath, who had always shown her kindness. And suddenly, she could not have said why, something in her frozen heart melted. Perhaps it was because she had been surrounded by the love and compassion of mainly female friends, and now this young man was offering her his sympathy. Perhaps his physical closeness stimulated the natural instincts of a woman to seek solace and protection from the opposite sex. But, for whatever reason, the tears that had remained stagnant and obstinate inside her for so long erupted in an unstoppable flow of misery, and she leant against Morgan's chest, sobbing as if her heart had, quite literally, broken.

Morgan's hands patted the air around her shoulders. Good Lord, he hadn't meant to upset her like this. He had meant to offer her comfort. He felt so ashamed, such a fool, but she was so drenched in grief that there was really nothing for it but to put his arms around her. And, oh! What a good feeling it would have been if only the reason for his embrace had been different.

'Oh, Miss Ladycott, Tresca, if I may be so bold,' he murmured. 'I'm so very sorry. I would not have upset you like this for the world. Please, forgive me. And know that if there is anything I can do to help, anything at all, you only have to say the word.'

To his dismay, he felt her stiffen and she pulled away, glaring up at him, the release of her tears having unlocked the burning spirit inside her.

'Oh, yes?' she snapped back with icy contempt. 'You wouldn't say that if you knew the truth.'

'The truth?' Morgan shook his head, totally bewildered. 'I don't understand.'

'Then let me tell you,' she spat, her eyes ablaze. 'Connor O'Mahoney, the man I love, is … is gone. And I'm carrying his child. Some people are sneering at me because of it, and those who want to help me actually can't do so. And I have no doubt that you can't or won't either.'

She tossed her head and strode off down the street, leaving Morgan staring after her, jaw agape and shaken to the core. Good Heavens above, he would never have believed it.

'I beg your pardon?'

Tresca's eyes widened with incredulity. Morgan Trembath stood before her in the dairy the following morning, his stance irresolute and twisting his hat in his fingers. Nevertheless, his voice was steady when he repeated his request.

'I want to prove to you that I meant what I said. I want you to marry me.'

Tresca stared at him, convinced she had misheard a second time, but knowing she hadn't. *Marry* him? A second later, she threw up her head in a sarcastic laugh.

'Don't make fun of me, if you please, Mr Trembath–'

'Morgan. And I'm not making fun of you. I mean it.' His eyes bore intently into her face and her bitterness stilled as she realized he was deadly serious.

'I've been thinking about it all night. Haven't slept a wink,' he went on in earnest. 'I've had feelings for you ever since you came into the shop asking for work. Only I was too timid to tell you. I was trying to pluck up the courage, but then Mr O'Mahoney came into your life, and it was obvious... So I had to stand aside. And I was so happy for you when he told me you were betrothed, though it broke my heart. But now...'

He hesitated, and his hand closed over one of hers. 'I know I can't measure up to Mr O'Mahoney. I'm just a dull little shopkeeper. But I do love you, and I can offer you a home and respectability for the child. I don't expect you to love me in return. And it would be a marriage on paper only, if you understand my meaning,' he added, blushing slightly. 'But it would make me a very happy man just to have you under my roof and to be able to protect you.'

He stopped, clearly flushed with excitement and a touch of embarrassment, and Tresca fixed her stare on him, totally astonished. Good God, he really did mean it. She pursed her lips, feeling her world turn upside down. As if she didn't have enough to cope with just now, she had this ... this lunatic to deal with.

'And what does your mother have to say about the idea?' she asked, trying to keep the scorn from her voice. 'As I remember, she seemed to consider Connor and me the dregs of the earth.'

'She doesn't know,' he answered, and Tresca thought she detected a flash of triumph in his words, as if he relished the thought of defying his mother for once. 'And she wouldn't until after the wedding. We could be married by special licence, so there'd be no reading of banns for her to hear.'

'And you'd expect her to welcome me into her family, her home, with an illegitimate child on the way?'

Morgan's mouth screwed awkwardly. 'No. But it wouldn't be illegitimate after we were married, would it? And you're so strong, Tresca. At least, you were before all this happened. You'd stand up to her, I'm sure you would. And ... and I'd be there, too. And once she realized she had no choice but to accept it, I'm certain that she would. But think about it. And if you decide not to accept my offer, well, I'll always be here for you. For there'll never be anyone else for me.'

And before Tresca had a chance to reply, he dashed out of the shop.

'Vera! Oh, thank God you're in!'

Tresca burst into Vera's room in an evident flurry of agitation. Vera glanced across at her, rejoicing that the old, spirited Tresca, buried for so long beneath her grief, seemed to have surfaced again. But what had happened to spur her into life again?

'Whatever's the matter?' Vera cried.

'I really don't know where to begin,' Tresca answered. 'Jane guessed about the baby the other night. But Mr Preedy overheard, and he said if I didn't leave, he would. Jane was so kind. She said she wanted me to stay on with her, and that she'd soon find another lodger. But, let's face it, she won't, will she? And certainly not such a reliable one. And it really wouldn't be fair on her, so I've been looking for somewhere else to live. But I can't find anywhere and there's only a few days before Mr Preedy will leave if I don't go first. And then, this morning, something quite extraordinary happened.'

'Extraordinary?' Vera frowned. It must indeed have been something extraordinary to have brought Tresca back to the ebullient, self-willed person she had always been before the tragic events that had decimated her life.

'Morgan Trembath's asked me to marry him.'

'What?'

'Yes. He knows about the baby, and he wants to help.'

'B–but marry him? And what about his harridan of a mother?'

'Oh, she knows nort about his crazy idea. But, Vera...' Tresca hesitated, her eyes deepening to an intense mahogany. 'At first I thought he must be deranged. But now I've had time to think about it, is it really such a crazy idea? Morgan's always been kind, and he's promised there'll be nort physical to the marriage. It'd solve a lot of problems for me–'

'And bring you a whole lot more. And his mother–'

'I'm sure I can cope with her. And it would give Connor's child a home. A good home. And a name. And surely I must put the child first? My own feelings mustn't come into it.'

Vera's mouth turned to a thin, questioning line. 'And what *are* your feelings?'

251

Tresca bit her lip. 'I ... I do like Morgan,' she faltered. 'And ... I could marry him. For the sake of the child. I must give him or her the best chance in life, don't you see? And ... because I don't know what else to do. Only...' She paused, and her throat closed up with the tearing agony that raked it. 'What if Connor comes back?'

All was quiet. Just the hissing of the coal in the grate. The heavy tick-tock of Vera's old clock on the mantelpiece. Then Vera took her friend's hands, watching the tears that ambled down her cheeks.

'Do you *really* think he will? It's been two months. If ... if he was still alive, he'd have sent a letter or *something* by now. And someone would have seen him. It's been in all the papers. Posters far and wide. And he wouldn't abandon you, we know that. Even if he'd had second thoughts about marriage, he would have done something to provide for you and the child. No. Much as it grieves me to have to say it, I ... I think we must accept that Connor is ... is no longer with us.'

Tresca had gradually bowed her head, but now she looked up again, her eyes swimming with anguish. 'Yes, I know,' she groaned, as a tidal wave of confusion rushed through her again. 'But ... what if...'

She stared at Vera, her face alive and intense with pain.

Slowly and deliberately Vera shook her head. And Tresca's heart buckled.

Twenty-Four

'Morgan, what are you doing back here?'

Charity Trembath's eyes hardened to steel as she stepped into the hall and spied her son with the young girl by his side. 'And what do you think you're doing bringing that ragamuffin into our house? Isn't she the urchin who had the gall to try and sell a used lamp back to us? And she was the strumpet consorting with that rough Irish navvy before he disappeared. Personally I don't know what all the fuss was about. The sooner all those ruffians leave Tavistock, the easier we'll all sleep in our beds. Now what *is* that hussy doing in my hall?'

Tresca froze to a pillar of ice. She had expected a hostile reception and had been scraping up her courage to face her mother-in-law of half an hour. But to hear her darling Connor spoken of in such derogatory terms was like running full pelt into a brick wall. The last few weeks had been bad enough, agonizing over Morgan's proposal, tossing and turning all night, weeping or dry with bitterness, a vision of Bella lying in a pool of blood ever in her mind – and the determination that she wouldn't end up the same way, no matter what. Finally she had taken herself up on to the moor to what had been one of her and Connor's favourite spots. And there she had said her farewell to Connor, and her heart had split in two.

She had begged Mr Preedy to give her a little more time, promising she would be leaving soon, but please would he not let on to Mrs Eilacott since she predicted that the kindly woman would be deeply upset. The sight of the dairymaid's misery had moved even the implacable Mr Preedy and he had grudgingly agreed. And so this morning, she had dressed in her best attire and packed her few possessions.

Jane knew at once that something was amiss. And when Tresca told her briefly what was to happen within the hour, she was appalled. Tresca couldn't possibly marry Morgan Trembath! He was a kind, gentle but spineless sort, totally under his mother's thumb. Tresca had a perfectly good home here with her, a home that would be loving and stable for the child. But when Jane had seen that Tresca's mind was made up, she had shut up shop, donned her hat and coat, and hurried down to the empty church with Tresca. Vera was to be one of the witnesses, and with a watery smile, Jane acted as the other so that Morgan wasn't obliged to engage a stranger off the street in exchange for a few shillings.

For a second or two as she had knelt by the altar, Tresca had felt Emmanuel's shadow brush against her shoulder. *That be right, my princess. Fight fer yersel', like you always 'as.* But now, standing before Charity Trembath, she felt herself wither. Had she made the most terrible mistake? No. She must hurl her misgivings aside and stand up to this woman who seemed to delight in belittling her hard-working, submissive son. Tresca took a deep breath, dragging the determination

254

from the depths of her broken soul.

To her amazement, before she could open her mouth, she heard Morgan's shaky voice beside her. 'Mother, I would thank you not to talk about my wife in such a manner.'

Charity's jaw fell open in disbelief. A second later, she snapped it shut so violently that her teeth gave an audible crack and her face turned puce. Tresca wondered – with curious detachment – if the woman might be about to suffer an apoplectic fit.

'Your *what?*' she gurgled at the back of her throat.

'You heard, Mother,' Morgan replied quietly, his lips thin and white.

'Oh, no, you don't! You can't marry *her!* I won't allow a son of mine–'

'Too late, I'm afraid. Tresca and I have just come from the church. Look.'

He took Tresca's left hand, where the plain gold band glinted on her third finger, and held it towards his mother. Tresca detected a flash of pride in the look he shot at her, but Mrs Trembath recoiled as if she had been forced to witness something vile and heinous.

'No!' she shrieked. 'You'll have to *un*marry her, then, won't you! Have it annulled! I won't have her in my house. I–'

Tresca saw Morgan swallow hard. 'May I remind you, Mother, that this is *my* house, not yours. The lease is in my name. And although you like to oversee certain aspects of the shop, I'm the one who works there all the time and makes the money to pay the rent on both the shop and

255

this house.'

Charity's lip curled, but then she gave a dramatic gasp and put her hand up to her brow as if she were about to faint. 'If only your dear father could hear you talk to me like that, he'd turn in his grave,' she moaned.

'On the contrary, in his will he very sensibly put everything in my name, as you well know. So I advise you to climb down off your high horse and accept Tresca as your daughter-in-law.'

Charity Trembath glared at her son, her lips knotted venomously. Morgan himself was still holding Tresca's hand. She could feel him trembling, and realized it was probably the first time for years he had defied his mother. The first time ever, perhaps, and she appreciated what it had taken for him to do so.

'Never!' the shrew hissed back. 'I won't have her bringing her wayward habits into *my* house.'

'Well.' Morgan nearly choked on his own words. 'You can move out if you wish. I'll grant you a modest allowance. Or you can live over the shop if you prefer.'

'How dare you treat me like this! I will not be driven from my own home by that ... that...'

'In that case, I suggest you start by putting a civil tongue in your head. Now, Tresca, let me help you out of your coat and then I'll show you round the house.'

Tresca silently obeyed, slipping out of her coat but without taking her eyes from the bitter woman who stood, hands on her hips and her mouth in a livid sneer. Tresca understood what a courageous stand Morgan had made and felt she

256

should say something to support him.

'I won't be any trouble, Mrs Trembath, really I won't,' she assured her in as polite a tone as she could muster. 'And I won't interfere in the house in any way. I'm sure you run it admirably.'

Charity snorted, and then she screamed hysterically as her eyes fell on Tresca's stomach, which had expanded rapidly in the past few weeks since Morgan's proposal.

'Oh my God, she's pregnant! Oh, Morgan, how could you, you little fool? You've let the slut ensnare you. B–but wait a minute. She must be, what, five months gone? She was seeing that Irish blackguard back then, wasn't she? So ... the child's not even yours. Oh, you damnable little whore!'

Her fingernails, extended like claws, shot towards Tresca's face, but Morgan grasped his mother's arm before she reached her target.

'Stop this at once! I happen to have loved Tresca from a distance for a long time, and I'm more than happy to help her now that she's, well, in trouble.'

'And I'm sure she's more than happy to accept! Well, I'm going up to my room to lie down. Just see what you've done to me, you ungrateful boy, and as for you–'

Tresca shut her eyes as the gobbet of spittle landed on her face. Perhaps she deserved it. She felt Charity push past her to reach the stairs, and Morgan went to follow her, but Tresca stilled his arm.

'No. Let her go,' she sighed. 'Give her time to get over it.'

257

Neither of them heard the words Charity mumbled under her *breath*. *'There's more than one way to skin a cat, you little minx.'* Instead, Morgan met the resigned look in Tresca's eyes and she watched him drag his hand over his nose and mouth as he let out a trembling breath.

'I'm so very sorry,' he murmured. 'I didn't think she'd take it quite so badly.'

'We knew it weren't going to be easy. And I'm the one who should be apologizing. For what it's worth, thank you for standing up for me.'

'And for myself. Perhaps it's something I should have done a long time ago.'

He gave a wry smile, and Tresca noticed, not for the first time, that Morgan was quite handsome when his habitually sombre face moved into a smile. She put up a hand to cup his cheek and he turned his head to kiss her palm. But inside her head she heard a quiet voice. *Aw, princess, what've you done?*

Dinner was eaten in leaden silence. Tresca knew that Charity was studying her through eyes narrowed with hatred, waiting, she felt sure, for her to make a mistake with her table manners. Tresca thanked God that she had always observed her betters, and Mrs Tremaine in particular had always been one to observe such niceties, even in her farmhouse kitchen.

The housekeeper, Mrs Lancaster, ladled soup into Tresca's bowl with what Tresca considered the shadow of a smirk on her face. She was right. In cahoots with her mistress, Mrs Lancaster had set out Tresca's cutlery in the wrong order so that

258

Charity could deride her over the dinner table. But when Tresca found that the positions of her soup and dessert spoons had been swapped, she silently replaced them correctly and then began to spoon the soup away from her within the bowl in the perfect way. She looked up briefly, and her eyes locked with those of her new mother-in-law. Tresca had guessed her game. The thwarted woman clearly knew it and was seething.

Morgan waited until the main course had been served before he attempted to break the stony atmosphere. 'Well, Mother, as it seems we are to be a family, perhaps you would at least show Tresca a little respect. If only for the fact that she has only recently lost her father, in addition to everything else that has befallen her.'

Charity crossed her knife and fork over her plate of food with deliberate precision and straightened her already rigid back. 'And am I supposed to feel sorry for her?'

'Oh, for heaven's sake, Mother, where's your Christian compassion?'

'The fellow died in the workhouse. Lazy and penniless in an institution that we hard-working people pay for.'

Tresca had been biting her tongue from the moment she had entered the house. Charity had taken every opportunity to criticize her, from her bundle of humble clothes to the way her springing curls refused to stay in place. She had taken it all on the chin for Morgan's sake, but now his mother's words made Tresca realize that in the short time she had been in the house, the witch must have sent someone, probably Mrs Lancaster, to find out what she could about Emmanuel so that she could torment her with it. It was simply too much.

'My father were in the workhouse because he were dying,' Tresca rounded on her mother-in-law. 'He had cancer and were too sick to do a full day's work. Anyone could find themselves in the same situation. Even *you*.'

She saw Charity's head jerk back slightly on her neck, but the spiteful woman retorted almost at once, 'I don't think so. Your father was an itinerant farm labourer, as I understand. Turned navvy when he couldn't get any other work.'

She nodded gloatingly as she picked up her cutlery once again. But Tresca could hardly contain the angry resentment that was boiling up inside her. 'I see you like to eat,' she somehow managed to comment in a steady voice.

To her satisfaction, Charity looked confused. 'Pardon?'

'You like to eat,' Tresca repeated. 'Meat, vegetables, bread, milk and cream. Without farmers toiling in the fields in all weathers, you wouldn't have food on your plate. Men who know their crops, refine their breeds of animals, see them safely through lambing or calving. It's all skilled work. Skills I doubt very much that *you* have. And do *you* know how to make the butter you put on your bread, or the cheese you eat? No, I thought not,' she concluded, seeing the horrified bafflement on Charity's face.

Beside her, Morgan warned out of the side of his mouth, 'I think that's enough. You don't want to rile her too much.'

260

'No, Morgan, she has to realize that I'm just as good a person as she is. And so were my father.'

'Huh! You can't even speak properly. *"He were, I were"*,' Charity mimicked.

'And how much difference does that really make? And if it really bothers you that much, I shall make a conscious effort to correct myself. I cannot say fairer than that. Now, I understand that this has all been a shock for you, but I promise you I will prove myself as good a daughter-in-law as you could wish for.'

'We shall see,' Charity scoffed, and forked a roast potato into her mouth.

The rest of the meal was eaten without another word being spoken. Afterwards, Tresca made an excuse to go upstairs since she felt if she spent another minute in Charity's company, she may well punch her on the nose. But just as she reached the bottom step, Charity flew out of the dining room after her.

'You may think you've won that round,' she spat, 'but there'll be plenty more that *I* shall win. One day I'll see you out of this house for good and Morgan will find a *decent* wife for himself. And while you are here, I promise I'll make your life absolute hell.'

Her shoes clicked on the tiled hall floor as she flounced away. Tresca watched her, and then fled up the stairs.

'Good night, Mother.'

'I can see nothing good about this night if you insist on carrying on with this charade. I assume you are going to do the gentlemanly thing and sleep in another room, seeing as the slut is obviously not in love with you? And hopefully you will come to your senses and have the marriage annulled on grounds of non-consummation.'

'That might be a trifle hard to prove, don't you think, as Tresca is already with child?' Morgan suggested. 'Besides, I happen to love her, and although Mr O'Mahoney was her true love, she is not without feelings of fondness towards me, and she knows what marriage entails.'

'I don't suppose the little whore cares. So go on. Ruin your life anyway. But don't come crying to me when it all goes wrong.'

'It won't,' he answered grimly, and turned into his bedroom.

Tresca was sitting by the dressing table in her nightdress, brushing out her hair. She was exhausted, her senses drained, but to see Morgan enter the room she had believed would be hers alone, locking the door behind him, made her heart thump in her chest. She turned, startled with fear as she watched him sit down on the edge of the bed, his head in his hands.

'M—Morgan, I thought you said—'

He lifted his head, wetting his lips as he met her gaze. 'I know. And it was my intention to sleep in the guest room. But Mother wants me to have our marriage annulled for non-consummation.'

'W—what?'

'So I want her to *think* we'll be cementing our marriage tonight. But don't worry, I'll keep my promise. But it does mean I need to sleep in here with you. On ... oh dear, I don't fancy the floor. So ... would you mind? I can put the bolster between us, see? Oh, Lord, this truly isn't what I planned.'

Tresca gulped, her heart rearing in her chest. It wasn't what *she* had planned, either. Could she really trust Morgan? Good God, she barely knew him! He had always been thoughtful and polite, but he was so very subservient to his dragon of a mother. And yet today he had done nothing but defy the old crow. Give her a dose of her own medicine, although his arguments had been couched in far more civil terms than hers had been. But now Tresca had little choice but to nod her consent.

'Thank you,' Morgan mumbled, and began to undress.

Tresca watched him, mesmerized by the day's events. He peeled off his upper garments first, and at the sight of his bare flesh, something in the very core of her yearned brokenly for the broad, powerfully muscled chest that had lit a fire deep down in her belly. Morgan was of a far slighter build, and yet there was a wiry strength to his shoulders that wasn't displeasing. Tresca pulled herself up short, suddenly aware that she was inspecting him, and she averted her eyes. She could hardly expect him to respect her privacy if she wasn't respecting his. If that was indeed what he planned to do, and it hadn't all been a deceptive ruse on his part.

She heard the creak of bed springs, and when she looked back, Morgan was snuggling down on his side of the bed. Dragging herself across the room, Tresca slid in beside him on the other side of the bolster. She had brought with her the pretty lamp Connor had rescued for her, setting it up next to her on the bedside table. Now she turned the wick down low, but didn't extinguish the tiny flame entirely. If Morgan tried to force himself on her, she wanted to be able to see enough to defend herself. Besides, the lamp made her feel that Connor was close.

Oh, Connor, I'm so sorry, she whispered to him inside her head. *I feel as if I've betrayed you, but I had to do it for the sake of our child.* She pulled the covers up to her chin and stared into the shadows.

Morgan emerged from the dining room having finished his breakfast before leaving for the shop. Work provided an unbelievable escape from the palpable tension that percolated through the house, and he pitied poor Tresca who spent more time there than he did. She went out as much as possible, visiting Vera or Mrs Edwards or any of her other friends in the street. Jane had a new dairymaid, but Tresca almost lived there, even serving in the shop. Charity Trembath could hardly object since she was nothing but a jumped-up shopkeeper herself – as Jane went to great and bitter lengths to declare!

Sometimes, if his mother wasn't going to be there, Tresca would accompany Morgan to the shop in West Street. Those were his favourite days, when he could look after her in a way that was impossible under his mother's scornful eye. Even when, with spring on the way, he had merely come home with a small bunch of daffodils still in bud for his pregnant wife, Charity had snipped off their heads in a malicious rage. But today Tresca was going to the shop with him, and being a mild, sunny day, he was planning on taking her for a stroll along the old canal at lunchtime. He was looking forward immensely to this humble pleasure and whistled softly as he climbed the stairs.

The door to the marital bedroom was open. As he reached the landing, Morgan heard a crash and the sound of shattering glass. Then a thin wail of despair which he recognized as Tresca's voice. He dashed to the doorway. Tresca was standing by the wardrobe, both hands over her mouth in horror, her eyes wild and bolting. Having started her daily round of cleaning, Mrs Lancaster was by the bedside table, waving her feather duster in the air, and Tresca's beloved lamp lay in fragments on the polished floorboards.

'Oh dear,' Mrs Lancaster pronounced, her voice laced with sarcasm. 'I seem to have knocked over your lamp. What a pity.'

'What's all this fuss about?' Charity demanded, appearing behind Morgan.

'Oh, just the lamp, Mrs Trembath.'

Morgan glanced over his shoulder at his mother, and the rage seethed inside him as he caught the supercilious, knowing look that was exchanged between the two women. He drew in his breath to say something, choking on his anger, but before he could think of any words, Tresca let out a strangling scream and stumbled to her knees among the broken pieces, trying frantically to scoop them up in her hands and put them back together. In a trice, Morgan was behind her, trying to stop her as already the shards of glass and china were slicing into her skin and blood was starting to drip from her fingers. She tried to fight him off, shaking in violent spasms, sobbing as she continued to scrabble among the splinters before Morgan managed to drag her to her feet.

'This is all your doing, isn't it?' he spat at his mother.

'No, it was merely an accident,' she purred back.

But she watched as Tresca turned to Morgan, weeping brokenly against his chest as he held her so very tightly, smoothing her hair and comforting her like a small child. Charity pursed her lips as she turned away. She might have achieved one of her aims – she had learnt how much the lamp had meant to her daughter-in-law – but she hadn't meant it to drive the bitch and her son closer together. Still, it was early days.

Twenty-Five

Tresca waddled over to the window. She prayed the baby would put in an appearance soon; it felt so enormous within her bulging stomach. When Dr Greenwood had examined her the previous day, he had patted her hand encouragingly as he had left the room.

'Send for me the minute her labour starts,' he had said to the young girl's stony-faced mother-in-law as she had shown him down the stairs. 'It feels like a big baby and it could be a difficult birth. But don't say anything to our little mother. I don't want her worried before it all starts.'

'Of course not, Doctor,' Charity had simpered.

Now, Tresca drew back the bedroom curtains to a grey, drizzling morning. What a pity. Friday the thirtieth of May 1890, the day of the ceremonies to open the new railway line. Connor would have been so proud to be among the crowd in his Sunday best, displaying his waistcoat with its umpteen shining buttons. Strange the way navvies vied with each other to have the highest number of the shiniest buttons. To Connor it would have been a mark of his seniority among the two thousand or so railway workers who had constructed this new line.

The knife twisted in Tresca's side. She crossed her hand over her stomach, realizing the baby's kicking had broken through her sad reverie. She had hoped against hope, but there was still no sign of Connor. He had disappeared without trace.

'Well, I must be off. You will be all right, won't you?'

Tresca brushed away her tears as Morgan came into the room. Dear, kind Morgan. She mustn't let him see. It almost seemed as if the child really *was* his. She recalled the day he had seen her skirt lift as the baby had kicked vigorously. His face had lit up like a young schoolboy's.

'Can I ... feel it?' he had asked hesitantly.

She had raised her eyes to his, such a wondrous, happy moment. 'Yes. Give me your hand.'

She could feel him trembling as she placed his

palm over the spot where she had just experienced movement. A second later, the baby had obligingly kicked again, and Morgan had laughed aloud, his eyes dancing in wonderment. They had put their heads together, joined in happiness.

The moment had drawn them closer together. As Tresca had grown larger and become more uncomfortable in bed, they had dispensed with the bolster. Morgan never once erred from his side, but had gone down to the kitchen in the middle of the night to fetch her some milk whenever she couldn't sleep. Dear Morgan. Even when his mother's acid tongue got the better of him, Tresca could only feel pity. He was doing his best, and without him God knew what might have happened to her. Quite often were the occasions when Tresca had been overwhelmed with gratitude and fondness, and brushed a kiss of affection on his cheek, making him blush.

'Yes, I'll be fine, Morgan, thank you,' she answered him now.

'Only I won't be able to come home at lunchtime. I'm expecting a large delivery and I need to be there. And Mother's planning to go to the opening of the railway this morning.'

'Yes, I know. I expect half the town will be there.'

'Perhaps not with the rain, but it'll be quite an event anyway. I understand they're bringing a train from Lydford with all the dignitaries on board. Stopping at Brentor first and then here.' Morgan's brow creased into a frown. 'You won't be going, will you? I don't want you being jostled about.'

'No, I don't really feel like it. I'll be able to see

the train going over the viaduct from the window here. So you get off to work and don't worry about me.'

Morgan dropped a kiss on her forehead and then hurried out of the door. Tresca turned back to the window, ignoring the tightening in her belly. She'd had this feeling many times over the last couple of weeks, but they were practice contractions, Dr Greenwood had said. But this morning they were stronger and more regular, and she was sure the baby wouldn't be long.

She heard the front door close and saw Morgan step out into the street below. She waved down at him as he glanced up and waved back. He had already turned away down the hill when Tresca's belly suddenly clenched so viciously that it took her breath away and she found herself bending over the deep windowsill to support herself. The pain brought tears to her eyes. Oh, please, Morgan, stop! But he had already passed beneath the viaduct and was out of sight.

It seemed an eternity before the cramping eased and Tresca released a tearing sigh of relief. Well, this was it. Her labour had truly started. She would have to get downstairs and ask Charity to send for the doctor. But she had scarcely reached the bed when the crippling pain came again, and she grasped on to the brass bedstead. Oh, Lord. And then she felt something snap inside her and a stream of something warm and wet poured down the insides of her thighs and into a puddle on the floor.

Her fingers closed even more tightly around the brass rod. She tried to call out, but she couldn't find the breath until the contraction had passed. Gingerly she hobbled to the far side of the bedstead, but as she eyed the distance to the door, the pain attacked her yet again, even more strongly than before. This time, she managed to cry out. No one came. It was half an hour later when she had crawled on her hands and knees to the door, that Charity finally opened it, dressed in her outdoor clothes, and stared down at Tresca in disdain.

'Get up off the floor, girl,' she barked.

'I – I can't–'

'For heaven's sake, it's only your labour starting.'

'But my waters have broken and it shouldn't be coming so fast. I'm sure we should send for Dr Greenwood–'

'Oh, don't make such a fuss. It'll be hours yet. Let's get you back into bed.'

She grasped Tresca's arm and hauled her to her feet, dragging her back to the bed. She pushed her down on to the mattress, lifted up her legs in one swift movement and then pulled up the covers, tucking them in so tightly that Tresca could barely move.

'You'll feel better now,' she said, her voice as cold as granite. 'Get some rest. You'll need your strength for the actual birth.'

'*Please*, Mother-in-law,' Tresca begged. 'I'm certain there be summat – *something* – amiss. The pains shouldn't be coming so quickly so soon and–'

'Nonsense. It'll be hours before you need the doctor. I was a day and a half with Morgan.

You're just being hysterical. Typical of your class.'

'Oh, no, I'm not, you mean old—'

She broke off as the agony ripped through her again and this time she scarcely managed to stifle her scream. Dear God, she was sure this wasn't right. Her fingers clawed at the blankets and she tried to draw up her knees, but the tightly tucked bedclothes prevented it. Her eyes stretched wide, savage with terror, as she gazed up at Charity's wooden expression.

'Mrs Lancaster and I are off to the opening ceremony,' Charity declared, pulling on her gloves. 'When we get back, we'll see if I need to fetch the doctor then.'

Tresca felt the strength drain out through her fingertips. Surely the witch wasn't going to leave her all alone in the house like this! How long would the proceedings at the station take? Could she possibly last that long? Oh, no, she could feel it coming again and bit down hard on her lip. But the torture was too great and she screamed aloud. No one heard her, though the empty house resounded with her cries.

She must, *must* fight this. When the contraction was over, she gritted her teeth and kicking her weak legs against the blankets, finally freed herself. The battle exhausted her, but after the next crippling pain, she threw back the covers. There was no way she could get downstairs to the front door and alert some passer-by. She was saturated in sweat, drowning in a weakness she had never experienced before. As she sat up, her head swam giddily, making her feel dizzy and nauseous. And when she glanced down, she gaped in horror at

271

the bright red stain spreading through her night-dress and over the sheets.

Oh, God. Bella. Dying alone in a pool of blood.

'No!' Her howl of terror spiralled to the ceiling.

The crowd at the brand new station applauded the speech by Tavistock's ex-portreeve and then a reply was given by a jolly railway official. The small band struck up again, masking the quiet hiss of steam coming from the gleaming engine waiting patiently by the platform like some massive gentle giant. Then the dignitaries climbed back on board, the driver pulled the whistle, and with a soft lurch, the engine's wheels began to turn. The train inched out on to the viaduct, gathering power as it disappeared into the cutting on the far side.

The spectators lingered for a few minutes despite the rain. Vera glanced around her. A few navvies had proudly watched the final act in the completion of the line they had toiled like slaves to build, but virtually all that hardy breed had moved on to pastures new. And where was Connor? Vera pondered sadly. Would they ever know what had happened to him? Poor Tresca. But her marriage to Morgan seemed to be a success in some strange way, and Vera was thankful for that.

There was Mrs Trembath Senior now with her housekeeper, each sheltering under an umbrella. Vera wove a path through the dispersing crowd, catching them as they turned away.

'Good morning, Mrs Trembath,' she addressed them politely, and Charity gave her an equally polite nod, for here was a young woman who

272

would have made Morgan a far more suitable wife than that trollop who had ensnared him and was carrying the illegitimate child of another man – and a coarse Irish navvy at that!

'A little short and sweet, the ceremony, don't you think?' Vera went on, feeling she must say something before she came to the question she really wanted to ask. 'Especially when the new line will be part of our lives from now on?'

'Personally I wish the viaduct didn't pass so near to our residence. Sadly, my dear departed husband took a ten-year lease on our property, but now I should prefer to live somewhere more suited to our status.'

Charity didn't add that despite being double-fronted and having an enormous garden, the house had never pleased her. Bannawell Street had always been one of the most overcrowded places in the town, with some very dubious residents. When it had provided popular lodgings for the navvies, it had been the last straw. At least they had all departed now – if only one of them hadn't left behind a brat that was going to be brought up as *her* grandchild. Still, if the girl and the bastard died while she was out – which she prayed fervently that they would – the status quo in their own house would be restored. Charity might even manipulate Morgan into finding a second wife in the young lady who stood before her now.

Vera, though, inwardly cringed at the woman's outrageous snobbery. 'Perhaps you would prefer somewhere like Watts Road?' she suggested, tamping down her true feelings. 'But may I ask how *young* Mrs Trembath is today?'

'She's well enough,' Charity replied, the lie coming easily to her lips. 'But in her condition, it wasn't wise for her to attend the ceremony. Now, Mrs Lancaster is to help me choose a new hat for the coming season. So, if you would excuse us?'

Vera watched as they headed off towards the town, and her brow dipped in a frown. Why would they go shopping when it was raining – and quite hard now? She had caught an odd, sly expression in Mrs Trembath's shifty eyes. And as Vera, too, set off downhill, she found herself hurrying. She overtook the two women, but instead of going down Drake Road, which had been built specifically to provide access to the new station from the town centre, she cut through Barley Market Street towards Tresca's home.

She knocked loudly on the front door and waited. Nothing. That was strange. She knocked again, but still there was no answer. Then she heard, very faintly through the open upstairs window, a thin wail of anguish.

She didn't know that inside the room Tresca was attempting to drag herself across the floor to the window to try and attract someone's attention. She felt so weak, the agony tearing through her almost constantly, blood still trickling down her legs and leaving a scarlet trail across the floorboards.

Vera desperately tried the door but it was securely locked. An instant later, she threw her umbrella aside and was flying down the hill, her feet hardly touching the ground.

274

Morgan paced grimly up and down, his heart screwed in anguish. Doctor Greenwood had been with Tresca for nearly three hours now and had sent for another physician to assist him. Vera, bless her, had found her way around the kitchen in Mrs Lancaster's absence and had supplied the two doctors with everything they requested.

The door opened and Dr Greenwood stepped into the room, rolling down his shirtsleeves as he came. There was a smear of dried blood across his snowy shirt-front that had seeped through the boil-washed apron he had worn, and Morgan's heart crashed to his feet. God Almighty. He hadn't heard a sound from upstairs apart from footsteps. No cry of a newborn infant. Surely it didn't mean both his darling Tresca and her child were ... were...

'Your wife is very poorly,' William Greenwood announced gravely. 'The placenta separated and she lost a great deal of blood, but we seem to have stemmed the flow now. She is still very weak and isn't out of the woods yet. But God willing and with careful nursing, she has a chance of surviving.'

Morgan felt the life force draining out of him, just as it had from his wife, and he collapsed into a chair, dropping his head into his hands. Oh, God, he had looked forward so very much to being a father, and now this. 'And ... and the child?' he stuttered.

'A boy. A big boy, too large for his mother. I had to use forceps, and even so, it wasn't easy. We had to revive the child, but he is holding his own. He will need a wet nurse, though. Hopefully we can keep Mrs Trembath's milk stimulated until she is strong enough to feed the child alone. But in the meantime – and I must reiterate that we are talking about if they both survive – the child will need supplementary feeding.'

Morgan nodded, on the verge of tears. 'Anything you say, Doctor.'

'I have someone in mind. And a nurse. And I would suggest a personal maid for the future as well. Your wife will need constant care. What I can't understand is why she was left alone when I had expressly told your mother to send for me the moment there was any sign of labour.'

'Nor can I,' Morgan murmured. 'I was at work, of course. I left Tresca with my mother and our housekeeper, but I understand from Miss Miles that they both went to the ceremony for the opening of the new railway, and as you see, they have not yet returned.'

'Well, because of them, your wife nearly died,' Dr Greenwood said, arching an eyebrow. 'So I suggest you employ someone more dedicated to her care in future.'

'Oh, I will, you can be sure of that!' Morgan told him, his voice vibrant with determination.

'Dear Lord, what on earth is *that?*'

'Mother, this is Lucy and she's coming to live with us.'

'Oh, for heaven's sake, Morgan, take it back to whatever gutter you found it in. You can't bring every waif and stray off the–'

Morgan's hands balled into fists. The anger he had felt over the birth of baby Callum had taken

276

hold with a force that astounded him, and he had found it increasingly easy to stand up to his mother. Now it felt almost alarmingly satisfying to interrupt and even defy her.

'I didn't find Lucy in the street,' he told her coldly. 'She happens to be a friend of Tresca's and she's going to be her personal maid.'

'Personal maid?' Charity scoffed. 'I hardly think she'd be suitable. Look, she's a cripple, or hadn't you noticed?'

'Lucy is quite capable of serving my wife and of helping her with Callum. And of protecting them from yourself and Mrs Lancaster, following your heinous conspiracy the other day. And I might have been employing another lady as well, a seamstress, if she hadn't already been employed in the Duke's summer residence at Endsleigh. If these people are good enough for aristocracy, then they will certainly be good enough for us.'

'Well, I can see the trollop upstairs really has turned your head.'

'I'd rather you didn't call my mistress by such a name, if you pleases, ma'am,' Lucy piped up, taking Morgan's lead, for really this kind gentleman, who had rescued her from the workhouse and was apparently Tresca's husband, was like a god in her eyes. She had, though, taken an instant dislike to Charity Trembath and was willing to put herself on the line to defend Tresca from her. Tresca, whose stay in the 'house' had provided the happiest time of her life.

'And on the contrary,' Morgan continued, 'Tresca has made me realize what a fool I've been all my life. If I have any further trouble from you or Mrs Lancaster, *you* will be the ones out on the street. Indeed, if I suspect the slightest action against Tresca, the baby or Lucy here, I will not only turn you out, but I will go to the constabulary. I'm sure there must be some law you can be prosecuted under for the way you put Tresca's life at risk, and both Miss Miles and Dr Greenwood would be witnesses to your felony.'

His voice had risen with barely contained fury, every word as clear as a bell to Tresca as she sat upstairs in bed, feeding Callum the little milk she had before passing him to the wet nurse's brimming breast. Morgan's raised voice filled her with guilt, for hadn't she destroyed his peaceful life? But then a wryly approving smile tugged at her lips. With each day that passed, Morgan was growing in her estimation – and in her affections.

Twenty-Six

The thunderclap exploded over the sleeping town like a roar from hell, and Tresca sat bolt upright in bed. At nearly seven weeks, Callum was going through the night, not demanding his morning feed until six o'clock. As her strength had returned, so Tresca's milk had become more abundant and they had been able to dispense with the wet nurse. Lucy slept with Callum in the spare bedroom that was now called the nursery, and would bring him into Tresca and Morgan's room whenever necessary.

Tresca had soon become used to feeding the baby in Morgan's presence. It was such a natural thing to do and it really felt as if they were a family. Like the true gentleman he was, Morgan would always avert his eyes, and on the couple of occasions he had accidentally caught sight of her, she was so enraptured in her child that she hadn't felt embarrassed. And after all, once Callum had latched on to her nipple, there was very little to see.

Now, though, it wasn't Lucy knocking on the door, was it? Dawn was breaking, so, being July, Tresca judged it was much too early for Callum's feed. Then a blinding flash tore through the room, flickering several times before it plunged the room back into gloom and another deafening crash made the windows rattle.

Morgan stirred and lifted his head just as the room lit up like a beacon again before another ear-splitting boom broke overhead.

'My, that's a storm and a half,' he declared, realizing Tresca was awake. 'Not frightened, are you?'

'No. But it is terrific, isn't it? I wonder if Lucy's all right.'

'I'm sure she'd come in if she needed to. We'd better try to get back to sleep. The little fellow will be wanting his feed in an hour or two, and I've got work in the morning.'

But it was so hot and sultry, and with the storm continuing to rage it was impossible to sleep. Then a deluge of rain began clattering on the roof and noisily overflowing the gutters, keeping them awake until it was light and Lucy finally brought Callum in for his feed.

'It's still coming down in stair rods,' Morgan reported from the window. 'The street's a river. I'm glad we live up the hill. If it's been raining like this on the moor, the Tavy will burst its banks by the time the water reaches the town.'

'You don't think there'll be flooding?'

'Wouldn't surprise me. I'll go in early in case there are any problems.'

Tresca looked up sharply. 'You will be careful?' she said in alarm, and realized in a blinding flash how much Morgan meant to her.

When he left shortly before eight o'clock, the rain had stopped and the street was full of people hurrying down to see if the unprecedented storm had produced any effect in the town. Tresca sighed. If there had been flooding, people would be suffering and she had seen enough of that. Bella, Assumpta, the workhouse inmates who had fallen on hard times – to say nothing of her own anguish. Losing her dear father had been hard enough, but for Connor to have disappeared at the same time had been crucifying. But even if he returned tomorrow, they could never be together. She was married to Morgan and she would remain faithful to him.

He seemed more confident now, though, she mused, and happier for it. Since his ultimatum, Charity appeared to have changed, too. At first she had showed grudging acceptance, but she had gradually softened, even becoming pleasant over the weeks. Oddly enough, she seemed to have succumbed to Callum's charms, handling him with a woman's natural care when Tresca – hawk-eyed – had allowed her to hold him, cooing at him, apparently besotted. Nevertheless, Tresca ensured Callum was never left unattended. Morgan, too, doted on the infant and guilt pricked Tresca's side as she watched them together. Morgan had done so much for her, and yet what had she done for him in return?

Her ponderings were brought to an abrupt end by a commotion in the hall below. She scooped Callum into her arms and, exchanging glances, she and Lucy hurried down the stairs.

Morgan and two other figures were coming in the front door while Charity and Mrs Lancaster arrived from the dining room. For once, they all shared the same feelings of astonishment as the three drowned rats dripped puddles on to the floor. Their soaked clothing was smeared with mud and some oily substance which looked to Tresca suspiciously like the peat residue that sometimes floated on the surface of water on the moor. Morgan was ushering the two strangers inside, grey-haired women who stared about their surroundings in utter bewilderment.

'River's burst its banks,' Morgan explained briefly. 'Forty foot of wall was washed away and Brook Street and Duke Street are flooded. I helped rescue several elderly people from Paull's Buildings. Including these two. They've lost everything. Not that they had much to lose in the first place,' he concluded under his breath.

Tresca bit her lip. Paull's Buildings were known to house some of the oldest – and poorest – residents of the town, many of them widows just managing to survive outside the workhouse. Unless the townspeople rallied to their help, they would doubtless have to end their lives, as Emmanuel had done, in the institution. Tresca shuddered at the thought.

'Come into the kitchen,' she said at once, meeting Charity's gaze. Her mother-in-law was clearly still shocked, but made no objection to having the strangers in the house. Tresca wouldn't have cared if she had. *She* was mistress of the house now, not Charity, and she would look after these two poor souls, no matter what.

'Mrs Lancaster, some large towels,' Charity amazed Tresca by demanding. 'Make some tea and I'll find them some clothes. They look about my size.' And with that, she followed Morgan who was making his way upstairs.

Tresca was totally taken aback. She couldn't believe this was the same Charity who had so recently wished herself and Callum such ill. But Callum was a little love and seemed to be weaving a spell over everyone, so all Tresca had left to do now was offer the two women reassurance.

She encouraged them to strip off their sodden clothes, have a swift wash and then be wrapped in warm towels. The shorter of them introduced herself as Madge. She was much quicker to accept the kindness she was being shown, and was soon sitting down at the table – dressed in some old clothes of Charity's, but still far better than anything she had ever owned – and sipping a hot cup of tea.

'Proper 'ero your 'usband were,' she declared.

'Water came swirlin' in, it did, just like that. Knocked Beryl yere off 'er feet. Then your 'usband appeared at the door. Us might've drownded if it weren't fer 'en. Riskin' *'imself* he were. But where us'll live now, I doesn't know.'

She glanced purposefully around the room and Tresca sucked in her cheeks. She would run upstairs and ask Morgan if they could offer the two women a temporary home, but, incredibly, Charity beat her to it.

'You can stay here,' she announced. 'One of you can share a room with my housekeeper and the other with our nursemaid, if you don't mind sleeping with my grandson.'

Her grandson? Tresca met Lucy's glance. Had Charity really changed so much in so short a time? It would certainly seem so.

'I'm just going up to my husband,' Tresca murmured, and hurried upstairs in a state of confusion.

Without thinking, she went into the bedroom without knocking. Although Morgan was dressed only in a clean pair of drawers, he didn't seem at all abashed, but Tresca had long realized there was an intimacy developing between them. Morgan was not unattractive, and Tresca recoiled from the spark of excitement that flashed inside her.

'It's chaos in the town,' Morgan told her, shrugging into a clean shirt. 'A crowd of people were on Abbey Bridge watching the water and they had to run for it when a tidal wave came down the river. I've never seen anything like it. The bridge withstood it, but the buildings either side were engulfed in seconds. People were crawling along planks from upstairs windows to escape, but if they'd fallen in the water, they'd have been swept away. The footbridge at the foundry went and a five-ton boiler was carried some distance downstream. So you can imagine how bad it is.'

Tresca had been watching him as he dressed, but her mind was only on the horrific conditions he was describing a hundred yards or so away. In his heroism, Morgan could have gone to a watery grave. In a sudden flood of emotion, Tresca stepped up to him and kissed him full on the lips. When she pulled back, Morgan blinked at her, a wry smile pulling at his mouth.

'I wish you meant that,' he mumbled.

Tresca's heart turned a complete somersault. Connor's disappearance over eight months ago had opened a bottomless chasm in her soul, and without Morgan she was sure she wouldn't have survived. But could he ever fill that gaping hole inside her? Did she *want* him to? She was still steeped in grief, so how could the thought of loving another even enter her head?

Oh, Connor, my darling love, where are you? Her heart cried out in despair as the broken turmoil swirled in her breast.

'I still doesn't trust 'er,' Lucy pronounced pointedly as she changed Callum's napkin one crisp December morning. Despite her crooked left hand, she managed such tasks admirably, even when Callum playfully kicked his sturdy little legs in the air.

'But she's changed completely since Callum arrived,' Tresca replied pensively. 'She plays with him all the time and yesterday she were feeding him bread soaked in milk. It were going all over the place but she were laughing like a drain. She were telling him all about Christmas, not that he understands a word.'

'I still thinks you'm too trustin',' Lucy grumbled, 'lettin' 'er take Callum out in his perambulator.'

'People can change, you know. Look how she were with Madge and Beryl.'

'Only cuz it made 'er look charitable, like.'

'Oh, I don't think so. They could've gone somewhere else while their home were being repaired, but she insisted they stayed here.'

'Well, I thinks you sees too much good in people. Not a bad fault, but you should be careful.'

Tresca gave a light chuckle. Lucy was apt to speak her mind and wouldn't have got away with it with most mistresses! She was about to tease her over it when she heard someone at the front door. Going out on to the landing, she heard Vera's voice talking to Mrs Lancaster in the hall and called her upstairs to the nursery.

'Good, I can have a hold of my godson, then,' Vera grinned as she bounded up the stairs. 'But first I need a word with you in private,' she added, dropping her voice. 'I've got something to tell you.'

Tresca's heart sprang into her throat. Was it to do with Connor?

With a trembling hand she opened the door to her bedroom.

'W–what is it?' she stammered, ushering Vera inside.

'It's your mother-in-law,' Vera began warily.

'Charity?' Tresca exclaimed, almost relieved. 'We were just talking about her. How she's changed. Lucy doesn't believe it's genuine, but I do. Perhaps it's having a baby around again. Morgan says she doted on him as a child and he thinks she resented him growing up.'

'Maybe. What I've found out could explain a lot, too.'

'Found out?'

'Yes. I was helping the reverend sort out some old parish registers and I found myself glancing through some of them. You'll never guess what I came across.'

Tresca's brow wrinkled with curiosity. Vera had said it was something to do with Charity – but what?

'The entry for Charity's marriage.' Vera nodded. 'Morgan was born in November 1862, wasn't he?'

'Yes. He were twenty-eight on his birthday last month.'

'I thought so. But his parents were only married in the July.'

'What!' Tresca's eyes might have popped out of her head. 'You mean–'

'There's more. Charity was a domestic servant. And the space for her father's details was blank.'

'So...?'

'I worked out roughly when she was born, and I found that entry as well. She was illegitimate. Father unknown.'

'My God, that's incredible. She always told Morgan her father died when she were little.'

'In her mind, she probably believed that was true. It's amazing what people can convince themselves of when they want to. It's my guess she struggled all her life. When she got married, it brought her respectability, even if Morgan's father was just a market trader back then.'

Tresca chewed on her lip, utterly dumbfounded. 'Morgan said his father built up the business from nothing.'

'With Charity pushing him all the time, no doubt.'

'You're probably right. They had a tiny shop in Duke Street before they moved to the big one they have now. They lived over it for quite a while before coming to live here.'

'Climbing the social ladder all the time. And Charity's guarded her new position with jealousy ever since.'

'And when I came along, it were too great a reminder of her own past.'

'I would say so, yes. People can be very strange sometimes. But things are much better now from what you say.'

'Yes. I've done my best to live up to her standards and she seems to be accepting me. But it's good to understand her attitude. It even makes me feel a little sorry for her.'

'You've a big heart, Tresca Trembath. I don't think I'd be as forgiving.'

'None of us is perfect. Life has taught me that.'

'Yes, but be careful all the same. Now where's

287

my godson? It was him I *really* came to see!' Vera
teased.

Tresca led her into the nursery, lost in thought.
She really couldn't take in all her friend had revealed. Good heavens, whatever next?

Twenty-Seven

'Asn't you folded they napkins yet, Tresca? I
doesn't know, you cas'n get the staff nowadays.'

Lucy's teasing tone reached Tresca's ears in a
happy song. She was standing by the nursery window with the untouched pile of freshly washed
towelling squares on the chair next to her. Outside, the long garden rose in several steep terraces
and on one of the middle levels, Charity was
sauntering along the gravel path, Callum in her
arms, pointing out to him the cloud of snowdrops
among the grass.

Tresca gave a deep sigh and absently picked up
one of her son's napkins. Charity really did seem
to love Callum. In fact, she seemed to love him *too*
much, if that were possible. But it was certainly
useful to have an extra pair of hands to cope with
the child's inquisitive nature as he crawled about
the house getting into all kinds of innocent mischief. Tresca refused to have him confined to the
nursery, but he was very much into opening cup-
boards to investigate their contents, which he
would scatter across the floor in a fascinating
array.

'Anither grand day for February, bain't it?' Lucy joined her young mistress at the window, and she too gazed across at Mrs Trembath Senior as she entertained the small child. 'So mild an' still.'

'I don't reckon it'll last,' Tresca replied contentedly. 'Winter could return just like that. The fresh air's good for Callum, mind, and Mother-in-Law's clearly enjoying it, too.'

A smile curved her lips as Callum, bored of the tiny white bells that bobbed among the green spiky blades, decided that the greying hair of the familiar woman who held him was far more interesting. His little hands made a grab at it and tugged. Through the slightly open window, Tresca caught her mother-in-law's faint chuckle and saw her blow a raspberry on to Callum's chubby fist. He screamed with glee and Tresca shook her head. Charity, whose own life had been a secret struggle, had found her peace at last.

A sharp pain of envy circled Tresca's heart. If only... She tried to stop herself. But no. She must voice the words in her heart. If only Connor was there to see his son. But he wasn't. Fifteen months now and still nothing. She should stop counting, stop hoping. Connor was gone. Something had happened to him. And if she was wrong and he suddenly turned up with some valid reason for his disappearance, what then? Part of her would hate him, blame him for deserting her, while the other part would still love him with a passion beyond her own comprehension. And where did dear, kind Morgan fit into the broken jigsaw that once had been her true and steadfast heart?

She turned from the window in a chaos of confusion as Lucy stated fiercely, 'Besotted wi' the babby, she is. Unnatural if you ask me.' And with pursed lips, the younger girl began to fold the napkins herself.

Down in the garden, Charity's sly glance saw Tresca move away from the window, and a poisonous smirk twisted her face. She grinned down at the child in her arms, chucking him under the chin, and he laughed back, his little face utterly trusting.

'I hate you, you little bastard,' Charity cooed at him, her voice soft while her eyes glinted malevolently. 'And one day I'll have my revenge. Huh! Don't understand a word I'm saying, do you, you little idiot?' Her lips curled back from her teeth in a lurid smile, and she glanced up at the window again. 'Get even with that trollop of a mother of yours, I will,' she promised with a smile that would have made the devil quake.

Tresca heard Morgan's key in the lock and something made her fly down the hall to greet him. She just felt so much more at ease when he was there, the glue that had bound her life together when everything had been falling apart. He returned her expectant smile wanly.

'Oh dear, have you had a bad day?' she asked sympathetically. 'You look tired.'

Morgan rubbed his hand over his brow with a deep grimace. 'Not really. But I've had a splitting headache come on this afternoon. In fact, I ache all over, especially my back. Would you mind very much if I went straight to bed? Make my excuses to Mother, would you? I really don't fancy facing her inquisition tonight.'

Tresca blinked at Morgan in alarm. It wasn't like him at all, so he must be feeling rough. 'Yes, of course. Oh, you poor soul. Shall I bring you up some laudanum?'

'Yes, thank you.'

He paused for a moment, and before Tresca could turn towards the kitchen, he lifted his hand to stroke her cheek. Then his mouth closed grimly, and Tresca watched him wearily climb the stairs.

Some time in the dead of night, Morgan's restless body woke her and she heard him groan softly as he attempted to turn over. She at once shifted round in the bed.

'Are you all right?' she whispered.

'No, I'm not. I feel bloody awful.'

The pit of Tresca's belly squeezed tightly. She had never heard Morgan swear before, so he must really be suffering. 'Sounds like influenza. I'll fetch you another dose of laudanum.'

'You couldn't refill the hot-water bottle, could you?' Morgan croaked into the darkness. 'I'm so cold.'

Cold? But Tresca could feel a scorching heat radiating from his body. She shot out of bed and wriggled into her dressing gown. 'I'll have to wait for the range to get up to heat.'

'You're an angel,' Morgan murmured as she lit the oil lamp and made her way to the door.

Downstairs in the silent, shadowy kitchen, the night closed in around her as she opened up the

291

vents of the range, willing the banked up coal to catch without delay. She waited impatiently, feeling strange and uneasy, and wishing for the millionth time that she could curl up safely in her father's arms as she had done as a child, and let the world and its problems fade away.

Back upstairs at last, Morgan muttered his thanks as he snuggled down with the refilled stone bottle. Tresca could feel him shivering beside her, but soon the laudanum did its work and he fell into a fitful slumber. It was Tresca who couldn't sleep now, listening to Morgan's occasional muttering in his fevered sleep. Tresca's mind was fully awake, pondering on how fate had led her to be sharing her life – and her bed – with a man who had, at first, been little more than a stranger. He had won her respect, her trust, and her affection ... but had he won her heart? His love for her had entwined itself about her soul, but could she return it? How could she when her true and passionate self belonged to another?

In the morning, Morgan was no better. The daylight hurt his eyes and when he tried to drag himself out of bed, he stumbled to his knees and Tresca had to assist him back into bed. Oh, Lord. It must be a bad strain of influenza. It would probably go through the entire household. A storm of fear broke over her. Callum. Everything must be done to keep the illness from him. He was nine months old and probably not strong enough to... Oh, good God, Tresca couldn't bear it if...

She stood at the door to the dining room where Charity was taking breakfast, and told her mother-in-law of Morgan's condition.

'Well, *I*'d better go into the shop today, then,' Charity announced, getting to her feet with a triumphant glint in her eyes. Tresca didn't like the expression on the older woman's face, but it was the least of her problems just now. 'It's about time I had some authority there. And I suppose *you*'ll want to nurse Morgan on your own,' Charity sniffed, lifting her chin haughtily.

'It would be wise,' Tresca reasoned cautiously. 'I'll isolate myself in the room with him. Perhaps Mrs Lancaster can leave food trays and anything else outside the door. We don't all of us want to catch it. Especially Callum.'

'Oh, no, especially Callum,' Charity repeated, and Tresca couldn't quite fathom the strange intonation in her voice.

It was on the third day that the rash appeared. Tresca had spent the night dozing in the armchair, and as the morning light filtered into the room, she crossed over to the bed where Morgan was stirring. As he turned to her, she recoiled in horror. His face was peppered in flat, angry spots.

'Oh, do you know, I feel a deal better this morning,' he smiled faintly at her.

'Oh, do you?' She hesitated indecisively, but felt she had to say something. 'I hate to tell you, but you're coming out in a rash.'

'Really?'

'Er, yes. On your face. And, look, on your hands. Oh, Morgan, I think I should send for the doctor.'

Tresca bit her lip. Whatever was it? She went to

the door and called out softly, hoping someone would hear her. She didn't want to holler in alarm as she felt like doing. The last thing Morgan needed was to know how worried she was.

To her relief, Lucy emerged from the nursery, already fully dressed.

'I need you to fetch the doctor at once,' Tresca told her without preamble. 'Morgan's come out in a proper fearful rash.'

Lucy blinked her eyes wide. 'I'll go directly. Callum's awake, so I'll 'ave the mistress take care on 'en.'

Within seconds she had rapped on Charity's bedroom door. The older woman opened it a few moments later, her face tight with annoyance at being disturbed when she was still in her dressing gown. But the landing soon became a whirlwind of activity and Lucy was out of the front door, grasping her hat and coat as she went.

Tresca shut the bedroom door, trying to take a calming breath. Lucy's gammy leg would prevent her from running to the physician's house, but Tresca knew she would go as fast as she could with her odd, lopsided gait. A river of emotion flooded through her. Morgan seemed better in himself, but his face was raw and inflamed. *Oh, Morgan, my poor love, whatever is it?*

The words went through her brain without pause, without hesitation. And somehow she was glad. Connor – and all he had meant to her – was a fading dream. But Morgan was the here and now, and Tresca's heart lurched with dread that whatever it was had struck him down might end up taking him from her.

294

It seemed an eternity before Lucy returned with the doctor. There were other physicians in the town, but since her acquaintance with Dr Greenwood in the workhouse, Tresca always considered him as their family doctor. She was surprised, then, when she opened the bedroom door to a much younger man.

'I'm Dr Franfield,' the stranger introduced himself. 'Dr Greenwood was already out on a visit and I'm his junior colleague. I was at his house when this young lady called,' he continued, smiling over his shoulder at Lucy. 'Now, if I can see the patient, please?'

He asked Morgan lots of questions, lifting one eyebrow slightly when Morgan reported the sore patches he had felt in his mouth the previous day. Then he gave his patient a thorough examination. He might be young, Tresca considered, but he certainly seemed very professional and possessed a kind and encouraging manner.

'Now, this might sound more alarming than it really is,' he said at length, 'but I believe we're dealing with a case of smallpox.'

Tresca stepped back, her hand over her mouth, and she saw the blood drain from Morgan's face. Smallpox! But surely...?

'I can't be sure for another few days,' Dr Franfield explained. 'If more waves of spots appear, then I will be proved wrong and it will be chickenpox. But the prevalence of the rash on the face rather than the trunk, and the fact that there are spots on the wrists and feet, would suggest smallpox. I've only recently returned from my seven years' training in London, and I saw several cases there, and there are strong similarities.'

'But ... how could he have caught it?' Tresca stammered, still in shock. 'I thought vaccination is supposed to protect you?'

'Indeed it does, which is why your husband's case will be mild. And why the likelihood of him developing any of the serious complications which can make the disease so dangerous will be absolutely minimal, as will any scarring from the rash. Our patient is feeling much better today, he tells me,' Dr Franfield went on, beaming down at Morgan, 'which is excellent news and quite usual as the rash appears. As to how he caught it, well, probably from someone who has also been vaccinated and has the disease mildly but hasn't developed the rash, which is actually more normal. So that person has no idea they have smallpox, but perhaps thinks they have a touch of influenza. So,' he concluded with a confident smile, 'the danger is very small indeed. However, I understand from your maid that you have a young child in the house. Has he been vaccinated?'

Tresca's blood ran cold and she saw Morgan sit bolt upright in the bed. Oh, God. 'Yes, he has. It's the law, isn't it?'

'Well, nowadays you can opt out by registering at the police station, but it's highly inadvisable. However, it would be preferable to keep the child away from his father or indeed from yourself, just in case. And do call myself or Dr Greenwood if the child shows any sign of illness.'

'Yes, of course. I've already been keeping the baby isolated. I've stayed in this room with my husband ever since he fell ill. We thought, like you say, that it were influenza.'

'Very sensible. I wish all my patients had your foresight. Now above all, I don't want you to worry. Keep the rash clean and dry. It will erupt in its various stages, I'm afraid. Wash your hands frequently with carbolic soap, and might I suggest clean sheets and pillowcases each day? Now if I may wash my own hands now, I will leave you in peace. Either I or Dr Greenwood will call every day, but please don't hesitate to contact us if you have any other concerns.'

A few minutes later, Tresca was showing Dr Franfield out of the room, her nerves still on edge despite his reassuring words. Dear God in heaven. And Morgan's poor face. He had never been what she would consider strikingly handsome, but neither was he unattractive. She had come to love – yes, *love* – those open, kind eyes, that firm, sensitive mouth. She must not let him down, must restore him to full health, the rock that she clung to, she realized now, like life itself.

The knock on the door startled her, and when she answered it, Charity was standing on the landing, fully dressed now, Mrs Lancaster on one side and a wide-eyed Lucy on the other.

'That nice young doctor has explained everything,' Charity announced. 'But just to be sure, I'm going to take Callum to stay at my sister-in-law's in Okehampton. We cannot risk the child developing the disease, however mildly. Just think if the poor mite ended up with a scarred face! And you will need all your strength to nurse poor Morgan. Now you know it makes sense,' she cajoled as she saw the alarm on Tresca's face. 'We must put little Callum first. Mrs Lancaster will send a telegram to my sister-in-law telling her to expect us later this afternoon. Mrs Lancaster will accompany me as she has been there before, and Lucy can stay here to help you.' With that, she swept into her own room, closing the door behind her, leaving Tresca and Lucy staring at each other in utter turmoil.

It was Lucy who regained her senses first. 'You'm never gwain fer let 'er take 'en, are you?'

Tresca's face contorted in anguish. What Charity had said was true, but... She turned into the room and hurried over to the bed again.

'Your mother wants to take Callum to her sister-in-law's in Okehampton,' she told Morgan. 'Do you think that's wise?'

'To Aunt Faith's? Oh, yes,' Morgan nodded firmly. 'She's a good sort. You can rely on her. Callum will be perfectly safe.'

Tresca went back to Lucy, chewing her lip. 'Morgan says Callum'll be fine there. And I've got to trust my mother-in-law, haven't I? She dotes on him, after all. And I must do what's best for Callum, mustn't I?' But as she turned back into the sickroom, she wasn't at all sure she had made the right decision.

Twenty-Eight

'Well, I'm pleased to say I can pronounce our patient cured.' Dr Franfield's serious face broke into a kind smile. 'And Mrs Trembath, you've shown no symptoms, which you would have done by now if you were going to catch it.'

Tresca met Morgan's gaze and both their faces echoed the doctor's relief. The past three weeks had been a nightmare and Tresca felt utterly drained, but now a dazzling light had shone through and dispelled the darkness. It was over, and life could return to normal.

'And you think being a dairymaid for so long might've helped?' Tresca asked as euphoria bubbled up inside her.

'Quite possibly. You were doubtless exposed to cowpox on occasion, and that is very close to smallpox. And you were vaccinated as a child. Very wise. I don't suppose vaccination will ever entirely eradicate the disease, but it would be nice to think that it might one day. Not in my lifetime, though, I don't suppose.' He sighed wistfully, but then the smile returned to his face. 'So it will be perfectly safe for your little boy to come home,' he concluded, picking up his medical bag. 'I'll see myself out unless I meet young Lucy on the way. And much as I have enjoyed your acquaintance, I do hope not to see you again soon. Not in my professional capacity, at least.'

He gave a boyish grin and happily left the room. Morgan was sitting in the armchair and Tresca took his hand, feeling the weight slide from her shoulders. He certainly appeared restored to health, and the marks from the rash had all but gone. There was just a tiny scar on his forehead and the slightest puckering of the skin on his right cheek, nothing at all disfiguring.

'Oh, I must send for Callum at once!' Tresca gave a sudden whoop of joy. 'I must send a telegram–'

Morgan caught her arm as she sprang away from him. 'My darling girl, send a *letter*. You're exhausted, running round after me. I can never thank you enough, and you know I can't wait to have Callum back, too. But give yourself some rest. A few days won't make much difference.'

Tresca hesitated, pushing her thumb against her mouth. 'All right,' she grinned. 'But I'm going to write straight away.' And she flitted out of the room in a whirlwind of excitement.

'Just 'ark at that there wind.'

Lucy voiced Tresca's thoughts as the windows rattled alarmingly in another ferocious blast. Tresca, Morgan and Lucy were having a cup of tea in the drawing room. They knew Charity would not allow such familiarity when she returned. Although Tresca could hardly contain her joyful anticipation at the prospect of seeing Callum again, she wasn't looking forward to Charity's presence, despite their recently improved relationship.

The mild February weather had given way to

the freezing temperatures of the following month. Today, the ninth of March, had witnessed a building wind. As night closed in, it was turning to a vicious, blustering gale that howled menacingly around the shivering town.

Above the clamouring wind, they caught an urgent knocking on the front door. Lucy leapt to her feet with a puzzled frown. A few moments later, a commotion had Tresca running out into the hall after her. Could it possibly be that Charity and Mrs Lancaster had returned with Callum?

Tresca thought she would explode with joy. Lucy was holding the front door, which was threatening to be wrenched out of her hands by the gusting wind. Tiny snowflakes were scudding in from the darkness outside, swirling in vigorous eddies on the tiled floor. On the threshold, Charity was struggling to close her umbrella which had turned inside out. A cab driver pushed past her, heaving her large trunk indoors and showering white dust from his broad shoulders. As he waited for his payment, Tresca wished he would hurry up, for surely Mrs Lancaster was outside with Callum in her arms.

Tresca couldn't understand it when he left and Charity pulled the door from Lucy's grasp, banging it shut behind her. Tresca blinked, shaking her head in confusion. Surely…?

'Where's Callum?' she demanded, battling to retain her hold on reality, for surely there was good reason . .

'It's good to be home,' Charity announced, ignoring her. 'It's all very well staying with one's sister-in-law—'

'B–but where's Callum? And Mrs Lancaster?' Tresca repeated as ice touched somewhere deep inside her.

'That ungrateful woman!' Charity dropped her umbrella into the hallstand. 'She left my employment a week ago. After all the years we've been together and all I've done for her.'

'Left your employment?' Morgan questioned, arriving at Tresca's shoulder.

'But where's Callum?' Tresca insisted, panic taking her by the throat.

Charity shrugged and fixed Tresca with a bemused frown. 'Callum did you say? I know no one of that name. Now then,' she went on, shaking her head dismissively, 'I need to freshen up, and then I'd like a nice cup of tea if Lucy will oblige.'

She began to climb the stairs, leaving the three young people staring at her, their mouths dangling open in horrified disbelief. Some dark, ominous fear blackened Tresca's soul, strangling her, pinning her down. Time fractured, bled. She could only watch, turned to stone, as Charity moved upwards as if nothing had happened, her face impassive. But ... but Callum...!

Tresca forced her paralysed lungs to take a breath and, breaking free from her shock, sprang up the stairs. 'What've you done with my baby?' she shrieked as she launched herself at Charity.

The look the woman turned on her froze her to the spot. Charity's face was a macabre mask, her features grotesquely contorted and her eyes gleaming with evil. She threw up her head with a bitter, deranged laugh and then, as her gaze rested on Tresca's dumbfounded stare, she

302

wrestled with her daughter-in-law's grasp on her arm. Towering over her from the next step up, she found some demonic strength and hurled the girl down the stairs.

Tresca heard herself scream as she tumbled downwards. It happened so quickly, she wasn't aware of any discomfort until several seconds after she came to rest with a dull thud on the hall floor. Pain seared through her wrist, and she became aware of Morgan cradling her against him.

'You bitch!' he cried in a furious voice so unlike his usual placid self. 'You—'

'It's what she deserves!' Charity sneered down at them, spitting with malice. 'She doesn't belong in this house, and neither does that bastard child of hers.'

'So what have you done with him? Where is he?'

'Somewhere you'll never find him! I want her to know what it's like to have your son taken away from you.'

'Taken away? What do you mean, you vicious old witch?'

'There, you see? You'd never have spoken to me like that before *she* came on the scene! Stolen you from me, that's what she's done. So I wanted her to know what that feels like.'

Charity's eyes had narrowed dangerously. But though she was biting back the agony in her wrist, Tresca had to fight back. 'I've done nothing of the sort!'

'Yes, you have! Wouldn't even let me nurse Morgan when he was ill—'

'But it were your idea to take Callum away. Now where is he, you—?'

303

Charity's eyes were ablaze, wild and brutal with madness. 'Wouldn't you like to know! He'll never come back to this house. Never!'

'But I thought as you loved 'en.'

Tresca glanced up in awed astonishment as Lucy slowly stepped past them, her voice cool and calm as she edged one foot on to the first step, then the next, inching her way towards the unhinged woman halfway up the stairs.

'Didn't believe that, did you?' Charity cackled viciously. 'It was just a charade to trick you while I waited for my moment. And now it's come and I'll not have any reminder of him in my house ever again!'

Lucy had almost reached her, but Charity suddenly fled up the remaining stairs and into the nursery. Gasping in pain, Tresca pursued her with Morgan on her heels, arriving just behind Lucy as the crash of breaking china reached them from inside the room.

They peered cautiously around the door. Charity had gone berserk. She had evidently hurled the pitcher and bowl to the floor. Now she had picked up the little chair and was smashing it on to the sides of Callum's cot. When she failed to inflict much damage, she ran over to the window and ripped the curtains from their rail with a yell of anger.

'Mother...' Morgan stepped forward in horror, but Lucy stilled his arm.

'No, leave her,' she whispered. 'Nort you can do. She'll calm down when she's ready. Seen the like afore, I 'as, wi' the imbeciles in the work'ouse. Go for months, proper normal like, then they suddenly snaps. I's afeared 'er 'ead's turned. Come on.' She quietly ushered them out of the room, taking the key from the inside of the door and then locking it behind her. 'Mr Trembath, sir. You needs to fetch the doctor. And the constable. I'll stay yere wi' Tresca.'

Tresca had been staring at her, blank with terror and so glad to have someone to tell her what to do. But stay there when Callum...

'No. I've got to look for Callum.'

'But you're hurt, and in this weather–'

Tresca's look silenced him, and he nodded in acceptance. Less than a minute later, they stepped out on to the street. The deafening gale was still screaming. Tresca would have been blown over immediately if Morgan hadn't caught her. They battled down the hill, trying to stay upright, blinding snow driving into their faces like icy needles. Hardly anyone else was abroad. They passed only one other person bent almost double in the fight to get home.

Another powerful gust knocked Morgan and Tresca against the building they were passing. Tresca yelped in renewed pain, but her cry was lost in the screech of the living, wilful thing that was hellbent on destroying everything in its path. They were plunged into darkness as the street lamps were blown out, and as they leant into the blizzard again they could scarcely see where they were going. There was just the roar of the squalling, heaving hurricane, the blackness of night, and the terror that somewhere out in this was Callum.

'Look out!'

Morgan wrenched her backwards as some huge object hurtled past them. Tresca could barely make it out. Was it a shutter torn from its hinges? Dear God.

'You should go back!' Morgan bellowed in her ear to make himself heard.

'No! You go on! I'm going to the railway station. They might know something.'

'No, I won't let–'

'Just go!'

She pushed him hard, pain burning through her wrist. But he knew nothing would stop her, and while he pushed on down the hill, she plunged across Pym Street towards the station. She forced her way through deepening snow, which in places was already piled a foot deep, stumbling, dragging herself up again. The wind took her breath away, tossed her like some toy, tore at her coat, whipped her hair across her face and stung into her eyes. Tears of desperation dripped down her cheeks. Oh, Callum! *Connor!* She hardly heard the great, rumbling clatter as the chimney collapsed in the gale, bringing bricks and roof tiles raining down about her...

'Tresca, my dearest, the inspector's here.'

Tresca scraped herself from the deep sleep where she felt safe and secure. The dull headache crept back into her awareness, reminding her of the appalling events of the last few days, and the blizzard which would surely go down in the annals of time.

The whole of the south-west had been decimated. At sea, ships had been driven on to rocks with many lives lost. On land, the hurricane had wreaked havoc, bringing down trees and telegraph poles and wiping out communications. Huge drifts of snow made roads impassable, cut off water supplies and literally stopped trains in their tracks. Windows were blown out, roofs ripped off and chimneys caused to collapse. Many people had lucky escapes – including Tresca.

'Dr Franfield had gone to Princetown and was presumably marooned up on the moor. So it was Dr Greenwood who came back with the inspector,' Morgan had explained, concern etched on his face. 'Mother was huddled in a corner, rocking herself back and forth in her own world. But as soon as they tried asking her about Callum, she became crazed again, lashing out, screaming. We had to hold her down while Dr Greenwood gave her an injection to calm her. They took her off to a police cell, but she'll probably end up in an asylum.'

'And Callum?' Tresca's lips were bloodless in her ashen face. 'Did she give any clues?'

She moaned in agony when Morgan shook his head, and she clung to him as he explained how he had gone in search of her and found her knocked unconscious from the flying debris from yet another collapsed chimney. She had been lucky not to have been killed, but she wished she had been. How could she live without Connor and now without his son?

'I'm afraid it's bad news,' the inspector said gravely as he stepped across to the couch where young Mrs Trembath lay, looking, poor girl, like death warmed up, her head bandaged and her

307

left wrist in plaster.

'I'm not sure my wife's in any fit state–'

'It's not about your son. I'm afraid we have no news there. Our enquiries have been severely handicapped by the effects of the storm. Telegraph wires are still down and travel is almost impossible. Mrs Trembath Senior must have been on the last train to get through from Okehampton, but we're doing all we can under the circumstances. It was odd, though, that she sent her trunk on an earlier train, but I'm sure we'll get to the bottom of it in time. No,' he paused, twiddling his moustache awkwardly, 'this is a different matter. We've found ... erm ... a body. Or at least some human remains.'

Tresca had been staring at him from the bottomless abyss she had tumbled into since Callum's disappearance. Once the inspector had said his visit had nothing to do with her son, she had sunk back down into its depths, but something in her personal horror made her sit up and listen.

'The storm brought down thousands of trees,' the inspector continued. 'One had come down in the Watts Road cutting. When the men went to clear it, they found the remains tangled up in the roots. Dr Greenwood examined it. He says... I'm so sorry to distress you further, but it would have been a male in his early thirties. A very tall and broad male with ... with red hair.'

The low gasp that slowly expanded Tresca's lungs almost asphyxiated her and she was so utterly grateful when Morgan put his arm around her shoulders.

'As you know, we believe something happened

by the scaffolding the night Mr O'Mahoney disappeared. Someone had fallen, whether by accident or foul play, we don't know. The body that has been found had several broken bones, consistent with such a fall, among them broken ribs which could well have punctured the lungs, and a cracked skull. If it was foul play, the perpetrators – and there must have been at least two to move such a large man – possibly tried to bury the body among the trees at the top of the cutting, but didn't make a very good job. Or perhaps the poor fellow was trying to save himself, somehow got to the top but then became disorientated, got tangled up in the tree roots and collapsed and died. I fear we'll never know the truth. But...' The inspector's voice became even softer as he looked down at the distraught young woman. 'We believe we know the identity of the deceased. I have his waistcoat, if you feel able...?'

Tresca groaned softly and her fingers tightened on Morgan's arm. She peeped out from the shelter of his embrace and nodded on a gasping sob as the inspector held out Connor's distinctive waistcoat with its many shining buttons.

The inspector left quietly, leaving Tresca weeping against Morgan's chest. He held her, not uttering a word since there were none to be said that could ease her pain as she cried until her heart would break – for another man. Very slowly, her tears subsided, but she still rested against her husband, feeling the warmth and comfort of him, the masculine love and support she craved.

'I knew ... he hadn't deserted me,' she finally croaked in a broken whisper. 'Sometimes ... I doubted ... but always, deep down, I knew...'

'I know, my love. He was a good man. I always liked and respected him myself. At least now you know what happened. Poor, poor fellow.'

A wrenching sigh lifted his chest, moving Tresca's head as she still clung to him. Oh, Connor. Had he gone down to the cutting in his euphoria over the prospect of becoming a father? He loved his work, and she could well believe it. Oh, dear Lord, what a cruel twist of fate.

She felt Morgan drop a kiss on the top of her head, and she melted against him as her tears began afresh.

Some days later, a letter, posted from Exeter the morning before the storm, arrived for Morgan from Mrs Lancaster, citing Charity's increasingly aggressive and erratic behaviour as the reason for leaving her employment – and please could she have a reference? Tresca scoffed in outrage. But as Morgan wistfully pointed out, his mother must have been acting strangely for Mrs Lancaster to have said so!

It hardly helped Tresca. She dragged herself through each day, tearing out her hair for news of Callum. Even at night she was tormented. Whenever she did manage to snatch a few hours' sleep, Connor drifted into her dreams, but when she reached out to him, his shadow faded away. In the cold light of day, grim acceptance was reluctantly stealing into her rebellious mind. There was a stillness where once her heart had beaten, but always, beside her, was Morgan, quiet, calm and supporting.

'Tresca, a constable's yere fer fetch you!' Lucy announced, bursting into the drawing room. 'And he's grinnin' from ear to ear!'

Tresca and Morgan exchanged glances, and Tresca's heart took a huge bound. Despite her bruised body, she was out of the front door in a trice, Morgan running to catch up with her. She didn't even stop to put on her coat, shrugging into it as she fled down the hill, ignoring the constable who puffed along behind her.

Her pulse was pounding like a traction engine as she flung open the door to the police station. She stopped then, and as the inspector's smiling face turned to her, the world ceased to spin. A tall, distinguished man was standing by the desk, and next to him a petite woman was beaming at her. In her arms she held a small, sleeping child, copper curls showing from beneath its warm bonnet.

Tresca almost collapsed, and would have done if Morgan hadn't arrived at that second and caught her. Callum! Her head still whirling, she sprang forward and snatched her son from the woman's hold.

Her mind was a blank. Just pure, unutterable joy.

'I was going home after delivering a baby in Mary Tavy,' she scarcely heard the middle-aged woman explain. 'I'm the local midwife, you see. I was hurrying down to the bridge. We farm on the moor above Peter Tavy on the other side of the river. And I found this little chap crawling along the lane. I know all the local children, and I didn't recognize him. So with the storm getting up, I thought the best thing was to take him home with me. And then we were snowed in up at the farm. This is the first chance we've had to come into town.'

'A miracle Beth found him–'

'Yes, and thank you from the bottom of our hearts, Mr...?'

'Pencarrow. Richard Pencarrow. And this is my wife, Beth.'

'And we've been able to further our enquiries, too,' the inspector put in. 'It seems that Mrs Trembath Senior left Okehampton on an earlier train than we thought. The same one, in fact, that her trunk was on. But having arranged for her trunk to be taken off at Tavistock, she changed on to the other line at Lydford so that she could break her journey at Mary Tavy.'

'So she arrived at Tavistock *South* Station?'

'Exactly. That's what confused us. So it was certainly premeditated. She was seen walking towards the river carrying the baby, but was alone when she returned to the station. Perhaps she was originally intending to abandon him up on the moor, but the breaking storm deterred her.'

'But how could she expect to come back as if nothing–?'

'Her mind's completely gone, Mr Pencarrow. She'll live out her days in a prison asylum.'

'Well, if you don't need us for anything else just now, I'd like to take my wife and our son home. We're...' Morgan paused, spreading his hands, '...so grateful. We can't thank you enough.'

There were handshakes all round, drawing Tresca from the rapturous dream that had enveloped her. Oh, thank you, God. Thank you, Mr and Mrs Pencarrow. But as she caught Morgan's wide grin, all she wanted was to get home where they belonged.

She relinquished Callum into Morgan's arms, since it was difficult for her to hold him with her plastered wrist, and they set off across the town square where a pathway had been cleared through the snow. Tresca clung to Morgan's arm, and as he smiled down, his love seemed to pour into her. Connor had been her passion, always would be. His death, and what he must have suffered, had broken her spirit. But in a way, it was a release. Now she knew the truth. That his love had been as true as hers. That he had never abandoned her. He had died loving her, and now, though her heart would take time to heal, she could move on.

She brushed away the tears she felt trickling down her cheeks. Tears of regret, but also of hope. And dear, *dearest* Morgan, who had taken his mother's insanity so well, was by her side.

He suddenly stopped, and in the middle of the square he bent over Callum's sleeping form and his lips found Tresca's, just for a moment, so soft and warm.

'It's wonderful to have Callum back,' he choked. 'We can be a proper family now. And ... one day,' he faltered, his eyebrows knitted, 'do you think he might have some brothers and sisters?'

Tresca blinked at him and her heart brimmed over. Slowly, she smiled through her tears.

'Yes, I think he might,' she whispered hoarsely.

Morgan's eyes travelled over her face and his hesitant smile answered hers. She linked her hand

313

through his elbow and they walked on towards Bannawell Street, the place where so many people had come and gone from her life – Assumpta and her young family; poor Bella; her dearest, darling Connor who would remain in her heart for ever; and her beloved father who had died in ignominy in the workhouse, but at least she had been with him at the end.

Yet through all the joy and all the sadness, Bannawell Street had become her home. She still had so many friends there, Jane, Elijah and his wife, Lucy, and Vera just around the corner. And of course, Morgan. And so, with peace in her heart at last, she walked towards the happy future that awaited her – with the man she knew she loved with a strong and steadfast heart.

Author's Note

Today, Bannawell Street is a quaint and desirable residential area of Tavistock. In the nineteenth century, however, it was known as one of the most overcrowded streets in the town with a reputation for 'colourful' characters. The inhabitants in my book are entirely fictional, although Jane Ellacott is based on her namesake, also a widowed dairy-keeper, who became the warm and homely lady in my story. The Solloways were the Workhouse Master and Matron of the time, reported to have been fair and compassionate. Mr Szlumper was Chief Engineer on the railway, and Mr Pearce ran a grocer's in Bank Square. I do not believe I have done them any injustice, but this book is not meant to be an accurate portrayal of any real-life person.

As for shops in the town, many of those mentioned did actually exist. The town's civic cemetery had recently opened, and the church in Callington Road did not become Catholic until 1952. The background events that affected the building of the railway have been followed as accurately as possible. The storm, the flood and the blizzard indeed took place and provided inspiration for the story.

The publishers hope that this book has given you enjoyable reading. Large Print Books are especially designed to be as easy to see and hold as possible. If you wish a complete list of our books please ask at your local library or write directly to:

Magna Large Print Books
Magna House, Long Preston,
Skipton, North Yorkshire.
BD23 4ND

This Large Print Book for the partially sighted, who cannot read normal print, is published under the auspices of

THE ULVERSCROFT FOUNDATION

THE ULVERSCROFT FOUNDATION

... we hope that you have enjoyed this Large Print Book. Please think for a moment about those people who have worse eyesight problems than you ... and are unable to even read or enjoy Large Print, without great difficulty.

You can help them by sending a donation, large or small to:

**The Ulverscroft Foundation,
1, The Green, Bradgate Road,
Anstey, Leicestershire, LE7 7FU,
England.**
or request a copy of our brochure for more details.

The Foundation will use all your help to assist those people who are handicapped by various sight problems and need special attention.

Thank you very much for your help.